It didn't make any sense to Cal.

Lindsey Hayes was a beautiful woman. Smart. Generous. Involved with everything and everyone in this upright, uptight little town.

Yet when she went home late every night, she went alone.

Cal thought about following her. Asking if he could sit with her on her porch for a while.

But he didn't move from the window. Because that wasn't really what he wanted.

What he really wanted was to bury his hands in her beautiful hair and taste the fullness of her mouth. To strip away the restraints between them, then ease himself into her and put an end to the fire burning under his skin.

But the fact that he would have settled for sitting with her on her porch kept Cal right where he was.

Because there was something dangerous about wanting to be with a woman that badly...

Dear Reader:

Romance readers have been enthusiastic about the Silhouette Special Editions® for years. And that's not by accident: Special Editions were the first of their kind and continue to feature realistic stories with heightened romantic tension.

The longer stories, sophisticated style, greater sensual detail and variety that made Special Editions popular are the same elements that will make you want to read book after book.

We hope that you enjoy this Special Edition today, and will enjoy many more.

Please write to us:

Jane Nicholls
Silhouette Books
PO Box 236
Thornton Road
Croydon
Surrey
CR9 3RU

The Rebel's Bride
CHRISTINE FLYNN

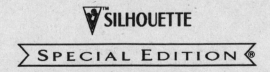

SILHOUETTE

SPECIAL EDITION ®

*Silhouette, Silhouette Special Edition and Colophon are
registered trademarks of Harlequin Books S.A., used under licence.*

*First published in Great Britain 1996
Silhouette Books, Eton House, 18-24 Paradise Road,
Richmond, Surrey TW9 1SR*

© Christine Flynn 1996

ISBN 0 373 24034 1

23-9611

*Printed and bound in Great Britain
by Mackays of Chatham PLC, Chatham*

CHRISTINE FLYNN

admits to being interested in just about everything, which is why she considers herself fortunate to have turned her interest in writing into a career. She feels that a writer gets to explore it all and, to her, exploring relationships—especially the intense, bittersweet or even lighthearted relationships between men and women—is fascinating.

Other novels by Christine Flynn

Silhouette Special Edition®

Remember the Dreams
Silence the Shadows
Renegade
Walk upon the Wind
Out of the Mist
The Healing Touch
Beyond the Night
Luke's Child
Lonely Knight
Daughter of the Bride
When Morning Comes
Jake's Mountain
A Father's Wish
*Logan's Bride

*The Whitaker Brides

Silhouette Desire®

When Snow Meets Fire
The Myth and the Magic
A Place To Belong
Meet Me at Midnight

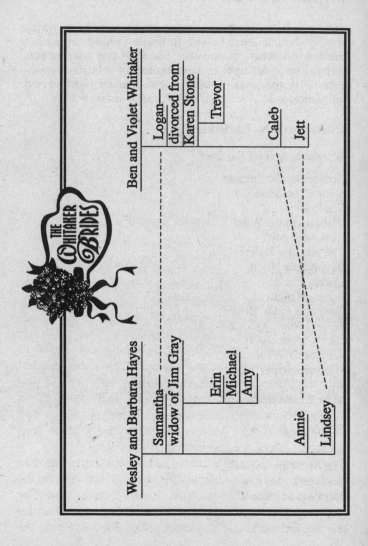

THE WHITAKER BRIDES

Wesley and Barbara Hayes

Samantha—
widow of Jim Gray

Erin
Michael
Amy

Annie

Lindsey

Ben and Violet Whitaker

Logan—
divorced from
Karen Stone

Trevor

Caleb

Jett

Chapter One

No one had told Lindsey Hayes that Papa Joe's was a bikers' bar. She had assumed that a place with such an innocent name was a pizza parlor. The sort of friendly neighborhood establishment she'd frequented when she'd briefly lived in New York. Yet, as she cut the engine of her sporty red Bronco and eyed a badly listing neon sign with a missing *J*, there was no way she could make the place out to be anything other than what it was. The shabby building with the metal beer logos bleeding lines of rust down its weather-grayed exterior was quite clearly a tavern. And a rough one at that. Motorcycles were parked three deep on either side of a metal-braced wooden door.

With more hesitation than Lindsey was accustomed to displaying, she glanced from the junkyard next door to the double-pump gas station across the two-lane highway. She had it on good authority that her sister's new brother-in-law worked weekends at a place called Papa Joe's on the old highway outside Austin. Since she'd driven for miles and hadn't seen any other establishment bearing that name, this had to be it.

Determined, though far less enthusiastic about her purpose than she'd been before spotting the forbidding-looking building, she slipped from her Bronco and started across the graveled parking lot. She needed to hurry. A shipment of summer whites waited at her boutique to be steamed and tagged and she'd promised herself that as soon as she got back, no matter what came up or who needed her help, she'd get that stock on the floor. Right after that, she would tackle the shirts she designed and sold to a specialty shop in Dallas. Since she was two weeks behind on that order, she could ill afford to waste any more of her time. The 110-mile drive from her home in Leesburg had taken the better part of two hours already. She wasn't about to make the return trip without attempting to accomplish her goal.

Half a dozen steps later, practicality overrode purpose. It wasn't often that Lindsey allowed obstacles to get in her way. Especially when it came to doing something for someone she cared about. She was, however, willing to make a slight exception for the row of Harley "hogs" flanking the door. The gleaming black gas tank on the nearest motorcycle had a skull and crossbones painted on it. The skull was cracked.

Lindsey might be determined, but she was no fool.

The gas station across the street had a phone booth. Thinking it wiser to call Papa Joe's from there and ask Cal Whitaker to meet her outside, she turned—only to whip right back around at what sounded like gunshot.

It wasn't gunfire that had her heart sliding to her throat. It was the slam of the tavern door against the wall. It had burst open with such force that it still rattled on its hinges.

The noise inside exploded out in a cacophony of shouts and loud music.

Stopped dead in her tracks, Lindsey felt her heart kick into double time. The narrow doorway was filled with flailing arms and legs, male bodies and dark leather. Heavy boots scuffled against wood and the rattle of a chain joined the sickening thud of fists meeting flesh and bone. A shout rose above the others from somewhere inside the smoky darkness behind the grappling men. A moment later, the sound of a grunt was followed by the sight of a foot-long knife arcing through the air. Flashing in the sunlight, it clanked against the Dumpster at the end of the building and spun to a stop by a silver-spoked tire.

Before Lindsey could discern how many bodies were involved in the melee, a leather-clad biker came flying toward her. He landed facedown at her feet, the curved scar at the base of his shiny, bald head grinning up at her like a smile. As she scrambled back, her disbelief vied with horror as another of the tavern's occupants came hurtling out. After half a dozen awkward steps, he landed on his knees next to the first guy. Two more frantic steps of her own and Lindsey backed into her Bronco's rear bumper.

She had reached behind to grope her way toward the passenger door handle, when the man on his knees rose, stumbled and swore. Swearing again, this time at her when he demanded to know what she was looking at, he grabbed the chain his prone companion used for a belt and hauled upward. The bald biker didn't want help. After shoving the guy back, he rose under his own steam and cut a staggering path to one of the motorcycles parked near the end of the building. The other guy, sending a curse toward the tavern, muttered something about finding another place to get a beer and followed.

Someone inside turned down the music.

Lindsey's heart was still pounding in her throat when her glance jumped back to the building. Only one person remained in the doorway. Tall, broad-shouldered and lean-hipped, he stood with the back of his hand pressed to the corner of his mouth. The black T-shirt molding his tautly muscled chest and arms had been partially pulled out from the waistband of his black jeans, and its neckband was ripped at one shoulder.

Lindsey felt a new form of hesitation assert itself. The hardness of his body spoke of a man intimately familiar with physical labor, and his dark hair was badly in need of a cut. But it was the ruggedness of his features that had her attention; features that were both forbidding and alarmingly attractive—in a decidedly raw, untamed sort of way. They were also a tad more familar than she liked. Even from the relative safety of twenty or so feet, she could see the steel in his expression.

Though she couldn't have imagined him looking any more unyielding than he did at that moment, that steel seemed to harden when he met her eyes. He didn't acknowledge her. He merely held her glance long enough to make it obvious he'd seen her, then turned his attention to the back of his hand after he'd withdrawn it from his mouth.

Scowling at it, he turned to spit bright red blood into a clump of grass struggling to grow at the building's foundation. By the time Lindsey had winced at the sight, he was pulling a red handkerchief from his back pocket to press to the corner of his mouth.

Fervently hoping this wasn't the man she'd come to see, she started toward him. The moment she did, he looked up.

His ice-blue eyes froze her in her tracks.

"I wouldn't come any farther if I were you, lady. You don't want to come in here."

His voice was a deep, intoxicating rumble. A little impatient. Definitely dismissive.

"If you're looking for a phone or something, use the one across the street."

The dampness from an earlier rain caused hinges to squeak when he started to close the door. Calling out a hurried "Wait!" Lindsey skirted the beastly looking bike blocking her path, only to stop again when she got close enough to see inside.

Behind him, two men in leather vests wielded cues at a pool table. Several more stood, sat or slouched along the dimly lit bar. He was right. She didn't want to go inside that awful place.

She pulled her focus back to the man separating her from the others.

Given the manner in which he had just removed two of the bar's patrons, she assumed he was the bouncer, the bartender or both. The fact that this uncivilized-looking male was apparently the one who kept the others in line made him all the more formidable.

"I'm looking for Cal Whitaker," she told him, hoping she only imagined how strongly his lean, strong jawline resembled those of the other Whitaker men she'd met. "Is he in there?"

Those impossibly blue eyes narrowed on her face. His scrutiny betraying as much insolence as interest, he let his glance run from the sun-streaked hair tumbling around the shoulders of her mauve jacket to the length of shapely leg exposed below the hem of her matching walking shorts.

She clearly didn't belong in the neighborhood.

"Who are you?"

"Lindsey. Hayes," she added. "He doesn't know me, but my sister is married to one of his brothers."

His expression had borne curiosity. After the way his eyebrow had arched with his inspection of her legs, it had even betrayed interest. Now she caught a decided chill. "What do you want?"

"To talk to him," she said, thinking that should be obvious. "Look, I don't need much time. Only a few minutes. Okay?"

For a moment he said nothing. He just stood there, watching her as if he couldn't decide whether he thought her foolish or brave for pressing her luck.

"Which brother?"

"What?"

"Which brother is your sister married to?"

"Logan," she returned, aware of the guardedness behind the question. "He and Sam...my sister," she explained, "were married last November."

His jaw went rigid.

Lindsey didn't betray by so much as a blink how Cal Whitaker's failure to attend the wedding had hurt her brother-in-law. Cal had known about the ceremony. He'd been invited to it. At the moment, though, she was more concerned with the vague, sinking feeling in the pit of her stomach. No matter how much she'd hoped otherwise, this was the man she had come to hire. It would have been nice if he'd identified himself instead of playing his little game of twenty questions.

"Did he send you here?"

"No. He didn't," she returned with a look that told him she thought the question a little ridiculous. If he knew anything at all about his oldest brother he'd know hell would freeze before Logan's stubborn pride would allow anyone to intervene where his brothers were concerned.

She didn't care to step into that particular mine field, however. At least, not until she was certain she could make that situation better and not worse.

"I'm here on business. I understand you're a carpenter." Behind her a motorcycle tried to start. Raising her voice over the engine's cough and shudder, she added, "I'd like to discuss a project with you."

"What kind of a project?"

"Can we discuss this someplace else?"

She wasn't sure he'd heard what she considered a reasonable request, given the present noise level. As she'd spoken, his glance had shifted toward a winter-bare pecan tree at the end of the building. The men he'd removed from the premises had mounted one of the bikes under it, and the earthshaking roar of its engine finally firing made hearing nearly impossible. Their departure wasn't what held Cal's attention, though. His focus was on the two choppers pulling in from the highway as the other motorcycle took off.

Uncapped headers snapped and crackled as the two newcomers backed off the gas and coasted their snorting machines to a stop behind Lindsey's Bronco. The taller of the two men, wearing a leather vest similar to those worn by the men she'd noticed inside, sported so many tattoos on his arms and torso that he appeared to be wearing a shirt. He killed his engine first. His companion, stockier and hairy in a faintly Neanderthal sort of way, wore a vest, too, complete with matching python on the back, and a handkerchief tied over his head. His most prominent feature was the row of silver studs rimming his right ear.

The walking work of art dismounted as his buddy punched the accelerator one more time. He noticed Lindsey just as the reverberating roar stilled to blessed silence.

An unholy grin revealed tobacco-stained teeth, and he planted his hands on his hips.

"Well, look what we have here, J.J. Papa's is picking up a little class. You coming or going, sweetheart?"

Lindsey felt her stomach take a sickening lurch as the men traded a glance and started forward. Bearing down on her like two cats toying with a trapped mouse, neither paid any attention to who might be watching. It didn't matter. This was their turf. Rules, as civilized people knew them, didn't apply.

The man called J.J. eyed her as if she were dessert. Pure menace leaked from his pores. "I dunno, man. She sure looks like she ought to be coming to me."

"Can't make up your mind?" the first guy taunted even as Lindsey blanched at the crass comment. "She can't make up her mind, J.J." He grinned at her, still talking to his friend. "What do you think we ought to do?"

"Maybe we should give the broad a little help."

Panic bloomed in Lindsey's chest. Ignoring the men was not an option. Neither was seeking the safety of distance. She had approached the tavern to talk to Cal, so the men were between her and her Bronco. Motorcycles, a Dumpster and two pickup trucks blocked escape behind her. To one side was the highway. To the other, the tavern. Incongruous as it seemed, that building and the formidable man in its doorway now seemed more haven than hazard.

Cal hadn't budged. As quickly as things were happening, it didn't occur to Lindsey that she should expect him to. In those awful, fragmented seconds she considered only that she was no match for either of the men in front of her, much less both of them, and that she needed to get away before either one of them touched her. But she was trapped. And the ape with the dirty bandanna on his head was reaching toward her.

Fear had washed the color from her features when, grinning, he touched the ends of her soft, shining hair. The moment she'd realized what he was going to do, she'd pulled her head to the side, trying to gain more distance, but she'd already backed up as far as she could. The handlebar of the bike behind her was stabbing her in the small of her back.

From the doorway came a low, succinct expletive. The profanity sounded irritated, impatient, as if the man who'd uttered it regarded the situation as something he truly did not want to be bothered with, but saw no way to avoid. Lindsey didn't care what he thought of it. Or her. All she cared about was that the ape with the earrings had dropped his hand and stepped back, and that her aggressors' attention had been diverted by the man coming toward them.

Cal had the stride of a predator. Controlled. Unhurried. Deliberate. He also had a grip of pure iron.

"You're freaking nuts, lady," he hissed on a whisper, shackling her upper arm with his strong fingers to pull her to his side. Letting go, he turned his forbidding expression on the duo, who'd just gone into battle stance. Both men had planted their feet apart and were flexing their loosely hanging hands.

"Take it easy, Rembrandt," she heard him say, his tone completely lacking the threat implied by his presence. "No one wants any trouble out here. Why don't you and your friend just go on inside and get a beer."

"I asked her a question. I got a right to an answer."

Cal seemed willing to concede that. He did not, however, seem willing to let the man get any closer to Lindsey.

The man he'd called Rembrandt had turned his challenging glare on Lindsey. As he did, Cal sighed—and promptly snagged Lindsey by the waist to haul her against his side.

"Answer him," he ordered her, his unwavering glance remaining fixed on the man glaring at his possessive grip.

Caught in that grip, it was all Lindsey could do to remind herself to breathe. He'd tucked her against his side, his arm solid across her back. Scared, stunned, she felt his fingers flex against her lower ribs just before the heat of his body began seeping into hers. The motion felt oddly like reassurance, which made no sense at all, given how put out he'd looked. More than likely it was just a signal for her to cooperate. Which she had every intention of doing, anyway. Not for an instant had she considered pulling back from him. His body felt like solid rock—absolutely, utterly unyielding. Like the set of his jaw. And at that moment all that mattered was that she also felt safe.

"I'm leaving," she managed to say, her voice not nearly as strong as she'd have liked.

Cal looked sympathetic. At the man. Not at her. "The lady said she's leaving. Sorry, buddy."

For one awful moment Lindsey was afraid the matter wasn't going to end all that easily. She didn't think Cal did, either. Though outwardly he looked relaxed, the tension in his body was unmistakable. She could feel it the entire length of her side, from where his hard thigh pressed hers to where her shoulder was trapped beneath his arm. At five-eight, Lindsey had rarely felt dwarfed by a man. But Cal had an easy eight or nine inches on her. Because of that, and because of how he'd turned her when he'd pulled her against him, her breast pressed the side of his chest and her stomach was flush with his hip.

Given the circumstances, she preferred not to think about their proximity. What she considered instead was that, in the blink of an eye, this man could shove her aside and his big hands could be fists. Rembrandt seemed aware of that, too. What with Cal's ripped shirt, the fresh scrapes on his knuckles and his bleeding lip, it was apparent that he wouldn't back down from a fight. From the size of his powerful body, it was just as apparent that he'd probably win.

It seemed to be his lip that had most of the biker's attention a moment later. That and Cal's possessive grip on his quarry.

"You could have said you'd already staked her out, man," he snorted, glowering at the way Lindsey's hand unconsciously gripped Cal's shirt. "I'm not fighting for no broad." A silver bracelet flashed as he hitched his thumb toward the door. "Come on, J.J. I'm thirsty."

Cal said nothing else. He merely held his ground while the biker tossed a derisive glare at Lindsey for wasting his time and turned to the door. Not to be rushed, his companion with the row of silver studs in his ear pulled a pack of cigarettes from his rolled-up shirtsleeve, shook one out and, snickering, sauntered off behind him.

For what seemed like an eternity, but was actually mere seconds, Lindsey held her breath while the men disappeared inside. The moment they did, that breath leaked out like air from a slowly deflating balloon. There wasn't a nerve in her body that wasn't suffering from a waning adrenaline surge. Her knees felt like rubber. Her palms were damp. And though a dozen emotions clamored for recognition, her only thought was of how vulnerable she would have been had it not been for Logan's brother.

"Are you all right?" he asked, his breath feathering the hair on top of her head.

He must have felt her sag against him, for his grip seemed to tighten. Realizing that she was leaning on him—and that she still had a fistful of his shirt—she let her hand fall as her glance jerked to his face.

She didn't know what she'd expected to see in his implacable features. She knew only that she hadn't anticipated concern. Yet it was there, guarded and grudging. But visible, nonetheless. She hadn't anticipated, either, how dangerous it would be to meet his eyes with him holding her as he was. The blatant intimacy of his hold had sent a message to her would-be assailants that had spoken far louder than a verbal claim—which had obviously been his intention. Now all she could think was that he knew exactly how to hold her to get the most contact from her body. He had every nerve in her body singing just holding her against his side. She could only imagine what he could do to her were he to pull her in front of him.

He was entertaining that very thought himself. She felt sure of it when his fingers brushed over her hip and his glance settled on her mouth.

Jarred as much by her own thoughts as the quick heat in his eyes, she ducked her head and eased back.

He'd already let her go.

"Thanks for the rescue," she said, torn between apprehension, gratitude and embarrassment. "I don't know what I would have done if you hadn't been here."

The concern she'd seen had already vanished from his expression. So had the heat. In their place was only the impatience she'd seen before. Now, however, it seemed directed at himself as well as her. "Forget it."

"No. Really. What you did was..."

"What I did," he interrupted, deliberately cutting her off, "was no big deal. I just happen to have a problem with guys who pick on people weaker than themselves. I'd have done it for anybody." A flash of anger, raw and real, darkened the depths of his eyes, only to turn back to impatience so quickly that most people wouldn't have noticed the change at all. "I'm not too crazy about people who put themselves in precarious positions, either. A woman like you has no business being in a place like this."

"I wasn't *expecting* a place like this," Lindsey informed him, wondering at the bitterness she'd caught in his voice. "And I don't need a lecture. If I'd had any other way to get in touch with you, I'd have tried it. This is the only place I knew to contact you."

"How did you know I was here now?"

"I called yesterday. The man who answered said you'd be in today after three."

He didn't really seem all that interested in her tracking abilities. Or that she was annoyed with his lousy attitude. He shoved his fingers through the deep brown hair reaching past his collar and glanced down at his watch.

"There's a diner down the road," he began, losing her completely. "It's on the left just before the junction, about a mile south of here. If you want to talk to me about a job, meet me there in ten minutes. I'll be on a break, so you'll have to make it quick."

He didn't wait to see if she agreed. Having designated where their conversation would take place, he headed back inside the dimly lit tavern and closed the door without so much as a backward glance.

Obviously he expected her to do as he'd said.

Lindsey had never appreciated being ordered around. She appreciated even less the way Cal had brushed off her thanks, then dismissed her so abruptly. But she wasn't going to stand there thinking about how pushy and rude he was while some other form of lowlife showed up. And she certainly wasn't going to dwell on why she could still feel the imprint of his hard body everywhere it had touched hers.

As unsettling as it was to consider, she felt as if he'd branded her.

* * *

The Highway 235 Diner was straight out of the fifties. It was the real thing, too. Not just a trendy, nostalgic version like the one Cal had worked on last year in Houston. The faded Coca-Cola sign at the end of the green Formica counter was as authentic as the old jukebox sitting just inside the door, and the squeaky black stools lining the counter probably hadn't been oiled since 1966.

The place smelled of coffee and chicken fried steak, which was the house specialty, according to the chalkboard hanging above the pie case behind the counter. It looked to Cal as if that was what the toothy waitress with the big hair had just set in front of the two truckers at the counter when he walked in the front door.

There was only one other person in the place. The woman he'd come to meet. She was sitting in a booth by the window.

Shaking his head at the waitress to indicate he didn't want anything, he stuffed his truck keys into his front pocket as he strode over to where Lindsey Hayes waited. She watched his approach, one hand on the glass of iced tea she'd ordered and a smile curving her lips. There was nothing overt about that smile. Certainly nothing that lived up to the potential of her very inviting mouth. But it managed to soften the wariness she was trying to keep from her eyes. She had incredible eyes, actually. They were a warm, coffee brown, at once languid and expressive. He'd seen determination in them, and fear. He'd been impressed by both.

"Are you sure you don't want something?" she asked, lifting her hand toward the plastic-coated menus when he slid into the booth. "Coffee?"

Her fingers were long and slender. Rather like the rest of her, he thought, deliberately raising his eyes to hers once more.

"I'm fine," he said, flatly dispensing with amenities. "What's the job?"

Lindsey fought the urge to sit back, to put some distance between her and the man whose presence seemed to fill the booth, the room. She'd lived in a lot of places in her twenty-seven years. Military bases and cities, mostly. And she'd always adapted. Since she'd moved to the country, she'd become accustomed to men who seemed a little rougher around the edges than their counterparts in uniform or in the city. Less polished. More . . . physical. But never had she encountered one anywhere who made her feel so protected one moment and so threatened the next.

Determined to keep her unease in perspective, she leaned forward, curling her fingers around the condensation-coated glass. This darkly attractive and somewhat impatient man was Logan's brother, and Logan, whom she adored, looked a little . . . dangerous, too.

"It's a couple of jobs, actually," she told him, her glance straying to the cut at the corner of his mouth. The small wound was still bleeding a little and the skin around it had swollen into the corner of his bottom lip. As painful as it appeared, she was certain it had to hurt. "I want to expand my clothing store into the empty space next door to my shop. And the outside needs a face-lift."

So he could see what she had in mind, she pushed across the table a drawing of what looked like an alpine chalet.

"Our town is attempting to draw tourists," she explained, aware of his less than complimentary frown at her design. "Since I head the revitalization committee, I thought I should set an example by being one of the first to make the transition to the Old World theme we've adopted. I'm also on a committee to restore our most significant buildings," she added, seeing no point in mentioning that she was actually a committee of one, since no one else had wanted the job. "That's the main reason I came to you. I understand you have an interest in restorations. We have a landmark that needs to be restored before the Fourth of July."

Refraining from comment, Cal pushed her drawing back to her, then touched the back of his hand to the corner of his mouth to dab at the cut. It didn't appear that he'd done anything so far to take care of it. Nor had he changed his torn black T-shirt. All he'd done to clean himself up was tuck his shirt back in and comb—or push—his hair straight back from his face.

"I'm a carpenter," she heard him say as he pulled a napkin from the metal dispenser between the salt and pepper shakers. "But if you're representing a town about a restoration, you're looking for credentials. That means you're looking for somebody else. I don't have any."

His tone was utterly flat, as if he expected her to look upon that lack as a failing that precluded further discussion of her offer. Avoiding her eyes, he touched the white paper napkin to the cut. It came away with a small stain of bright red blood.

He swore under his breath and dabbed at it again.

Lindsey swore, too. To herself. The rough, dry paper was only making him bleed more by pulling off the blood that had managed to clot.

"We can't afford someone with credentials." There were four settings of utensils on the table. From the one in front of her she picked up the spoon and dipped it into her glass. "But we do need someone with skill. You have the skill, but not the credentials. Therefore, I don't see where we have a problem."

Ice clinked against metal and glass. "Even if you don't restore the bandstand, my shop still needs remodeling," she continued, snatching a napkin from the dispenser herself after she'd located the cube she wanted. "I have no idea how long either project will take. But it's a hundred miles from here and sixty of that isn't on freeway, so I would hardly expect you to commute. The empty apartment over my shop comes with the job, if you're interested. It's not much, but it wouldn't cost you anything. Here."

A faint frown creased Cal's forehead when his glance shifted to the half-wrapped ice cube she held out to him.

"Put it on your lip," he heard her say.

The frown shifted to forbearance. He knew what to do with it. He'd just been wondering where this job of hers was—until she'd caught him off guard with her gesture.

With a muttered, "Thanks," he reached for her offering.

"I can only imagine how the other guy must look right about now," she quietly told him. "His lip was bleeding worse than yours."

Cal didn't necessarily appreciate that information. "I didn't want to hit him."

"In that case, I'd really hate to think what would have happened had your heart been in it."

Her voice was soft, her smile faint. In no mood to be charmed, he gave her his best let's-get-on-with-it glance and touched the cube to his mouth.

The ice stung like hell.

"You said a hundred miles." His concession to this new assault on his body was little more than the faint hardening of his jaw. He was sick of split lips, bruised ribs and trying to keep the peace with men who were always spoiling for a fight. "Where is this job?"

He saw her lean forward and cross her arms on the table. There was grace to the movement, though he couldn't honestly say he'd ever considered such a thing about a woman before. Not sure why he'd considered it about her, he focused on the sudden hesitation in her expression.

That same hesitation was in her voice when she spoke. "In Leesburg," she finally said, looking as if she were bracing herself for a less than favorable reaction. "My sister is director of the chamber of commerce there. The town has adopted her plan to revitalize the town."

"The sister that's married to Logan?"

Lindsey nodded.

They wanted to restore all of the public buildings, she hurried to add. At least, that was what Cal thought she said as she went on about the funds the town had raised from an Oktoberfest it had held last fall. The town intended to raise more funds with an Independence Day celebration, which was why she wanted the bandstand finished by then. Cal wasn't really listening, though. Not now. Once she'd mentioned Leesburg, his interest had taken a hike.

He'd grown up not far from that tightly knit ranching community. But there was nothing there for him anymore. There never had been. His parents were dead. Logan had the ranch. And Jett, his youngest brother, was off chasing down a dam to dig or a bridge to build, even more rootless than himself. Cal, at least, had an apartment. It wasn't much, but it was a place to return to from wherever his latest construction job had taken him or, lately, when he came off shift at Papa's, since construction was so slow. Jett had only a post-office box.

Not that the brothers ever wrote to each other. Or even talked, for that matter. Cal only heard from Jett when Jett was passing through on his way somewhere else. The last time had been three months ago, when Jett had called to pass on an invitation to Logan's wedding. Before that, Cal hadn't talked to him in ten or eleven months.

He hadn't seen Logan in seventeen years.

The ice had soaked the paper napkin. Wadding the napkin into a ball, he dropped it into the empty ashtray. A moment later his hand was on the table as he prepared to push himself out of the booth. "You're wasting your time. Thanks for the offer, but I'm not interested."

Lindsey's hand landed on his. "The town is twenty miles from the ranch. Logan only goes in once a week, so it's not likely you'll run into him . . . if that's what you're worried about."

The waitress had plugged the jukebox with a string of old Bobby Vinton tunes. "Blue on Blue" had followed "White on White," and the lament of a broken heart mingled with the low-keyed conversation of the men at the counter. Cal was far more aware of the woman across the table from him. Seeming suddenly self-conscious, she glanced to where her pale, slender hand curved over the back of his darker, rougher one. Slowly she drew her fingers away.

Suspicion fairly dripped from his tone. "Why did you come to me about this?"

"Why?"

"The reason," he elaborated, not about to trust the innocent confusion in her expression.

That she had been so quick to address the cause of his reluctance made him more than a little uneasy. He wasn't accustomed to anyone knowing him well enough to read him the way she just had. Certainly not well enough to zero in on the reason he hadn't been home in so long. But with her sister married to Logan, she undoubtedly had access to the Whitakers' less than illustrious family history. People nowadays called the sort of family he'd grown up in "dysfunctional." Not being the politically correct sort himself, he preferred the more straightforward term of "screwed up." Not that he thought about family at all. Or had. Until she'd shown up.

"Come on. Tell me why me instead of someone else," he insisted when all she did was sit there looking uncomfortable. "There are lots of carpenters looking for work."

"I don't know how to put it without..."

"Just say it," he cut in.

"I don't want to offend you."

Her sensitivity was commendable. But unnecessary. "I don't offend easily. Who's this offer from?"

"From me," she returned, as puzzled by his insistence as she was annoyed with his attitude. "I came to you because of a conversation I had with your other brother. Jett," she emphasized, so Cal wouldn't shut her out the way he had at the mention of Logan's name. "It was at Logan and Sam's wedding. I was complaining about how few skilled carpenters there were in the area and how much it would cost to bring someone in to remodel my shop, when he told me about you. Then, when Sam and I were talking about the bandstand a couple of weeks ago, I remembered Jett saying you'd worked on restorations before. He also said you'd been laid off from your job. I thought that if you were still looking for work, I might be able to get you for less than I could someone else."

It didn't matter to Cal that she'd been bargain hunting. Every muscle in his body was tensed to keep going—to walk out the door and forget every word she'd said anyway. But he was torn between practicality and the fierce need to protect himself; a need that was such a part of him that he hadn't even realized it was still there. Until now. He didn't consider how quickly the walls had come back up, though, or how deeply the resentments ran. His only thought was that if he didn't protect himself, there was no one who would.

The thought burned like acid. He couldn't remember anyone sticking up for him. Ever. Not even his big brother.

Yet what this woman had just offered was a way to get something he'd just about given up hope of having.

"How much are you paying?" he asked, his voice tight.

The caution in Lindsey's expression was echoed in her voice as she named two separate figures, one for each project. "Are those amounts all right with you?"

Cal didn't answer. Not right away. He simply sat there, his eyes hard on her face and his jaw clenched, while he tried to figure out how someone who looked so soft could hit so hard. One moment, the soothing, seductive tones of her voice had elicited thoughts of midnight whispers in a darkened bedroom. The next, she'd quietly resurrected memories he'd long ago chosen to bury, making him feel exposed, vulnerable. Those were feelings he didn't appreciate at all.

But he needed that money. The figures she'd named were more than he could earn tending bar in a year, and he was getting tired of chasing all over the state for another construction crew to join. The thought of going back to Leesburg put a knot the size of a brick in his gut, but there was something he'd wanted for a long time now. And what she'd just offered could easily help him get it.

"It'll do," he conceded, an unwelcome hint of uncertainty battling his harsher emotions. "Where's this store of yours?"

Had it not been for that uncertainty, the terseness of his question would have compounded the second thoughts plaguing Lindsey about what she was doing. But that hint of vulnerability, spare though it had been, was enough to confirm what she already suspected.

It would be a risk for Cal to go back to Leesburg. He hadn't said a word about it, but it was clear from his reaction a moment ago that the thought of seeing Logan was what had held him back just now. Lindsey knew all about emotional risks, and about how a person's sense of self and security could be devastated when those risks didn't pay off. That was why she couldn't fault his hesitance or his defensiveness—even though she had no idea what had happened between the brothers.

Uneasy with the empathy she felt, she dug through her purse for her billfold, then placed a dollar on the table for her tea and slid her business card across to Cal. "I'm in the old Merchants' Building on the south side of the town square. I'd appreciate it if you'd call me as soon as you can start."

He barely glanced at the card before slipping it in the pocket of his T-shirt. "How soon do want me?"

"As soon as you can make it."

"How's tomorrow?"

Lindsey's eyebrows rose in surprise. He was obviously a man who didn't put things off once he'd made up his mind. "That would be terrific. But what about your job here?"

"Joe's got other bartenders." None were as big as he was, though. That was why Joe scheduled him so often. "I'll work my shift tomorrow and get down there around seven tomorrow night. That'll give me an early start the next morning."

That suited her fine. She would have told him that, too, had he not scowled at his watch just then—which reminded her to check her own.

It was a two-hour drive back to Leesburg. With a grimace, she realized she was supposed to be at her nephew's basketball game in an hour and a half.

Preoccupied now with wondering if she should call her sister and tell her she'd be late, or just show up late as usual, she was halfway to the door when she remembered that the game wasn't tonight after all. It was tomorrow night—which meant Cal would need a key.

She hadn't realized that Cal was so close. One moment, her attention was on her keys as she started to remove one from the ring. The next, she had turned, the keys were clattering on the floor and she was flat against a wall of rock-solid chest.

He caught her by the arms to keep her from falling back. But she didn't quite hear what he said. It was probably just as well. His tone hadn't been complimentary.

The apology that sprang to her lips died in place when she looked up.

She would have been better off if she'd fallen. In the space of a heartbeat, she'd become aware of the heat of his hands seeping into her and the quick curiosity in his eyes as they narrowed on her face. Specifically, on her mouth. Through the soft cotton of his shirt, she felt the steady thud of his heart.

A gentleman would have set her back. And he did. But Lindsey swore she felt his fingers tighten as if he intended to draw her forward—just before he sucked in a deep breath and stepped away.

A moment later, he'd picked up the keys from the scuffed linoleum. Lifting her hand, he folded them into her palm.

"You dropped these," he said in a tone so bland that one of the customers at the counter chuckled.

Lindsey ignored the men at the counter. She couldn't see them anyway. Not with Cal's body blocking her view.

Her quiet "Thank you" wasn't as even as she would have liked. Annoyed with herself, she calmly straightened her shoulders. "You'll need a key," she told him, trying to pull the ring apart. "I won't be there when you arrive, so you can let yourself in to the apartment."

She was shaking. It was unnerving enough that he'd managed to scramble her senses simply by holding her long enough to make sure she had her footing. It was even more unsettling to have his effect on her be so... visible.

Without his saying a word, his hand covered hers. Strong, and maddeningly steady.

"It's the gold one," she said, thinking how sore his knuckles looked. "I'm usually in the shop by eight, so just let yourself in and I'll catch you when I get there."

"Is the old Feed and Hardware still there?"

She said it was, certain from his decidedly businesslike tone that he'd asked because that was where he would buy the lumber and supplies he'd need.

"What about Arnstadt's?"

Arnstadt's was the local drugstore. She told him that was still there, too, though she wasn't quite so certain why he'd asked about it. In the moments before he pocketed the key and handed her back the rest of them, she knew only that hiring Logan's brother might not have been such a hot idea after all.

It didn't take long for her to discover she wasn't the only person in Leesburg of that opinion.

Chapter Two

"How are you ever going to get caught up if you start remodeling now?" asked Louella Perkins. Bangle bracelets jangling, she snapped a lid on Lindsey's coffee-to-go and set it next to the cash register. "You never have time to do anything fun as it is."

"Fun?" Lindsey grinned. "You mean ogling cowboys and giggling with the girls out at Greasewood Flats?"

"Don't give me any grief about Greasewood," Louella muttered. "I know it had a reputation for a while. But it's calmed down. You ought to try it again. I hear there's a real cute fiddler in the band they've got playing there next weekend."

"I can't. You just said I don't have any time as it is."

Wiping her hands on the apron covering her peppermint-striped uniform, Louella pursed her bright-coral lips. Had it not been for the smile she was suppressing, she might almost have looked annoyed. She'd been trying to fix Lindsey up for the past three years. A person would have thought she'd given up by now.

"I know that's what I said. And with your niece not working for you anymore, and that new girl you hired home with a sick little one, you're only going to get further behind on your orders. Shouldn't you wait till the timing is more convenient?"

Even as she posed the question, Louella hit a button on the cash register. She never failed to offer the latest gossip, a willing ear or an opinion with whatever she served friend or customer. This morning, business being slow now that the shingle-mill rush was over, she'd been ready with all three.

Although all Lindsey was interested in was her coffee, her usual, easy smile was in place when she handed over a dollar bill. "I've given up on ever finding a convenient time," she admitted, rather wishing that Erin, her niece, hadn't become so involved in school activities that she couldn't work for her anymore. Camille was good. She just wasn't as reliable as Erin had turned out to be. "I've needed more space since the day I bought that shop. Once I get the wall knocked out between it and the space next door, I'll have all the room I need."

"Along with all the dust and noise and inconvenience of working in the middle of a remodeling project," Louella helpfully reminded.

A vision of tarps covering racks of clothing and motes of sawdust swirling over her floors immediately replaced the image of updated merchandise displays and space for the specialty items Lindsey designed. Refusing to think about how disruptive the project would be until after she'd had her coffee, Lindsey muttered, "Except for that," and automatically dropped the change she received into the charity jar by the register.

"So, who'd you hire?" Louella wanted to know before Lindsey could make her escape. "That fellow from over in Lownsdale Essie told you about?"

The odd thump of Lindsey's heart coincided with the ping of a bell. The cook had an order ready. Presumably for the two elderly "regulars" sharing a newspaper at the opposite end of the café's flamingo-pink counter.

"Ah...no." Coffee in hand, Lindsey edged toward the swinging glass door that opened onto the street. At eight o'clock in the morning, there wasn't yet much traffic on the tree-lined, two-lane thoroughfare. But, then, in this sleepy little town, there seldom was. "I got Logan's brother. Cal."

The waitress, who was a prominent member of the local grapevine, had already turned to pick up the order from the service window above the grill. When she turned back, she had a plate of pancakes and sausage links steaming in one hand, a plate of grits and eggs in the other and a frown on her face that did nothing to alleviate the sense of unease Lindsey had been dealing with ever since she'd left Austin yesterday.

"Cal Whitaker?"

At the sound of the bell, both the men at the counter had glanced up. Now they, too, were frowning.

Herb Albrecht, the more senior of the two gentlemen, directed his bulldog scowl at Louella. Not because she had his breakfast and wasn't serving it, but because, being hard of hearing, he hadn't caught what was being said until Louella had moved closer.

"What about Cal Whitaker?" he demanded in a voice as rusty as the old iron bench he and his cronies routinely occupied outside the barbershop, weather permitting.

"Lindsey hired him." With a nod, the waitress indicated the slender young woman standing at the far end of the counter. "To remodel the Country Boutique."

Herb leaned over the counter to squint through his spectacles at Lindsey. "You're that new gal, aren't you? The one that started up the chamber of commerce?"

"That's her sister," the man next to him muttered. "Samantha is her name. She's the short one that married Logan Whitaker. This here's the gal who bought May Bradley's dress shop a couple of years back."

Herb's squint deepened as his gaze returned to Lindsey. "You hired that troublemaker? Ain't he the one who went to jail?"

"That was the youngest one," his companion snapped, sounding as if he wished Herb would keep his facts straight. "And he didn't go to jail. As I recall, Logan got the judge to send that one into the army or some such thing. Caleb was the middle boy."

Keeping his frown in place, though most of it was hidden by his bushy gray beard, the man everyone knew simply as "Gramps" glanced down the counter himself to Lindsey. "What did you go and hire him for, miss? Don't you know his kind ain't nothing but trouble?"

"His kind?" Lindsey repeated, as unprepared for the men's reactions as she'd been for Cal himself when she'd met him yesterday. "I'm not sure what you mean."

"I mean," Gramps explained, quite patiently, "that he's not from what you'd call quality stock. There's a saying about a bull being only as good as his sire that I'd keep in mind if I were you. His daddy was as mean a drunk as they come. From what I hear, Cal grew up to be just the same. Can't tell you how many times the sheriff busted up a fight with the RW's cowhands when they'd come into town after they'd been drinking. They aren't the same bunch Logan has working for him now. But back then, that middle boy would be right there with 'em, already looking like he'd been caught in a tangle before they even arrived.

"Except for Logan and his boy," Gramps qualified, possibly because he remembered her relationship to the man, "I can't say much to recommend any Whitaker. Logan might be a bit of a loner, but at least he knows about honoring his responsibilities."

"It's for sure the one you're talking about doesn't," Herb piped in. "Fact is, I wouldn't be surprised if he doesn't show up at all."

On that point, Gramps agreed. "Even if he does," he went on, "there's the possibility he won't finish what he starts. That's a trait of folks who don't think about no one but themselves, you know. Nothing is important to 'em but what they want."

The certainty in Gramps's expression only added to the apprehension Lindsey had been struggling with. Yet, given that Cal Whitaker had most definitely not been thinking of himself when he had rescued her from the creeps outside Papa Joe's yesterday, she had no choice but to take exception to Gramps's conclusion.

"I'm sure you must have reasons for what you say," she conceded, not sure if it was caution or challenge stiffening her back. "But when I met him he seemed . . ." Defiant? Difficult? Dangerous? "All right," she lamely concluded.

"He might have been on his best behavior."

She didn't think so. "Would you mind telling me why you feel the way you do?"

He didn't seem to mind at all. In fact, if the way he straightened his stooped shoulders was any indication, he was quite pleased to share the reason for his rationale.

"I don't know if Herb here remembers," he began, motioning to the man whose gnarled hands were folded very prayerlike and pious on the counter, "but I recall that Roy over at the gas station gave the boy a job pumping gas a few years back. That was before Roy's daughter married Glen and Glen took over the place," he added to Herb, as if to prompt his friend's memory.

"Anyway," he went on after the gray head next to him started bobbing in confirmation, "Roy's pa got sick and he had to take him down to the hospital in San Antonio. Roy left Cal to close up that night and open for him the next day. But the boy got bored and took off without locking up and never came back the next morning, either. When Glen got back that night, he found the place had been sitting wide open all that time just begging to be robbed."

Herb gave a final nod. "Boy had no sense of responsibility."

"Did pretty much the same thing over at the shingle mill, too," Gramps added. "Saw that firsthand, since he was on swing shift, same as me. He didn't walk off like he did at the gas station. But he only worked three days and quit. Couldn't stick with anything."

From what Lindsey had heard, it had to be at least ten years since Gramps had retired from the mill. "How long ago was this?"

He scratched at his iron-gray beard, then shrugged as if the actual number of years didn't really matter. "I don't know for sure. He might have still been in high school. Must have been," he decided, ruminating a little more. "It was before his old man died."

"Then you're talking about something that happened sixteen or seventeen years ago." Cal was thirty-four, seven years older than her. She had discovered that the day of

Sam's wedding, when Logan had put Sam's name next to his on the family tree in his mother's Bible. "Have you seen him since?"

"Can't say that I have." He turned to the man beside him. "You?"

"Nope."

Lindsey glanced from one man to the other, wondering how they could dismiss the impact seventeen years would have on a life. "A person can change considerably in all that time."

Herb snorted.

Gramps wasn't quite so concise with his response. He didn't exactly scoff at the concept, but the way he shook his head at her did indicate he thought her a little naive for a city girl.

"Never known one that changed that much. But you believe what you want. All I know is that if I hired him to do something for me, I wouldn't go paying him without seeing his work first."

Having spoken his piece, he turned his attention to the waitress busily watching them both. "You going to give me them grits, honey, or are you waiting for 'em to sprout? I'm not getting any younger sitting here, you know."

Looking as if a fire had just been lit beneath her, Louella sprang to attention and slid the steaming plate in front of him. The pancakes were placed in front of Herb, who was muttering about not needing any riffraff in town. Moments later, having refilled the men's coffee and dropped the pot back on the burner on her way down the counter, she scooted over to where Lindsey was contemplating the steam vent in the lid on her coffee cup.

Because Lindsey refused to subject her taste buds to her own coffee any more often than necessary, she usually grabbed her morning dose of caffeine either at the café or at the bakery next door to her shop. This morning she wished she'd opted for the bakery, instead. Essie, its owner, would have been too busy this time of day for anything other than a quick "Good morning." Now, between Louella and the two old coots critiquing their breakfasts, news of her having hired Cal would be all over town by noon. Judging from Herb's and Gramps's reaction, that news would not be well received.

With a glance toward her customers, Louella motioned Lindsey into the tiny alcove by the swinging kitchen door. Though they were out of earshot, the waitress lowered her voice to a near whisper. "I take it you don't know very much about Cal?"

"Not really. No," Lindsey amended, since that was closer to the truth. "All I think I've ever heard anyone say is that he was the one who flattened the side of the old fruit stand out on the highway with his truck."

"Your sister has never said anything about him?"

Lindsey shook her head, her misgivings growing when she considered that Sam didn't even know what she'd done. Yet. She wouldn't think about her oldest sister's reaction to her decision just now, though. With Sam at a meeting in Austin until the day after tomorrow, she had plenty of time to worry about how she'd break the news to her—provided she got to her before someone else did.

"I was a couple of years ahead of him in school."

"You knew him?"

The coral beads in Louella's dangling earrings danced as she gave her head a shake. "Not really. I just knew him from around school. But I never talked to him. My little brother knew him, though," she added, now that she thought about it. "Jack had wood shop with him. I remember because Jack made Mom this pretty carved jewelry box, but nobody believed he'd made it 'cause Jack was all thumbs and the box was so perfect. He finally admitted that Cal had helped him with it. But it wasn't like they were friends or anything," she hurried to qualify. "I don't think Cal had any friends. The only person I ever really saw him with was his little brother. He was real belligerent. Real standoffish.

"I'm not saying he's still like that," she had to add, not wanting to seem as narrow-minded as the men bickering over their breakfast. "I mean, I agree with you that people can change. But what if that change is for the worse?"

It looked as if there was something more Louella wanted to say. But she was needed back at the counter. Her customers were arguing over whether grits contained cholesterol. Doc Weger had apparently told Gramps he was supposed to watch his.

Since neither man knew for sure, Herb wanted Louella to check the nutrition label on the can the lye-soaked corn had come in—which meant whatever else she had to say would have to wait. That was fine with Lindsey. It wasn't at all like Louella to warn her away from a man, and Lindsey had already heard enough to put a knot the size of a lemon in her stomach.

That knot grew to the size of a Texas grapefruit over the course of the day. Gossip about who Lindsey had hired started with a buzz around ten o'clock that morning and had become the topic of conversation by the time she flipped the sign on the Country Boutique's front door to Closed at five o'clock that afternoon. With few exceptions, all the women who had stopped in to browse the racks of the only exclusively women's shop for miles had wanted to know if what they'd heard was true. Many had an incident to share, most involving some scrape Cal had allegedly gotten into, or recalling how he wouldn't show up

for school for days at a time. That he'd managed to grad-
uate at all was nothing short of a miracle. At least, that was
what she heard from Muriel Jennings, who taught En-
glish and history at the high school, and had had all the
Whitakers in her class at one time or another.

Muriel had come in with Rita Brunnell, who worked
part-time at the drugstore. Although Rita had never had
anything to do with Cal personally, she'd added her two
cents' worth by informing Lindsey that she'd definitely
heard all about him, and that she simply couldn't believe
Lindsey had sought him out. But those who knew Lindsey best were more willing to cut her a little slack where Cal
was concerned. After all, she couldn't possibly have known
how bad his reputation had become before he'd disappeared following graduation. Lindsey was still something
of a newcomer to Leesburg herself. At least she was by the
standards of a community that counted longevity in de-
cades. Some families had no fewer than three generations
living in and around the picturesque little town. Having
been there for only three years herself, she was still very
much the new kid on the block.

What her friends didn't know was that Lindsey, who
had worked so hard to fit into their small, tightly knit
community, had been something of a rebel herself as a
teenager. As much as she could have been with a navy
colonel for a father and two older sisters riding herd on
her, anyway. She knew what it was to want to break free
and test one's own wings. She'd had the hangover from
hell at the tender age of sixteen to prove it, too. Along with
what had to be the longest grounding on record for sneak-
ing out her bedroom window to TP the car of the creep
who'd dumped her friend two days before the biggest
dance of the year.

In the overall scheme of things, her transgressions were hardly court-martial quality. Not the way deserting a post would have been—which was what Cal had done when he'd purportedly ditched his job at the gas station. But Lindsey could certainly understand how a person could get into a little trouble. Not that she condoned fighting or shirking one's responsibilities. It was just that there was something missing from the accounts of his misdeeds.

I just happen to have a problem with guys who pick on people weaker than themselves.

Pulling herself back to her task, she pinned another section of fabric to the T-shirt she was appliquéing. She didn't know why she could still hear his words so clearly; the bitterness in them, the deep-seated resentment. But she hadn't been able to forget them. Or the look in his eyes. Something about the fierceness of that statement—about him—just didn't quite fit with the picture the townspeople were painting.

Or maybe it fit all too well.

The thought was unsettling. Even more so was her next thought. She'd seen a hint of that same resentment in Cal's eyes when she'd mentioned Logan.

Shaking off the discomfiting realization, she smoothed out a patch of lace. She couldn't imagine how the man her sister had married could be responsible for the animosity Cal harbored. Logan was a good man. Her sister wouldn't have married him otherwise. What she was going to do, Lindsey told herself, flipping on the tape player above her worktable, was turn her attention to more immediate concerns. And what concerned her most at the moment, was how people were going to react to the rather rebellious-looking man she had hired.

She only hoped she hadn't invited any real trouble by asking him here.

She was still hoping that when, two hours and four lace-and-denim-embellished shirts later, she heard the slam of a truck door—and the heavy thud of boots on the outside steps that led to the apartment upstairs.

The volume on the tape player was lower than usual, the bluesy notes of a sax barely audible over the hum of her sewing machine. Even then, preoccupied as she was, it took a moment before the muffled noises registered. When they did, she closed her eyes and sucked in a deep, steadying breath.

Herb had been wrong. Cal had shown up.

The back of the old two-story building was as dark as pitch, a circumstance that made it nearly impossible for Cal to see once he was halfway up the stairs. With the moon obscured by clouds, the only light was the patch from the multipaned window below him. For all the good it did.

The least she could have done was turn on a light.

Already feeling far less than welcome, Cal headed back down the narrow wooden steps. He'd caught a glimpse of Lindsey through that window moments ago. She'd been sitting with her head bent, her back to him and her hair shining softly in the overhead lights. When he reached the bottom step and glanced toward the window now, all he could see was a sewing machine and a wall covered with bolts of cloth, ribbons, lace and stacks of some sort of garment in various stages of assembly.

When she'd said she owned a clothing store, it hadn't occurred to him that she'd actually make some of what she sold. As polished and pretty as she'd looked, he'd thought her more the type of woman whose husband had bought her the store to give her something to do. She hadn't been wearing a ring, though. Thinking about it now, she sounded pretty independent, too.

The thought was shrugged off as he kept on going. He didn't knock on the door next to the window, which he supposed he should have done to let her know he was here. In no mood to talk to her, to anyone, he headed straight back to his truck and yanked open the driver's-side door.

He'd just reached inside to turn on the headlights, when the light next to one of two back doors came on. An instant later, that door swung inward, and the woman he hadn't decided if he should bless or curse appeared at the threshold.

She stood with one hand on the knob, her head cocked. All Cal noticed was her hesitation, and the wariness in her eyes when her glance moved from the low ponytail covering the collar of his worn leather jacket to the toes of his harness boots.

The muscles in his jaw jerked. Looking away before she could, he told himself he might as well get used to seeing that sort of guardedness around here. He'd received the same reaction ten minutes ago from the owner of the steak house out on the highway. Thelma, who'd looked ninety the last time he'd seen her and hadn't changed by a wiry gray hair since, had squinted at him for a full ten seconds before flatly announcing that she'd heard he was coming back.

That was all she'd said, but the moment she'd spoken, heads had turned fast enough to snap necks. Hearing the quick murmur that had spread through the place, he'd suddenly lost his appetite. Instead of dinner, he'd bought a local paper from the stack by the cash register, making it look as if that was all he'd come in for, and left.

Hating that this woman was eyeing him with that same caution, when she didn't even know him, hating even more that the means to his goal had to be in this jerkwater town, he slammed the truck door and picked up the duffel he'd dropped beside it. He'd tried everything short of driving backward to avoid the tension that had come just thinking of being back in this place. But that tension had built with every mile closer he'd come. Now he could feel the tightness coiling every muscle in his body, and the last thing he felt like doing was making polite conversation with a woman who looked as if she was about to be swallowed whole. If he still drank, he'd head for the nearest tavern. He was unwilling to allow this place that much control over him. Right now he just wanted to get some sleep.

He'd just cleared the front of his truck, when he glanced up to where Lindsey stood in the light of the doorway. His stride slowed. There was no wariness in her expression at all now, nothing of the caution he'd imagined he would see. Just a surprisingly open smile.

"Hi," she said, pushing one hand into the pocket of the loose dress that hung in a straight line from shoulder to midcalf. "Sorry about the dark. I didn't realize how late it was getting or I'd have turned on the lights."

He didn't make transitions quite so easily. His expression remained as hard as flint. "I didn't think you were going to be here."

"Neither did I. That's why I gave you that." Letting her fingers slide from the knob, she pointed toward the key in his hand. "My nephew's game was canceled because half the team is out with the flu, so I stayed to get caught up."

"Don't let me disturb you."

She was about to tell him he wasn't. But it was a lie she couldn't quite manage. He *did* disturb her, though not the way he'd meant. She could feel the tension snaking from his big body, taunting her, demanding a response. Forcing her eyes from the death grip he had on his bag to the unyielding and defensive set of his jaw, she had the feeling she knew why he seemed so tense, too. She didn't doubt for a moment that he would have been happier had she not been there, but it wasn't that. It was this town.

There was an edginess about him that was as unsettling as it was familiar. Not only because she'd sensed that same disquiet in him when they'd talked about his coming here yesterday. It was familiar to her because she'd experienced that same uneasiness herself, that feeling of being totally out of place. She'd felt that way every time her father had been transferred to yet another base and she'd had to struggle along with her sisters all over again to make new friends. To fit in. To be accepted.

It was that same feeling she sensed in him now. Of being in a place where he didn't feel he belonged.

She didn't have to know why he felt that way to sympathize with him. She only knew she wouldn't wish that awful feeling on another living soul. "I'm glad I stayed," she told him, hoping to relieve what she could of his discomfort. "I know you aren't starting until morning, but my plans are right inside. If you'd like to look at them."

Cal started to shake his head, to tell her he just wanted to get his truck unloaded and crash for the night. At least, that was what he'd intended to do before he saw the compassion in her quiet smile.

"Yeah," he muttered, unwillingly drawn by that soft expression. Faced with an evening with nothing other than his dark thoughts for company, he decided studying the plans didn't seem like such a bad idea. "If they're handy, I'll take them upstairs with me."

"Come on in, then. I'll get them." She backed up, only to stop before she turned. Her head tilted slightly. "How's your lip?"

He hadn't expected the question. Or the concern.

"Better," he mumbled, wondering if she had any idea what it did to a man to have a woman look at his mouth as if she wanted to reach out and touch the tender flesh.

Her glance fell to his hand. More specifically, the bruises across his knuckles. But instead of asking about them, she only gave him a faint little smile that did extraordinary things to the nerves at the base of his spine, and stepped inside.

He watched her turn, the fluid motion drawing his eyes to where her casual denim dress swayed against her long legs as she moved away. He'd seen that shapeless style on other women and given it no thought whatsoever. He'd have given it no thought now, if he hadn't known how firm and slender she was beneath that concealing fabric.

He allowed his thoughts to get no further than that. It was going to be a rough night as it was without remembering how her body had felt against his. Not that he'd been able to forget.

Needing to concentrate on something else, he dropped his duffel inside the workroom and closed the door. The soft scent of gardenia filling the room didn't help his efforts at all. That scent was the same essence she had worn yesterday. It had sent a jolt of pure heat straight to his groin when he'd inhaled it.

The enticing fragrance, innocently seductive, seemed to be coming from the small lace sacks of petals, leaves and buds someone had assembled on one of the worktables on the far side of the room. The table next to it held pieces of fabric and the sewing machine he'd seen her at earlier.

"When did you buy this store?" he asked, thinking it safer to consider the changes in the town rather than the changes taking place in his body.

"A couple of years ago." A bolt of cloth lay across the top of a poppy-red metal file cabinet. After propping it next to a headless mannequin, she began rummaging through a stack of files the bolt had anchored. Organized she was not. "This was May Bradley's shop for nearly thirty years. But I suppose you know that," she added, still digging. "I worked for her for a while, then bought her out when she retired."

"What happened to the appliance store next door?"

"It moved over to Main."

"You must have bought the entire building then, if you're going to go knocking out walls."

Lindsey's quiet "I did" sounded preoccupied. Which was rather how Cal thought she looked.

From where he stood in the middle of the inadequately lit space, he saw a frown flit over the porcelain-smooth skin of her face as she tossed one file aside and reached for another. From the size of the stack, it appeared to him that she hadn't filed so much as a scrap of paper in months.

"I don't know what you noticed coming in," she said, continuing her search, "but I don't think much else has changed since you were here last. Has it?"

He could have sworn she'd been reading his mind. "I doubt it," he muttered, thinking that, as he'd driven down Main Street, it hadn't appeared to him that anything had changed at all. Stores still apparently buttoned down for the night promptly at five o'clock and the sidewalks rolled up right after that. The only activity had been around the Lone Star Tavern. Judging from the half-dozen trucks nosed into the hitching posts in front of it, there hadn't even been that much going on there.

Yet, despite appearances, a few changes had taken place. If nothing else a woman who was far more intriguing than anyone he'd ever known in this town had bought up the dress shop. What he couldn't understand as his restlessness took over and he began prowling the cluttered room was what a woman like her was doing in a place like this to begin with.

"You're not from around here." He made the observation as a simple statement of fact as he picked up a roll of ribbon and set it down again. Her polished voice lacked the drawl that would have identified her as being a native. She sounded like the Midwest. Or maybe California. Her voice, the almost soothing quality of it, had been one of the first things to impress him about her. That and her legs. "Where are you from?"

The metal drawer closed with a solid thud. "Everywhere," she told him, thinking of the dozen military bases her family had lived on before she'd turned eighteen. "Nowhere," she amended, because she'd never lived in any one place long enough to think of it as home.

She glanced over to meet Cal's frown. "New York," she said finally, since that had been her last address before Leesburg and his expression made her think he wanted her to narrow it down.

Lindsey found her plans buried under the order form for belts and purses she'd meant to mail off three days ago. Ready to explain that the renderings were far from architect quality, since she'd drawn them herself, she turned to face him.

Cal had come to a stop by the wall where she stored extra lingerie. But it was the wall intersecting it that had his attention. The one she'd papered with her designs. If the expression on his face was any indication, they were not his cup of cappuccino.

"Some of those are pretty outrageous," she had to admit, certain from his deepening scowl that he found the designs impractical. Between the ruffles on the spring collection she'd proposed for Gianni and the wildly plunging necklines and backs of the evening gowns that had actually been produced under a top designer's label, there wasn't much represented on that wall that would be worn by the average female.

Leather creaked faintly as Cal reached out to lift the edge of a sketch.

With her initials exposed, he turned his apparent disapproval to her. "These are yours."

"I had to make a living somehow."

The lines in his wide brow disappeared. "I wasn't being critical." The paper silently fell back into place. Cal knew zip about women's clothes. Even less about making them. But he recognized the hand of an artist and the sketches looked professional. "Is that what you do?" He motioned toward the sketches. "Make that kind of stuff?"

"Not anymore. A person has to be in Dallas or New York to be a player in high fashion."

"So why aren't you there?"

"Because I'm perfectly happy right here," she returned ever so reasonably. "I'm not setting the industry on fire with my creations, but I've found a niche that allows me to own my own shop in a town I really like." Her shoulders lifted in an elegant shrug. "What more could I want?"

"To be somewhere else," he told her, looking at her as if she were certainly intelligent enough to have figured that one out herself. "Leesburg is the sort of place people move from. Not to."

Lindsey didn't move. She didn't even blink as she held his implacable stare. Yet she retreated from him as surely as if she'd just walked out of the room. "I suppose that depends on what you're looking for. Doesn't it?"

She didn't want an answer. She didn't need one. She was fully aware of how much he disliked what she cared so much about, and the last thing she wanted was to get into an argument with someone she barely knew. She also didn't want him to ask why she felt so strongly about a town she'd never even heard of until she'd driven through it on her way to somewhere else, and how she'd come to settle in such an obscure place. From the intent way he watched her, she had the feeling he'd see right through the decidedly incomplete version of the truth she always offered when asked that question. She simply wasn't up to admitting that, much as she suspected he had done when he'd left Leesburg so long ago, she'd been running away.

She already identified with him far too closely as it was.

"Why don't I show you the apartment?" she offered, wishing he wouldn't look at her as if he could see right through her. "I've put clean linens out and the kitchen has the basics. But one of the burners on the stove doesn't work and the faucet that says Hot is really Cold..."

"I'll figure it out. You don't need to show it to me."

"I don't mind."

"I do."

She tilted her head back, wanting to see his eyes. "Why?" she asked, only to realize that meeting his eyes had been a mistake.

She could see a question in them, his curiosity over her not-so-subtle evasion. She'd halfway expected that. What she hadn't anticipated was the way that curiosity turned to frank appraisal when his glance traveled over her face, down the length of her body, and came back to settle on her mouth.

"I just don't think it's a very good idea, that's why. Just show me where I can store my tools. I don't want to leave them on the truck."

The look in his eyes had left no question about why he didn't want her upstairs. Or maybe the look had been more indicative of what he would have wanted had he gotten her up there alone.

Not sure if she should feel shaken or grateful for his tacit warning, Lindsey pulled her eyes from his and handed him the file she held. She'd intended to explain how to piece the papers together to get the whole picture. Deciding he could figure it out for himself, she strode across the thread-strewn floor and snatched a single key from a wall peg.

She told him he could put his equipment in the empty space next door and unlocked the outside door next to hers so he could go in. The moment that was done, she returned to her workshop to try to accomplish something—anything—while she listened to the sounds of saws and sawhorses and heaven only knew what else being unloaded and set up on the other side of the wall.

It was a half an hour before she saw Cal again. He didn't knock. He just walked into her workroom and picked up the duffel he'd left there.

"You can lock that door now," he told her on his way back out. "What time do you get here in the morning?"

"Eight."

"I'll be here."

"Wait!" she called, stopping him at the door. "Would you answer something before you go? Please?"

He hesitated, but only for an instant, before he turned to face where she sat with a soft-pink shirt wadded in her lap. "What?"

She had to know. Only because she couldn't understand why anyone would be willing to come to a place when it so obviously disturbed him. Unless he'd come to face old ghosts. "Why did you take this job?"

For a moment, she didn't think he was going to answer. He simply stood with his broad shoulders filling the door, his fist clutching his bag and his eyes boring into hers as if he couldn't believe she'd had the nerve to ask such a thing.

"Because there's something I want to buy," he finally said—and left her with the deflated hope she'd harbored that, maybe, he'd come with some thought of seeing his brother.

Chapter Three

Lindsey usually loved mornings. Ever since she'd moved to this place of earth-scented air and wide-open vistas, this place of drawled greetings and people who called her by name when they saw her on the street, she had felt a sense of anticipation with each new dawn. A sort of eagerness that she'd thought she'd lost.

This morning, however, as she hurried along the shadowed path between the bakery and her store, her level of anticipation left a lot to be desired. As for eagerness, she couldn't have managed that one had her life depended on it. She had looked forward to remodeling her shop ever since she'd bought it. She'd spent hours, months, drawing and discarding interior plans for the sales area and her workroom. Once the town had decided to restore itself, she had thrown herself into that with equal fervor, burning the midnight kilowatt night after night while she researched original building plans and authentic alpine facades, drafting her ideas for a place that would attract the tourists the town sought. Now all she could think about was the man she'd hired.

The postman had just told her he'd seen the sheriff in front of her store with Cal about a half an hour ago. He couldn't tell what they'd been discussing, but he'd said Cal had looked madder than a rabid hound.

"You're late."

The disembodied voice, deep and disturbing, came from above her as she cleared the arbor of wisteria rooted at the corner of the modest little building. Glancing past the meandering vine that, come spring, would nearly overtake the back of the structure, Lindsey felt the steam leave her stride.

Cal's dark-blue truck was parked right where he'd left it last night, a few feet from the building's side-by-side back entrances. A weather-grayed stairway angled to the ground between those peeling white doors. Cal himself was sitting on the narrow landing at the top. The rabid hound the postman had compared him to would have looked friendlier than he did.

Already caught off guard, Lindsey watched him give the twig he'd shredded an impatient flick and sent it arcing through the air.

Unconsciously, she tightened her grip on the white sack in her hand. "'Morning," she offered, though the abbreviated greeting had no effect. "I didn't know if you'd be here."

"Why wouldn't I be?"

"I just heard that you and the sheriff had ... a problem."

"And which did you think had happened?" His tone matched the chill in the foggy morning air. "That I'd been arrested, or that I'd split?"

"I didn't know what to think," she quietly admitted, as uncomfortable with his challenge as with the bitterness in it. "I wasn't sure what had happened. I'm still not."

In the face of her logic, Cal said nothing. He simply remained where he was, sitting in the shadow of the eaves with his booted feet planted wide on the warped step below and his hands dangling between his knees. Though it wasn't yet forty degrees outside, he hadn't bothered with his leather jacket. Or any jacket, for that matter. His only concession to the cold was a long-sleeved henley shirt a few shades darker than his faded blue jeans. Even then, he hadn't bothered with the buttons, and the sleeves were shoved to his elbows in pure defiance of the weather. A metal box, tomato red and covered with scratches, sat on the step below his boots. He obviously hadn't put it inside with the rest of his tools last night. The file she'd given him rested on top of it.

"What happened," he finally explained, snapping off another piece of winter-bare wisteria from where it twined down the handrail, "is that the sheriff saw me checking out the exterior of your building. He said it looked to him like I was casing it. Trying to break in," he added, in case she didn't catch his drift.

"Did you tell him what you were doing?"

The glance he sent her was remarkably patient. "What do you think?"

Her expression mirrored his.

"He knew damn well what I was doing," Cal muttered when her silence told him she wasn't into playing guessing games. "It was just a convenient excuse for him to flex his muscles."

"Why would he want to do that?"

Cal snorted, shaking his head. "In case you haven't noticed, the people in this town have a very narrow tolerance for folks they don't regard as being as lily pure as they are. Let's just say he wanted to remind me that I'm not the town's favorite son.'' A withered brown leaf trembled on the bit of vine in his hand. It turned to dust between his fingers. "Where's your car?"

Given the circumstances, now was not the time to point out that his view of the people around here might be just as narrow as theirs. Or to wonder if he'd lumped her into his tidy little generalization. She didn't trust his change of subject. The edge remained in his tone, controlled, like the anger causing it.

"At home," she told him, far more concerned with the fury he was trying to suppress than his interest in her vehicle.

"Are you having trouble with it?"

"No," she returned, puzzled.

"Then why didn't you drive?"

"I live over on the next block. You can see the roof of my house right through there." Lifting her hand, she indicated a maze of skeletal pecan trees in the orchard down the street. On the far side of that block, visible through the branches, was the stone chimney and pitched roof of her little white house. "Unless I have errands to run, I don't usually drive to work. Why?"

"I just thought that might have been why you weren't here when you said you would be."

Cal didn't give Lindsey a chance to say anything else. Wanting only to get to work, he stuffed the file under his arm, snagged his toolbox and jerked himself upright. It didn't matter why she had left him cooling his heels. She was here now. What had happened with the sheriff didn't matter, either. Or so he told himself, much as he'd always done when he'd been accused of yet another transgression by one of the town's good citizens. Had he truly earned his reputation, he'd probably have never survived to leave this place. As it was, there had been times when he'd wondered if he would.

Damp wood creaked in protest as he stalked down the stairs. Prompted by his descent, Lindsey turned to slip her key into the door. It rankled her that the local authority had treated him as if he were still seventeen, but it was hard to feel bad for him when he'd just made it sound as if she'd left him stranded for hours.

The familiar scent of gardenia greeted her when she pushed open the door and walked into the even more familiar clutter. Her workroom always tended to look as if a tornado had whipped through it. But this morning when she flipped on the lights to reveal the colorful chaos and she set her sack on the marginally empty space at the end of the worktable she didn't make her daily vow to get a handle on the mess. She was too aware of the crystal-blue eyes on her back to care.

The metal toolbox jangled when it hit the floor. Following that jarring sound came the heavy thud of the door as Cal closed it. To Lindsey, it felt as if he'd just closed the door on a cage. The room suddenly seemed even smaller than it was. Confining. Inescapable.

"What time do you open?"

"Nine o'clock. I would have been—"

"It would have helped if you'd been here on time," he cut in, as his brooding frown landed on his watch.

The accusation in his tone caught Lindsey with her heavy purple jacket halfway unbuttoned. He was trying to put the incident with the sheriff behind him; to bury it, or accept it as a matter of course. She appreciated the effort. The only problem was that he hadn't moved beyond the anger that had come with it. He'd simply focused that anger on her.

This was the second time he'd mentioned her lack of punctuality.

"What is it you want?" she asked, no longer willing to forgive his brusqueness. She understood his agitation about the sheriff. He had a right to feel it. But she refused to bear the brunt of it. "If it's an apology, that's what I was about to offer. You deserve one. For a couple of reasons. But if you're looking for an argument, you'll have to look someplace else. I'm sorry about what Sheriff Hollis did. As long as he's been sheriff around here, I'm sure he knew exactly who you were. Just as you said. Like everyone else by now, he also had to know why you're here."

Cal had done nothing wrong. Yet he'd been treated as if he had. Therefore she could hardly fault him his anger. She had the feeling, though, that he'd done nothing to help the situation. When she'd asked if he'd explained to the sheriff what he'd been doing, Cal had deliberately skirted her question. At the time she'd thought he was merely baiting her with his cryptic response. Now she couldn't help thinking that he hadn't defended himself to the sheriff at all. He'd merely stood there in defiant silence and let the man think whatever he wanted.

For some reason, Lindsey couldn't help but wonder if he hadn't always been a little like that.

"I'm sorry for what he did," she repeated, feeling rather certain of her suspicion. "But my being here on time wouldn't have prevented what happened. I'm not that late."

Cal didn't move. Confronted with the fact that the events of the morning obviously mattered more than he wanted to admit, he stood with one fist gripping the file and his eyes locked hard on hers.

No stranger to stubbornness herself, Lindsey met his unyielding expression with a respectable imitation of calm.

It looked to her as if Cal must have seen the match as a draw. Something that looked suspiciously like resignation washed some of the hardness from his features.

"If I'd wanted a fight," he told her, the bite leaving his tone, "I could have had one with the sheriff. I'm sure that's what he was hoping for. All I want is to get to work." He placed the file on the table next to the sack. "You hired me to do a job. For that, I need to talk to you about which area you want me to start on, and I need to get some money. It's just that I couldn't do either until you got here."

I wouldn't go paying him until you see his work, Gramps had said.

"For lumber," Cal added, the edge threatening to creep back into his tone with the hesitation that crossed her face. "That's a bearing wall you want torn out. I can't start anything until I've got material for supports. And I'll need a key. I'd just as soon not have to wait around for you to let me in every day.... If you don't mind."

Lindsey felt her own irritation ease up. He hadn't been able to do anything until she'd arrived—except sit and stew over his encounter with the sheriff. She'd only been fifteen minutes behind schedule. Being in a place he didn't want to be in to begin with, that fifteen minutes might well have seemed like an eternity.

"You won't have to wait again. And I'm sorry I was late," she said, because she really had tried to be on time. "I was at the bakery, waiting for fresh coffee." And skirting questions about him, because Essie had seen the strange truck parked out behind their neighboring buildings. She'd pounced on her the moment Lindsey had appeared in front of the pastry case.

Then the postman had shown up.

The sack crackled as she reached inside and extracted two lidded foam cups. She set one within his reach, upset with herself because her hand was trembling, upset with him because he'd caused that reaction.

"There are a couple of muffins in there, too," she told him, determined to get beyond the morning's less than auspicious beginning, "in case you don't want to go over to the café for breakfast." She hesitated, her voice softening. "It can be kind of crowded over there this time of the morning."

His eyes flicked to hers, narrowing with curiosity before darting quickly away. He hadn't expected her to know he had no desire to go to a place where conversation would screech to a halt the minute he set foot inside the door. Or where he wouldn't be able to eat a meal without eyes focused on the back of his neck. But his quiet "Thanks" indicated he was as uncomfortable with her insight as he was with her hospitality.

"About the materials," he reminded her, and watched her turn away.

"You can get whatever you need at the Feed and Hardware," she told him, stuffing her jacket behind a rack of jackets she had no room for out front. "I think you can, anyway. It is the only place around here to buy lumber. Just get whatever you have to have and ask Gil to put it on my account. He's knows I've asked you to help me."

To help me. Not to work for me.

"And if he doesn't have it?" he asked, curious at her choice of words.

"Then I'll give you a check for the rest. Or you can order whatever it is and I'll pay for it. I've never had anything remodeled before, so you'll have to tell me what you need me to do."

She had no idea what sort of items he would require. She could construct a garment out of tissue paper if she had to, but her knowledge of building construction was limited to what could be accomplished using her large fabric shears for a hammer and a knife for a screwdriver. She told him that, too, without apology, and asked how long he thought the job would take. After all, he also had the building to reface and the bandstand to restore, but they could talk about those later.

"Right now," she told him, "I just want to get the inside done so the worst will be over with. I've run out of space out front, but what I really need is more work room. I can barely maneuver in here."

Cal could hardly dispute her last statement. He didn't see how she could find what was here already, much less find space to put more of whatever all it was she created. But what struck him was that her idea of the worst part of the project was the polar opposite of his. As far as he was concerned, working inside the building would be a picnic compared with having his back exposed to the vultures circling the town square.

What struck him, too, was that Lindsey had no compunction whatsoever about him doing the job however he saw fit—and that the scent of her was driving him crazy. She smelled like a summer night. Warm, provocative.

The realization that she trusted him to do right by her had actually managed to ease the tightness in his shoulders. But when she moved in front of him, the fresh fragrance clinging to her hair elicited another sort of tension entirely. That tension made him restlessly aware of the shape of her mouth when she looked up to ask if he wanted to tour the rest of her shop. It also had him sucking in a breath of scented air when, having said he thought that might be a good idea, his glance drifted to the gentle swells of her breasts.

The skin exposed by the vee of the long, coral sweater she wore over her slacks looked satin smooth, and incredibly, invitingly, soft. Her breasts would be that same tawny color, he thought. Or maybe a bit paler, given the faint dusting of freckles that betrayed a certain indulgence in the Texas sun. But it wasn't imagining the texture of her skin that caused the sharp jolt of heat in his gut. It was the thought of how perfectly she would fit in his palms.

The band of silver on her turquoise bracelet caught the light when she slowly raised her hand. Fingers splayed, her palm came to rest just below her throat.

The movement was distinctly protective. So was the look in her eyes when his glance darted back to hers. He'd be a fool to believe she didn't know what he was thinking about. But instead of being encouraged by the awareness that she couldn't keep from her eyes, he was wondering what in the hell he was doing.

He had no business considering anything *but* business with this woman. She was a means to an end, the signature on a paycheck. It didn't matter that he couldn't remember the last time he'd been with a woman. Nor did it matter that something about this particular woman had him feeling as if he were pacing inside a cage. He wasn't about to complicate or jeopardize this job. Even if he was interested in anything beyond a quick tumble between the sheets, her life was square in the middle of a town he had about as much use for as a toothache. As soon as he finished what she'd hired him to do, he would forget this place even existed.

The sharp ring of the telephone pierced the taunting silence. With a start, Lindsey's hand snaked up to cover the pulse already beating a little too erratically at the hollow of her throat.

"Excuse me," she murmured, backing up. Motioning in a wide arc, she offered him as gracious a smile as she could muster. "Go ahead and look around while I get that. The light switch for the front of the store is right on the other side of that curtain."

Yeah, he thought, seeing the relief sweep her features at the reprieve. As soon as he was finished, he'd be out of there. And she'd be more than happy to see him go. She might trust him with her project, but that was about as far as it went. A woman like her—a respectable lady who owned a dress shop in an upright, uptight little town— would have little to do with a man like him.

Lindsey had two telephones in her shop: one out front on the antique jewelry case that served as her sales counter, and a portable model. The base of it was on the rolltop desk in her workroom, but the receiver was, as often as not, buried elsewhere.

Tracking the electronic ring to her sewing machine, Lindsey answered with a deliberately bright "Country Boutique" and watched Cal shove aside the curtain that separated workshop from store. Pale-peach chintz was still swaying to a close behind him when she heard her assistant's voice on the other end of the line.

Mentally crossing her fingers, Lindsey fervently hoped the woman wasn't calling to ask for another day off. She really needed Camille today. Not to help her get caught up on her orders. Not even to help move and cover displays. The task would be a pain, but Lindsey could manage by herself. She needed the divorced young mother to be a buffer between her and the man whose presence threatened her in ways she couldn't begin to define.

But Camille wasn't coming in. Her three-year-old was still home with the flu. Which meant that Lindsey, because she wouldn't open for business today, would be alone with Cal.

Not that being alone with him was something she needed to feel concerned about. Though the man had a definite knack for rattling her composure—deliberately, she was sure—it was only a matter of minutes before it became abundantly clear he had nothing on his mind other than what he'd been hired to do. It was equally apparent that he didn't intend to waste any time doing it.

Within minutes, it also became clear that Cal had probably never before set foot in a women's boutique—though it was impossible to guess his thoughts when she found him frowning at a display of beribboned baskets filled with sachets and socks.

Her merchandise was a collection of the practical, the nostalgic and the feminine, most of it displayed on or in antiques. Many of her customers didn't want to travel to cities to shop, so she carried a little of everything—from everyday wear to wedding gowns, though she usually special-ordered the latter from catalogs for local brides. Tucked throughout the various displays were dozens of tiny treasures: miniature picture frames, floral tea cups, bath soaps, lotions and lace handkerchiefs. There was a charmingly cluttered feel to the place, but unlike her workroom, there was nothing haphazard about the placement of any item.

At least there wasn't before Cal got going. His expression deliberately blank when he looked from Lindsey to the filmy scraps of lace dangling from the drawers of a dresser, he asked her to shove everything inside the drawers and close them so he could move the thing away from the wall. He also wanted her to close up the two antique armoires angled at the corners of the wall he was to remove. Having muscled those into the middle of the room, his brawny frame and work clothes looking decidedly out of place among the laces and ribbons, he turned his attention to measurements, calculations and drawing a couple of diagrams before he headed out the back door—telling her on his way to drape anything she didn't want dust on.

As he passed her, she also heard him mutter something about not understanding why she hadn't draped everything already, since she'd known yesterday that he was coming. But he was talking to himself, not her, so she didn't have to tell him she hadn't done it because she hadn't had the time. Which was the truth. As far as it went. To be totally honest, she would have had to admit she hadn't felt completely confident that he would show up, and she hadn't wanted to do all that work for nothing. But he hadn't asked. And since he didn't break a single, long-legged stride as he headed out to his truck to go to the Feed and Hardware, Lindsey didn't have to say a thing.

Cal spent less than an hour at the hardware store. Lindsey knew that only because she heard the crack and clatter of wood hitting the floor in the vacant space next door when he unloaded his truck. Wanting to make sure he hadn't had a problem with Gil, she stepped out the back door of her workroom to talk to him—only to find herself posing her question to his back when he hefted a stack of long boards to his shoulder and walked right past her.

"Everything was fine," he mumbled tightly, and disappeared inside before she could do much more than wonder why she'd bothered to ask.

Everything was not fine. Lindsey didn't doubt that for a moment. It was also certain that Cal wasn't going to confide why it wasn't so terrific, either.

Ten minutes later he was off for the rest of the lumber he hadn't had room to haul the first time.

Two minutes after that Samantha Whitaker walked in the front door.

"Sam," Lindsey greeted, smiling at her sister across a rounder of blouses as the bell over the door chimed a second time. "I didn't think you were due back until this afternoon."

The door, with its grapevine wreath still shuddering, had just closed behind the petite blonde who'd conquered Leesburg—and its wealthiest, most reclusive rancher—last fall. It had been Lindsey's idea that Sam move to Leesburg after she'd become widowed. She'd been convinced Sam would be the perfect director for Leesburg's chamber of commerce. And she was. What Lindsey had really cared about, however, was that there were now two members of the Hayes family living in the same state.

"I couldn't stand being gone," the newly married mother of three admitted with a self-deprecating smile. "One night away from Logan and the children was enough. The seminar got boring so I came home last night." Taking in the draped and boxed displays, she wrinkled her nose in confusion. "What's going on?"

Light glinted off the gold clip that held Sam's pale hair so sedately at her nape. The style was so... Sam, Lindsey thought. Her eldest sister was always so composed. So together. Both of which Lindsey never had been. Sam was so much more fragile looking, too. She and Annie both were. But, then, they were both petite. Which again Lindsey was not.

Lengthy though the list was, enumerating her short-comings wasn't high on Lindsey's list of priorities at the moment. What was, was that Sam apparently hadn't yet heard about Cal.

The thought came with a certain relief as Lindsey met deep-brown eyes very much like her own.

"Remodeling," she began, opening another one of the plastic sheets Cal had given her. "There's going to be dust all over the place when that wall comes down, so I've got to cover everything. I'll be closed for a few days...until we can hang plastic sheets for a temporary wall while the new side is finished out," she explained, slipping into the par-lance Cal had used. "In the meantime, I'm going to get caught up on my orders."

"That'll be a first. You've been behind on those since I moved here. I can't understand why, but you thrive on be-ing disorganized."

"I do not," Lindsey good-naturedly insisted, thinking it wouldn't have hurt her sister to have a little more faith. "The bandstand is going to be done, too," she went on. "Right after my shop is finished. As much trouble as we were having finding someone to do it, I was afraid we'd never have it finished in time for the Independence Day celebration. Now we will."

A delighted smile lit Sam's face. "Really? That's won-derful! But I thought the guy Essie recommended hadn't done restorations before."

Plastic crackled as Lindsey shook out the sheet and Sam snagged the other end to help. Together they lifted it over the rack.

"He hasn't. And the estimate he gave me was out in the ozone. The shop is doing well, but I could never afford to pay what he wanted. I got someone else."

"Who's that?"

"Logan's brother."

The plastic fell silently in place.

"Oh, Lindsey." Sam's shoulders dropped. "You didn't."

Lindsey hated it when Sam did that. Said "Oh, Lindsey" as if she didn't have the brains God gave a grasshopper. It always made her feel like she was twelve.

"I told you what Jett said, Sam. Remember? You even agreed that we needed someone like Cal because the town can't afford to pay an expert."

"I know what I said," Sam returned with patience. "I also know that when we talked about it, I told you that I wasn't sure it was a very good idea...even if he would agree to it." Which she obviously never dreamed he would do. "I know you mean well, and I appreciate that you're working so hard for the town, but there's so much more to consider here than just getting some carpentry work done."

"You mean Logan."

"Yes, I mean Logan."

"He's part of why I did it," Lindsey countered, holding firm despite her second thoughts. "We both heard him ask Jett if he thought Cal would ever set foot on the ranch again. And we both saw his face when Jett said no. You told me yourself that he misses him."

Something shifted in Sam's eyes—understanding for her sister, compassion for her husband. Frustration that the situation hadn't just been left alone.

"Lindsey. Please," Sam began, rubbing her forehead as if a pain threatened there. "I know what you're trying to do. You've always been the peacemaker in the family. And heaven knows every family needs one. But sometimes there are situations that just can't be resolved."

"Theirs might be if they'd talk about it. They're brothers."

They were family. To Lindsey, that was enough said. For a moment, she thought it was enough for Sam, too. Growing up as they had, Sam, Annie and Lindsey had stuck together like gum to a shoe. That didn't mean they hadn't argued, or taunted, or gone for days in a pout not speaking to the offending sibling. Especially since Lindsey, being eight years younger than Sam and two years younger than Annie, was often being baby-sat and bossed around. What it did mean was that they had always been there for each other, that they were accepted just the way they were.

They just didn't always see eye-to-eye on everything.

Like now.

The way Sam rubbed her forehead didn't bode well for agreement. "I wish it were that simple," she said with a sigh. "But they've been estranged for years. You can't just arbitrarily pull two people together after that long and expect everything to work out. I don't know what the problem is exactly. But it's not just a misunderstanding or an incident that can be explained away."

"I'm sure it isn't just a misunderstanding," Lindsey quietly agreed. She had glimpsed pain beneath Cal's brooding features. The kind of soul-deep hurt a man who appeared to possess little beyond his pride and the tools in his truck would be likely to acknowledge. "You said their mom died when Logan was young, and from what I've heard in the past couple of days, it sounds as if their father was a real peach. From the stories going around about Cal, I have the feeling there wasn't any stability in their lives anywhere."

It came as no surprise to Sam that people had been talking. Gossip was what people did in Leesburg. Like Lindsey, Sam had taken Essie's advice from the very beginning by ignoring half of what she heard and seriously questioning what remained. But there was one thing about talk in a small town that usually proved out. With few exceptions, there was usually a grain of truth at its core.

"You seem to have the same picture I do," Sam conceded, adding what Logan had told her about Ben Whitaker—that he'd been a hard drinker with a hair-trigger temper. Except that he hadn't always been that way. "It was only after their mother died that Logan ever saw his father take a drink," Sam told her. "I guess it got worse as the boys got older."

"Maybe that's why Cal got into all those fights. Maybe some of those fights were with Logan," Lindsey suggested, thinking that could easily have been his way of lashing out at the lack of security or support in his life. Only, that didn't make all that much sense to her. She would have thought that the brothers would have pulled together, leaned on each other. Not drifted apart.

Sam wasn't thinking about Cal.

"You're going to have to tell Logan he's here, Lindsey. He needs to know. To be prepared in case he runs into him when he comes into town. I don't want him hurt."

Though Lindsey couldn't fault Sam's protectiveness, it made her decidedly defensive.

"I don't, either. I don't want either of them hurt," she added, then checked herself because that latter thought shouldn't have been so acute. "It's not as if they're going to suddenly find themselves face-to-face somewhere. Cal already knows Logan only comes into town on Tuesday. He'd have to be deliberately looking for him for them to see each other."

"Do you think that's likely to happen?"

Considering the responses she'd gotten from him thus far, Lindsey could only offer a quiet "No."

Sam looked relieved. Or maybe it was just exasperated. Whatever it was, she spent an inordinate amount of time studying her manicure before she reached for her purse.

"I've got to get to the office."

"Sam..."

"I'll tell him myself, Lindsey. I don't know how he'll react. But I'll tell him."

Lindsey blew out an cxasperated breath of her own. The last thing in the world she wanted was to have her sister upset with her. She hadn't done anything wrong. All she'd done was remove some physical distance between the brothers. It was up to them to close the gap that remained.

"Cal should be back any minute," she said, thinking how useless it would be to say she'd only tried to help. "Do you want to meet him?"

Lindsey had never known Sam to be anything but gracious with strangers. But her sister was also fiercely protective of the people she cared about. Despite the fact that Caleb Whitaker was her brother-in-law, Sam didn't know him from Adam. But she loved his brother. And by staying away for seventeen years, Cal had hurt the man she loved.

"I don't know, Lindscy. I'll have to think about it."

With that, Sam headed for the door and her office on the other side of the square. She didn't offer her usual, breezy "Catch you later" on her way out. She just gave Lindsey a look that said she really wished Lindsey hadn't put her in this position—and that, if it got right down to it, the only side she could be on was Logan's.

If Lindsey hadn't already met the man who was, at that moment, pulling up to her back door, she might very well have felt the same way.

Chapter Four

A Closed sign didn't mean much in a small town. A tap on the window from someone with a familiar face couldn't be ignored. And when people on the outside couldn't see someone they knew was supposed to be inside, they either went to the back door or resorted to the telephone.

Lindsey's had been ringing more than usual all day.

Her present caller was one of her customers, a pleasant enough lady who knew Lindsey was a soft touch for calendars, raffle tickets and the chocolate-almond bars the kids sold to raise money for various school activities. Unfortunately, Lindsey's hope that the woman's call was only to push a fund-raiser was quashed within six seconds of picking up the phone.

"Lindsey?" May Beth began, sounding terribly conspiratorial. "I just heard from Babs that Rita told her Camille is still home with her little one and you're there alone. Are you all right?"

"I'm just fine, May Beth," she assured her, wondering how Rita had known about Camille—unless Dr. Weger had phoned in a prescription for Camille's little girl. Since Rita worked at the pharmacy, she knew to the aspirin who had bought what for which ailment. "Considering the mess this place is in," she qualified, dubiously eyeing her ghostly displays. "I have just about everything covered or boxed up, but I don't know how much longer I've got before the dust starts."

For the past six hours, she'd heard the muffled buzz of Cal's saw as he'd attacked the wall from the vacant space next door, the rip of wallboard being pulled down and the occasional window-rattling bang that told her he'd felled a particularly large chunk. By now he'd surely removed most of the far side of the solid partition that divided her little building in half.

May Beth was glad for her progress. Or so she said. But even as Lindsey listened to the woman explain that the remodeling wasn't what she'd been talking about when she'd asked if she was all right, a crack appeared in the wallboard. The crack grew along what appeared to be a seam. A moment later, a piece of the boutique wall fell in. Followed by another.

Lindsey was now looking across her jewelry display case at bare studs. From beyond those exposed two-by-fours came the sound of heavy boots on cement, the sound fading toward the back door.

It wasn't that newly exposed three-foot gap that broke her train of thought, however. It was May Beth's remark about being alone with "that man" that required Lindsey to stop wondering if Cal had even stopped for lunch.

"I'm perfectly fine," Lindsey told her. "Really," she insisted when the woman offered to bring her children over and keep her company. "I appreciate it but there's no need.

"I'm positive," she added, wondering what people thought was going on in her little shop. "He isn't doing anything but working."

Not so certain that May Beth didn't sound vaguely disappointed with that bit of news, Lindsey promised to call if she got to feeling uncomfortable and needed company. A moment later, having thanked the woman for her concern, she replaced the receiver and blew out a beleaguered breath. As she did, she glanced across the stack of colorful scarves beside her—and saw Cal through the yard-wide opening he'd created in the wall.

He was watching her. He said nothing, though. He simply stood with his legs braced, his broad shoulders filling most of the space and a long black crowbar dangling from his hand. The late-afternoon light filtering through the display window sparked off the bits of dust dancing in the sunbeam. It also caught his features, removing shadows that would have provided an excuse for the darkness clouding his expression.

"That wasn't the first call you've had like that, was it?"

"No," she told him, refusing to insult him by pretending she didn't know what he was talking about. "It wasn't."

"How many have there been?"

"Does it matter?"

"Very little matters to me," he emphasized tightly. "All I want to know is if you're worried about being alone with me. I don't know what all you've heard, but I can guess."

He didn't defend himself by denying his reputation. Or explaining it. But, then, she already had the feeling he thought defending himself would be useless.

Maybe, she thought, it was because he didn't feel anyone would listen.

"I don't believe everything I hear."

A bit of the edge left his voice. "But are you worried?" he insisted, determined to get his answer.

For several very long seconds, the only sounds to disturb the sudden stillness were soft strains of a classical concerto coming from the tape player in the back room. But the music Lindsey always played had lost its soothing qualities. The air seemed to vibrate with the tension radiating from Cal's body as he held her eyes, waiting. It reached toward her, pulling at her midsection, demanding responses she didn't want to feel. Didn't trust.

Yes, she was worried. "No," she told him.

He didn't believe her. But he didn't seem interested in telling her so. Not verbally, anyway. He merely held her glance in a way that made her think he knew it was only her stubbornness offering the assurance, but that he appreciated the assurance anyway.

A moment later, he lifted the crowbar to the wall above his head. His jaw working, he wedged it between the stud and the wallboard.

Iron-hard muscle bunched in his arms, the tendons standing out against his bronzed skin. Sweat stained the underarms of his shirt, and when he stepped through the opening and turned to get better leverage on the crowbar, she saw that same dampness darkening the back of his shirt.

The tremor in her hand slithered to her stomach.

Lindsey's first impulse was to pick up the scarves she needed to fold and finish the task in back. Her second was to root herself right where she was. To leave would be to give credence to all the talk, to allow the rumors and innuendos influence over her. It would also make him believe she felt the way all the others did. That he was still the irresponsible rebel they'd said he'd been. He'd known people were talking, too.

Even as tough as he seemed, and despite his assertion that nothing mattered to him, what he'd overheard had to hurt. Pulling a disappearing act right after she'd told him the talk didn't make any difference to her would only add salt to his wounds.

So Lindsey stayed where she was. And after she finished the scarves, she pulled out her phone book and called the mothers of the kids on the high-school volleyball team to let them know she'd taken over car-pool duty for Peggy Foster until after Peggy had her baby. Lindsey would be driving five of the kids, plus the equipment, over to Dry Creek for their game on Thursday.

As for tonight, Lindsey had promised Sue Albrecht, who taught home economics at the high school and was married to crusty old Herb's grandson, that she'd come by to talk to her about a class Sue wanted her to teach. Prom was coming up in May and several of Sue's students wanted to design their own prom dresses. A meeting with Sue was why Lindsey had to leave at five o'clock, long before Cal was ready to call it quits for the evening.

He didn't even glance at her when she said she had to go. He just gave her a nod and proceeded to jerk down another hunk of wall.

"How late did you plan to work?" she finally asked, thinking he should at least take a break for dinner.

"I hadn't thought about it. Just leave my key on your desk. I'll lock up when I leave."

"Do you want me to bring you anything?"

"Yeah. You can hand me that wedge over there. And there's a roll of duct tape in my toolbox. You can get it for me before you go."

She'd meant food. But she didn't press. The man had a one-track mind. Get in. Get the job done. Get out. The General Sherman approach to task management. Thinking Cal also bore a strong resemblance to Sherman's tank, with that impenetrable armor of his, she considered giving the method a try herself.

Cal had been hard at it when Lindsey left that evening. Arriving at ten minutes after eight the next morning, she found him carting what he'd torn down the day before out to his truck to take to the dump. His schedule was the same the next day, minus the drive to the local landfill. He worked from dawn until well after dusk, leaving only for more materials and, once, to stop by Meier's Market. From what Lindsey could tell, he spent the rest of the time alone in the apartment above her store.

In a way, Lindsey couldn't blame him for not venturing beyond his limited neutral zone. Considering the wide berth the locals were giving him, he'd hardly been made to feel welcome.

That discomfiting thought was warring with thoughts of the conversation she'd had with Sam yesterday, when Lindsey spotted Rita Brunnell with her hands against the boutique's front display window. With the afternoon sun angled as it was, the windows facing the square reflected the bandstand, the trees and the cars parked along the curb, making it difficult to see very far into the store. That was why Lindsey thought nothing of what the thirty-something pharmacy clerk was doing when, crossing the street, she called out to her.

"I'm over here, Rita. I just ran over to the café for a second. Go on in if you want." Fighting the breeze for control of her hair with one hand, Lindsey lifted the carryout container in her other toward her shop. "The door's open."

The woman with the coppery corkscrew curls jerked back so fast, a person would have thought she'd been stuck with a cattle prod.

"Oh, my heavens, Lindsey," Rita gasped. "You scared the daylights out of me." Looking far more embarrassed than startled, she let her hand fall from where it had landed over the embroidered *Arnstadt's Drugstore* on her mint-green tunic. "I was just trying to see how much progress he's—you've," she quickly corrected, "made in there. Louella said he's been working in there for three days straight."

"If you mean Cal," Lindsey replied, wondering why people couldn't refer to him by name, "he has. Why don't you come in and see what he's done? You can check out the new dressing room he's building in back."

"Oh, I'd love to, Lindsey," the woman told her, looking as guilty as sin itself, despite her smile. "But I really don't have time right now, and I wouldn't want to keep you from your lunch." Unable to hold Lindsey's eyes, her glance fell to the wisps of steam escaping the cardboard container. It smelled suspiciously like meat loaf, the café's blue-plate special. "You're obviously running late yourself if you're just now getting around to it."

The meal wasn't for her. Lindsey was not, however, going to mention that to Rita. "It has been hectic lately" was all she said.

"I can only imagine," the woman cooed, ever so sympathetically. "Your sister said she's hardly seen you all week. She was in for shampoo and shaving cream on her lunch hour," she confided. "I believe she's been awfully busy, too. She must be. I asked how her brother-in-law was, but she said she hadn't had time to meet him yet."

That Rita had asked Sam about Cal was not a comforting thought. For a number of reasons. "She has been busy" was all Lindsey allowed.

"I just think that's so odd," the woman continued, oblivious to the guard that had just slipped over Lindsey's normally open expression. "I mean, she's just across the street. Much of the time, anyway. And he's right here. It would only take a moment for her to drop in, one would think."

Rita was clearly fishing. But Lindsey wasn't sure for what. She did know, however, that Sam wouldn't have discussed family with this woman. Whatever she had said to the pharmacy clerk had been minimal at best—which was probably why Rita was here now.

Sam had used the minimalist approach when she'd called last night, too. Only then she'd said plenty.

Logan said it's up to Cal, her sister had told her. *He's not going to push him. But any time he wants to talk, he's willing. I just really wish you hadn't done this, Lindsey. If Cal doesn't see him, Logan's just going to be disappointed all over again.*

At least Logan wasn't upset with her. As unhappy as Sam was with her, she'd also made a point of mentioning that.

"I could have sworn I saw her over here just a few days ago," Rita was saying. "You'd have thought she'd have run into him then."

"That was probably the day he was buying lumber," Lindsey returned, determined to treat the matter as insignificantly as her sister undoubtedly had. Thinking Rita must spend her entire day with her head cranked toward the drugstore window, she offered a bland smile. "Would you like to meet him?" she asked, because she knew Rita never had.

From the way Rita's eyes widened at the suggestion, a person would have thought Lindsey had just asked her to disrobe in public. Shock had her stammering, "Me? Oh, well, I . . . well, no. Why would I?"

"Didn't you say you'd asked Sam how he was?"

A hint of pink crept up from her white collar. "Well . . . yes."

"If you met him, you could see for yourself."

Though Lindsey's logic was as reasonable as her tone, she knew that was not at all what the woman wanted. Watching Rita fumble for another excuse while her flush deepened, she also now understood what Rita had been doing looking through the window. She hadn't been checking out the progress of the shop or trying to see if Lindsey was inside. She'd been trying to see Cal.

As obvious as that was, so was the fact that, while Rita had wanted to catch a glimpse of him, she didn't want to be in a position where she might actually have to speak to him.

The burning feeling in Lindsey's chest made no sense at all. When she'd met Cal, he'd been tossing bikers out the door on their ears. The man was as solid as a tree, as big as a small mountain, and he possessed the disposition of a bull elk. Yet she actually felt the need to protect him. Or maybe it was just defend.

"You know, Rita," Lindsey said, her tone dropping the way it tended to do when she was irritated, "Cal isn't doing anything but minding his own business. That's all he's done since he got here. Maybe everybody else should just try doing the same.

"I'll see you later," Lindsey added as the woman's mouth dropped open. Then, before she could add anything else for the woman to repeat, she turned away and reached for the door's brass handle.

* * *

It was about time, Cal thought when the chime over the door sounded and he glanced up to see Lindsey entering the boutique's front door. Through a gap in the milky-white plastic partition he could see her shove her wind-blown hair back from her face, her skin flushed from the cool air. He'd wondered how much longer she'd stand out there visiting.

Unbidden, a knot of heat curled in his stomach.

He'd been watching her for days. Not overtly. Not the way he was now as she stopped, took a deep breath and sent a decidedly uneasy glance in the general area of where he was working. But he'd been aware of her with a constancy that was becoming as frustrating as he found the woman herself.

He now understood why she was always late. She was constantly going in three different directions at once—which ultimately meant she got nowhere. He'd asked her this morning—six hours and fifteen minutes ago, to be exact—to mark where she wanted the electrical outlets for her display lighting. Within a minute of his request, she'd received a call from the woman who supposedly worked for her, and he hadn't seen her since.

Though he'd yet to meet the phantom Camille, he knew from what he'd overheard of conversations from the other side of the plastic wall that the woman's child was no longer sick. Camille was now having car problems, however. Lindsey had therefore spent half an hour on the phone trying to talk the woman into dumping her present heap, which, from the sound of it, had a regular reservation on the rack at the local mechanic's, and buying something more reliable. Right after that, Lindsey had become sidetracked in her workroom—presumably packing up the shirts she'd told Camille she'd take to her to work on. She never had come back to do what he'd asked.

Considering her penchant for disorganization, he supposed it was understandable that she looked a little harried, or hurried, or whatever it was making her frown as she approached the gap in the plastic. Given his present state of frustration with her, he doubted his expression was any more inviting.

The plastic sheet made a brittle rattle as she widened the gap to step through.

"May I suggest something?" he asked the moment she stopped a few feet from where he was working.

The smell of freshly cut wood mingled with the scent of warm male as Lindsey passed behind Cal to set the cardboard container on the end of the sawhorse. "Sure," she told him, the intriguing combination of scents sensitizing already raw nerves. Pushing her fingers through her hair again, she looked around the stripped-out space, seeking the diversion he'd offered. She'd taken all his suggestions so far. "What do you have in mind?"

"Try doing one thing at a time. At least until I get this finished."

Her hand fell, confusion sweeping her features at the forced patience in his voice. "What are you talking about?"

"The way you operate. Try finishing one thing before you start something else, will you?" Looking as if he couldn't understand how she accomplished anything at all, he turned back to the door he was building for the dressing room he'd finished framing last night. "I asked you this morning to mark the outlets. I can't hang drywall until you do."

Beneath his dark T-shirt the muscles in his back bunched and tightened as he lifted another length of wood to a pair of sawhorses. She was holding him up again. He needed to attach the electrical boxes to the studs before the new walls could go up. He'd told her that this morning—while she'd been infusing herself with caffeine because she'd been up half the night working on shirts.

Lindsey closed her eyes, willing calm. "Sorry," she breathed, remembering now what it was she'd meant to do before Essie had come over and asked her if she could help her fix the lining in her coat. "I'll do it right now. Do you want me to mark those things or the drawing?"

She'd motioned toward the studs. "Those things," he muttered. "Use this."

He withdrew a flat carpenter's pencil from the tool belt slung low on his lean hips. He had a black bandanna tied around his forehead to keep his dark hair out of his eyes, and the black T-shirt straining over the muscles of his shoulders had a Harley-Davidson logo on the back. There was no denying he looked forbidding. Or maybe she thought, *forbidden*. Whichever it was, his appearance only increased her agitation. It didn't matter that she found him more compelling than she should. It was the impact his appearance had on everyone else. In a town peopled by conservative men in cowboy boots, western-cut shirts and curl-brimmed hats, Cal's overlong hair and bikerlike clothes were just other reasons for people like Rita to feel uncomfortable about him. In a town like Leesburg, conformity counted.

Reaching for the pencil he held out to her, she couldn't help wondering why he couldn't be just a bit more cooperative. It wasn't that he had to conform. He just didn't have to be so blasted . . . defiant.

She hadn't meant to snatch the pencil away from him. Yet as irritated as she suddenly was with him, all the talk and herself, she didn't seem to have a choice.

That quick irritation wasn't lost on Cal. But before he could do much more than wonder what had happened to cause it, she had swept by and his focus had been diverted. The turtlenecked tunic she wore was the same deep pink as her slim denim skirt—and that skirt was slit from midcalf to midthigh.

It was the flash of leg afforded by that slit that had his attention when she sank to her heels by a stud ten feet away. The woman was at once as modest as she was seductive and the dichotomy, like a few others slowly revealing themselves, intrigued him far more than he liked.

"Done," she told him a couple of minutes later, and held out his pencil.

Meeting her eyes, he quietly studied her face as he took it and slid it into his tool belt. She was upset. She was doing her best to hide it. But Cal could tell she was. He worked too hard to keep his own feelings in check not to be aware of the struggle.

That he'd noticed wasn't the problem. He noticed a lot of things about her. What bothered him was that her agitation shouldn't have made any difference to him one way or the other.

"What about the floor?" he asked to keep from wondering what was bothering her. Even before she'd yanked the pencil from his hand, he'd felt something wasn't right. She hadn't just seemed in her usual hurry when she'd come in. As he thought about it now, she'd been upset even then. "I wanted to talk to you about it yesterday, but every time I tried there was some teenager over there showing you material or trim or something for some prom project."

The light of curiosity suddenly alleviated the perturbed look in her eyes. Telling himself the change shouldn't matter to him so much, he nodded toward the partition.

"Those sheets are made out of plastic. Not cement. Unless I've got power tools running, it's pretty hard not to hear conversations. So, what about the floor?" he continued, curious in spite of himself about why, with all the talk of boyfriends he'd also heard from the girls, he'd yet to hear Lindsey or anyone else mention a man in connection with her. "If you want anything other than the plankboards on it now, you're going to have to order it pretty soon. I don't want to have to wait around for it to get here if whatever you decided on is out of stock."

The man was impossible, she thought as she waded through the wood shavings to retrieve the container she'd brought with her. "You won't have to wait around," she assured him, unable to imagine why she'd felt any sort of need to protect him. "I think I just want it refinished. But I'll get back to you on it. Soon," she promised, and held the container out to him. "Here. It's probably cold by now."

"What's that?"

"Your lunch."

His frown was swift.

Already annoyed, she was in no mood to put up with any of his guff. "You're entitled to breaks," she said. "Take one and eat it."

"I'll eat tonight."

"Fine. But what's supposed to keep you going until then?" She pushed the box to within an inch of his middle. As she did, she unabashedly ran her glance from his broad chest, over his flat abdomen and down his powerful-looking thighs. "A body needs fuel, Whitaker. Especially when it's being pushed the way you're pushing yours. And you need to take a break. I insist on it."

"As my employer?" he asked, his voice deceptively mild.

"Yes."

"You're pulling rank?"

"If I have to."

"What if I don't cooperate?"

If he didn't choose to cooperate, she didn't have a snowball's chance in the Sudan of making him. Refusing to back down from the challenge glittering in his eyes, she chose the one approach he couldn't refute: logic.

"I know you're in a hurry to get this done," she told him, far more sympathetic with his situation than he seemed to realize. "But you won't get anything accomplished if you let yourself get run down or exhaust yourself to the point where you start making mistakes or get careless. Redoing mistakes is only time-consuming, but if you fall off a ladder and break something, you'll just be stuck here that much longer."

Cal didn't appreciate the lecture. He appreciated even less that there wasn't much about her eloquently delivered argument that he could refute. But he'd already worked past the point of hunger, pushing himself as he had yesterday and the day before and making himself ignore the demands of his body. For food, anyway. Two meals a day got him through. The rest of the time he worked. As for those other demands, his formidable control seemed to have taken a hike. Even though he was exhausted, thoughts of this woman reminded him of needs that had him pacing a rut in the floor of the damnably tiny apartment.

"I just want to get this done," he stated, catching a whiff of something hot and delicious.

Lindsey was already aware of the fatigue he refused to admit to. It was in the faint lines around his eyes, lines that were more deeply etched than they had been a few days ago. But now it had entered his voice.

"I know you do," she told him, at a loss as to what drove this man, more confused still by the need she had to understand him. It made no sense to her that he would be willing to come back to this place after all these years, simply because there was something he wanted to buy. She couldn't imagine, either, what that something would be. "But you're not going to get it all done today."

A distinct gnawing sensation in his stomach got the better of his stubbornness. Preferring to think it was the smell of the food and not her concern that made him reach for the box, he muttered, "You don't have to feed me."

He didn't expect her smile. But suddenly it was there, pulling at the corners of her lovely mouth. It was the same easy smile she so readily bestowed on her friends, the one he'd heard so often in her voice and in the lilting laugh that sounded to him like magic about to happen. Magic because sometimes when he heard it, he almost felt like smiling himself. Almost.

"I'd do the same for anyone putting himself in such a precarious position," she told him, the smile fading from her mouth but staying to warm her eyes. "Don't think anything of it."

There was a vague familiarity to her words, but Cal didn't have time to consider why, as she turned at the sound of the chime over the door and disappeared through the gap in the plastic. He considered only that he was hungry and that, since she'd brought him the food, he might as well eat. It felt too foreign, too dangerous, to think she might actually be concerned about him. For a woman's concern—anyone's for that matter—wasn't something with which he was at all familiar.

What he was familiar with were the stares that followed him through Leesburg Feed and Hardware the next morning. He wasn't there but a few minutes. Just long enough to pick up light-switch covers and the paint Lindsey had selected a couple of days ago. But it was long enough to make Cal forget about the fatigue that had settled in his bones. Between the restlessness of his sleep the past several nights and pushing himself as hard as he was, he was beginning to feel as ancient as the two crusty-looking, gray-haired old coots staring him down from either side of the nail barrel.

Cal did his best to ignore them, then turned his attention to the man behind the cluttered counter. Gil, the tobacco-chewing owner, didn't seem to think as much of his presence as the two old men who'd cut their conversation short the moment he'd walked in. But Gil had been dealing with Cal all week, so he wasn't that much of a novelty to him anymore.

"Got Miss Hayes's order all ready to go," Gil told him before Cal could ask. "Just sign here."

"Put these on it, too."

The older man eyed the switch covers Cal tossed onto the counter. Pushing the brim of his seed cap back with his pencil, he gave a shrug—which Cal assumed meant that the man had decided the purchase was in line with what Cal was doing for Lindsey—then reached past the garishly ornate antique cash register for his receipt book. A moment later, having written out a new receipt so he wouldn't have to change the old one, he shoved both slips of paper toward Cal and slapped the pencil down on top of them. "I'll get the paint."

Cal didn't bother to feel offended by the man's strictly business attitude. He preferred it, especially given the comment Gil had greeted him with the first time he'd walked into the eclectic old store.

Gil hadn't said "Hello" or "Heard you were back." He'd just given him a narrow-eyed once-over before informing him that he bore a fair resemblance to his older brother.

Cal hadn't asked if that was good or bad. But the glare he'd sent in the store-owner's direction when he shoved a list across the counter and asked him to fill it for Miss Hayes had put an end to any other remarks along that line that the man had been prepared to make.

"You're the middle one, ain't ya?"

The question had come from over by the nail barrel. Turning to the old men flanking it, Cal tried to decide if he knew who he was. Seventeen years could put a lot of mileage on a face, but there was nothing even vaguely familiar about either the withered-up old guy with the bald head and bulldog scowl or his companion with a beard like a well-used gray mop.

"The middle one what?" he asked, thinking he never had known many of the locals. He'd escaped from the ranch as often as he could, usually in the company of one of the younger ranch hands, who would sneak him beer out the back door of the Lone Star. The only adults he'd known were the few he'd had to deal with directly.

"Whitaker boy," the one with the face like an aging mutt mumbled.

He was thirty-four years old. And they still referred to him as a "boy."

Yeah, Cal thought, his weariness seeming to increase as, refusing to indulge the nosy curiosity, he turned back to the scarred counter. I'm the middle one.

"Not too sociable, is he?" he heard the guy whisper loudly to his pal. "You sure he's the middle one?"

"'Course I'm sure" came the even quieter reply.

"Well, aren't you going to ask him?"

"Ask him what?"

"What we were talking about yesterday. Why he ran off and left Logan to work that ranch all by himself. You said you never could understand how anyone with a lick of responsi—''

"Lord Almighty, Herb," the man with the beard muttered. "Just because you're deaf as a post doesn't mean the rest of the world is."

"I was just reminding you of what you said" came the disgruntled but still loudly whispered reply. "And there's nothing wrong with my hearing. Got new batteries just last week."

"Well, you might try putting them in."

Cal didn't hear the other guy's reply. He tuned the men out, ignoring their bickering much as he tried to ignore the insinuation that he'd run out on some duty he supposedly had to that godforsaken ranch. Or, even more absurdly, some duty he supposedly had to his family. His family had been a joke. And the brother they seemed so sympathetic toward had never given a damn about him.

Those stomach-knotting thoughts had barely surfaced before they were banished. It was hard enough being where he couldn't avoid reminders of the years he'd tried to forget. But he wasn't about to consider the reasons he'd left when he did. That was why Cal forced himself to concentrate on deliberately slowing his breathing, mentally gaining the control he'd lacked in so many ways all those years ago.

He'd done a pretty decent job convincing himself that what he'd heard hadn't mattered at all, by the time Gil reappeared with a heavy carton and set it on the counter. Inside were four separate gallons of paint.

"I've got three more boxes in back," Gil said, panting more than sounded healthy. Pulling a red handkerchief from the back pocket of his jeans, he ran it over his ruddy face. "Might be easier if I just stack 'em on the loading dock and you pick 'em up there."

"Where are they?"

"Back with the feed."

"I'll bring the truck around. Just leave them where they are and point them out to me when I get there. I'll get them myself."

Cal thought Gil looked a little surprised before he mumbled "Obliged" into his handkerchief as he made another swipe. But Cal didn't acknowledge the man's gratitude. He just tucked the forty-pound box beneath his arm and struck out for the door without so much as a glance toward the old goats shaking their heads at him.

He didn't get very far, though, before the guy with the malfunctioning hearing aid piped up again. Cal had only made it to the seed display before he heard the man tell his buddy it was hard to believe that nice little Hayes gal was going around defending him the way she was doing. After all, it was obvious enough from his split lip that he hadn't changed the way she'd said he could have.

Chapter Five

A man could fool the world, but he couldn't fool himself.

Cal couldn't remember where he'd heard that. But he was faced with the truth in that axiom less than five minutes later—which was all the time it took for him to load up the paint, drive the two blocks over and one down to Lindsey's boutique and start unloading the boxes into the unoccupied half of the store. At the Feed and Hardware he'd shoved the boxes into the truck bed instead of sliding them, slammed the tailgate into place instead of just shutting it. Now he was repeating the process, only in reverse.

The tailgate came down with enough force to snap its hinges.

He'd done one hell of an impressive job of deceiving himself. Somehow he'd actually thought he'd gotten past it all; that he'd buried the feelings of helplessness, confusion and anger he'd lived with every day of his life in this place. He'd been eighteen when he'd left. Legally, physically, a man. A man who'd never been a child. But the years between then and now hadn't killed the feelings he'd worked so hard to forget or slaked the memories. Despite himself he remembered feeling defeated every time he'd tried to figure out some way to get himself and his little brother out of the hellhole they'd been raised in after Logan had made his escape and trotted off to college. Those awful feelings had merely lain in wait for him at the county line, ready to jump on, jump in and remind him of how little control he'd once had.

It would have been so easy to leave. To simply pack up his tools and burn rubber all the way back to Austin.

He wouldn't have been at all surprised to learn that was what the people around here might expect him to do. Yet, despite what people thought of him, he'd never once taken the easy way out.

He understood responsibility all too well, and he'd never voluntarily left a job unfinished in his life. He'd been prevented from honoring commitments when he was younger, but there was no one to dictate his choices to him now. He'd told Lindsey he'd remodel her shop and restore the bandstand, and he would keep his word. Other than his tools, his word was the only thing of value to him. And when he left, it would be on his own terms.

The conclusion didn't make him feel any better. Nor did the fact that Lindsey was watching him set the last box down, much harder than necessary, atop one of the others.

The slight arch of her eyebrow was her only comment about his mood. "Is it the right color?"

Cal dragged in a deep breath and turned his back to her. "I guess so," he returned, shoving his hand through his hair while he tried to focus on which piece of wood he wanted from those stacked along an unfinished wall. "The sample taped to the box looks like the color chip you gave me."

Before he'd left, Cal had hung the dressing-room doors. Preferring to use his energy on something more productive than anger, he decided to cut moldings next and turned, wood in hand, just as Lindsey stepped through the gap in the plastic.

Her glance bounced from the boxes he'd stacked in the middle of the room to his less than welcoming expression. He didn't have to be psychic to know she was wondering why he'd been manhandling her paint.

"You didn't eat lunch, did you?" he heard her ask, her tone faintly chiding.

It wasn't a question. Wondering how she knew, wondering, too, if she had any idea what the quiet concern in her eyes did to him, he looked away with a tight "No" and laid the length of molding on the table saw.

He caught the briefest hint of hesitation. "I didn't think you had. You weren't gone long enough to have stopped anywhere. It doesn't look like you brought anything back with you, either."

"I didn't."

"Then you can have mine." She set a paper sack on one of the boxes of paint. As she did, he noticed a small swath of fabric dangling from her hand. It was the same pale-peach color she'd chosen for her walls. "It might improve your mood."

"I doubt it," he muttered, snagging his clear safety glasses from where he'd hung them on the arm of his table saw.

"You didn't consider a thing I said yesterday, did you?"

"Of course I did." Stubbornly he focused only on the second of the two conversations they'd had yesterday afternoon. "You said you wanted to keep the floor the way it was because you like the way it looks. I've considered that and decided to just sand it and seal it. Unless you now have something else in mind."

What she'd actually said was that the rustic look of the plankboard floor gave the place a feeling of warmth and hominess—words he'd never before considered and would probably never hear again without thinking how odd it was that someone who looked as if she belonged on a yacht draped in one of the slinky gowns she'd once designed would be so drawn to such things.

She tipped her head to one side, her expression intent, curious. It was only her tone that held exasperation. "I wasn't talking about the floor. Are you just naturally obtuse or do you have to work at it?"

"It comes naturally. Look," he muttered, curious himself but not wanting to be. "You don't need to take care of me."

"I'm hardly trying to take care of you," she informed him. "But somebody should. If that's what you've been getting by on," she said, pointing to a wadded-up potato-chip bag and candy-bar wrappers in a pile of wood shavings, "you're certainly doing a lousy job of it."

The words were barely out of her mouth before she closed her eyes and drew a deep breath. Feeling every bit as exasperated with herself as she did with him, she mumbled a quick "I'm sorry. That was out of line. I was only trying... I'm sorry," she repeated, deciding to spare him the explanation she wasn't sure she understood herself. "If you'll just let me borrow a screwdriver or something, I'll check that paint to make sure it matches and get out of your way. I won't hold you up anymore."

He should just let her check her paint and go. At least, that was what Cal told himself as he obliged her by pulling the requested item from the tool belt draped over a sawhorse and handing it over. Had she been anyone else, that was exactly what he would have done, too. But the woman who took the tool from him with a quiet ''Thank you'' had never shied from his glance as everyone else did when they saw him. She never let him push her away quite so easily, either. Though heaven knew he'd tried. Now, faced with his latest attempt to keep her at arm's length, he felt the full weight of the chip he carried settle on his shoulder.

She wasn't like the rest of the people there. He'd known that from the moment he'd met her. And while he questioned her taste in towns, it was wrong to treat her as if she had anything to do with its judgmental attitudes.

Cal had set one of the boxes apart from the others. It was next to it that she lowered herself and peeled back the lid of the carton.

Crouching on the opposite side, he reached for the screwdriver when she started to pry at one of the silver lids. ''Let me do that,'' he said, his voice gruff with guilt.

''I can manage.''

''I'm sure you can.''

''Then let me do it. I don't want to keep you from your work.''

''Lindsey.''

It was the first time he'd ever called her by name. And she didn't seem to appreciate the exasperated way he'd uttered it. Or maybe, Cal thought, what she didn't appreciate was the way his hand had closed around hers on the handle. He really couldn't tell what was in her expression when her glance jerked to his. He met her eyes only long enough to realize it hadn't been a good idea to get so close to her. With only the width of the box separating them, he was close enough to see the fine grain of her skin, the exquisite softness of her mouth and the way the delicate bones in her throat moved when she swallowed.

Without a word, she relinquished the yellow-handled screwdriver, her hand slipping slowly from beneath his.

He shouldn't have felt the loss of that contact. But he did. Far too fiercely. Not knowing what to do about it, he busied himself with prying off the lid. ''You can't tell if it'll match this way,'' he said to her, unable to imagine why he suddenly felt the loneliness that usually only came late at night, when there was little he could do to avoid it. ''It'll dry lighter than this.'' He pointed his chin toward a scrap of wood on the floor near her foot. ''Dip that into it.''

He caught the flash of a gold earring as she swept her hair back from her face and reached for the stick. They were surrounded by the scents of construction dust and fresh wood shavings and the new smell of wet paint. That was all he should have noticed. But now all he noticed was the play of light in Lindsey's hair, the scent of summer she wore that never failed to conjure images of how perfectly her body would fit beneath his and the dull ache of loneliness centered in his chest.

Seconds later, Lindsey stood to find a place to lay the stick to dry and Cal was tamping the lid back onto the can.

''Thank you,'' she said again and offered him a smile he knew he didn't deserve.

He hasn't changed the way she said he could have...hard to believe she's been defending him....

The old man's words came back to Cal, words he'd dismissed because he didn't know how to feel about what Lindsey had done.

He still didn't know how he felt about it. Part of him was surprised. Another part felt skeptical. If she'd defended him, certainly it had only been in connection with her reasons for hiring him. But even at that, he didn't like the idea that hiring him had caused difficulties for her.

"No problem," he returned, wondering what he could say to redeem himself for the way he'd been acting. He still considered it a miracle that he hadn't told both of the old men back at the Feed and Hardware to go to hell. But his irritation with them wasn't her problem, and it hadn't been right for him to take his frustrations out on her.

"Look, you didn't need to apologize for what you said before. You're right. I could use a break." He could use some company, too, because at that moment he really didn't want her to leave. But he'd settle for an answer. "Would you explain something to me first, though?"

"If I can," she replied, hesitating.

"Why have you been defending me?"

The question, like his subtle apology, caught Lindsey completely off guard. "Who said I was?"

"Are you saying you haven't been?"

Lindsey opened her mouth. And promptly closed it again.

Cal reached for the sack. Then he reached for her hand.

"Come on," he muttered, pulling her toward the back door. "If I'm going to take a break, you will, too. You can tell me what's going on while I eat."

It was breezy outside. The wind brushed across the knee-high grass in the open lot behind the store, causing it to sway like a field of wheat. The view wasn't much from the steps, which was where they sat, Cal taking the fifth one up and Lindsey the second from the bottom. But it was that field and the sagging barbed-wire fence dividing it from the graveled utility area that had Lindsey's attention when she sat down. It was the same view visible from the apartment upstairs. The only view.

She should have suggested he take his break somewhere else. Someplace that would have given his spirit a break as well as his body. Since she'd asked him to come to this town, she'd felt somewhat obligated to try to make his stay easier. But she didn't know where he'd feel comfortable.

"All I did was suggest that someone mind her own business when she started asking about you," she said, watching him unwrap his sandwich. On the way out, Cal had told her what he'd overheard and asked what would have prompted the old man's remark. Lindsey was certain that it had been her conversation with Rita. From Cal's brief descriptions, she was equally certain that Gramps and Hugh had to be the men he'd encountered. "I don't think that qualifies as defending you."

To Cal, given that she'd made that statement on his behalf, it most certainly did. "Why did you have to suggest it to begin with?"

Lindsey didn't want to answer that. If she did, she'd have to explain about Rita hearing that Sam hadn't met him yet, which would lead to him learning that she and her sibling had differing viewpoints on his presence in Leesburg. The last thing she wanted right now was to create a bigger roadblock between him and Logan. If Cal knew Logan's wife wasn't crazy about his being here, it might seem as if his brother was fortifying his camp. Whatever the brothers' problem was, it didn't need to be further complicated.

There was another reason Lindsey didn't want to answer. If she did, he might ask why she appeared to be leaning toward his side of the fence. That was something she simply couldn't explain. To him or to herself.

Not particularly pleased with that circumstance, Lindsey pulled her attention from the bird resting on the sagging barbed wire and angled her back against the rail post.

Cal sat with his booted feet planted eighteen inches apart above her. Glancing past the hole in the knee of his jeans, she watched a quarter of the sandwich disappear in one bite. The man clearly ate only to refuel.

"Because she was poking her nose where it didn't belong," she finally told him, reducing the situation to its simplest terms. "And it got rid of her. Your lunch was getting cold."

She could feel him pause. "This was yesterday?"

At her nod, Cal's eyebrows drew together, the look in his eyes that of a person whose memory has just been given a nudge. "That's why you were upset when you came in?"

That he'd noticed her state of mind made Lindsey hesitate. Or possibly it was his hint of disbelief that made her pause.

"I happen to have a problem with people who try to make something out of nothing. Okay?" Rita had never even met him. "Especially a person who doesn't believe in giving others a chance."

It was apparent he thought her a tad idealistic. "You ought to realize by now that people around here don't know how to mind their own business," he informed her before the first half of the sandwich became history. "They'll also believe only what they want." Swallowing the bite, he popped the tab on the cola he'd pulled from the sack. "Jumping to conclusions is easier than considering possibilities, and if facts tend to get in the way of what they want to believe, they just ignore them."

He tipped his head back, the strong cords of his neck convulsing as he took a long pull on the soft drink. His position prevented her from seeing his eyes. But she didn't need to. The resentment in his voice spoke volumes.

She wished she hadn't heard it. She wished she could just let it go.

She might as well have wished she could stop breathing. "What was it they ignored about you?"

Her voice had been quiet. Caution mixed with concern.

The can dangled from his fingers when he rested his wrist on his knee. For several very long seconds, he stared at the top of it, concentrating as if he might find the answer to some unfathomable mystery in the contour of the pull tab.

"It doesn't matter," he finally said, something tormented hiding in the depths of his quiet voice. He set the can on the step beside him. Carefully. The way he appeared to have considered her question. "I had a certain reputation when I left and that's all that matters around here now."

It did make a difference. To her. She didn't want it to, but there had been something beneath the hard edge and the attitude that had drawn her from the moment she'd met him, an inherent integrity that bespoke strength and a deep-seated kindness that he either deliberately choked back or had forgotten how to express. It didn't seem anyone saw beneath the tough-guy image but her.

But, then, he didn't let them.

"It doesn't seem you've given them any reason to think otherwise since you've been back."

"Maybe I don't give a damn what they think."

"Maybe," she agreed, wondering how often he had had to tell himself that before he started believing it. "But maybe if you give them a chance, they'd give you one."

The bird on the fence gave a halfhearted chirp and hopped down to peck for night crawlers. From above her came only the sound of silence.

It was followed a moment later by the crackle of the paper bag being wadded into a ball.

"I've got to get back to work," he announced, as if she hadn't said a thing. "Thanks for the sandwich."

At the dismissal, she dropped her glance to his harness boot, planted solidly on the step just above where her elbow rested. She couldn't help thinking that the toes of those heavy boots were as beaten and scarred as his soul—and the soles were as thick as his head.

He was already on his feet when Lindsey looked back up. Recognizing a brick wall when she encountered one, she had just started to rise, too, when his boots hit the bottom step and his hand materialized in front of her.

He had a working man's hands. Hard and calloused. Strong. Just as he was. It made no sense that she would find his grip as reassuring as she did. As compelling. Yet, as he drew her to her feet, she was struck by the same sense of security—that feeling of being utterly safe—that she'd felt when he'd tucked her against his side in front of a biker bar.

Just like that time, the feeling lasted all of a few seconds before she became aware of the heat simmering beneath the surface of their every encounter.

She'd thought he would let her go the moment she was on her feet. He did no such thing. With one easy tug, he brought her to within a foot of his solid body. His eyes grazed her face, then settled on her mouth.

"If anyone starts in on you about me again," he said, looking as if he were wrestling with priorities when he met her eyes. "Send them to me to deal with. From what I've seen, you're well thought of here. There's no sense making things difficult for yourself by defending someone who won't be around that long."

There was a vaguely protective quality to his thoughtfulness. And something that sounded strangely like a warning. But the determination in his eyes caused her to overlook both, along with the heat where his thumb brushed her palm. "I don't always do things just because they make sense."

He couldn't dispute that. "I mean it, Lindsey."

"Could you please say my name without growling it?"

"Would you please not be so damn stubborn? I'm trying to help you out here."

"Lindsey?" called a decidedly concerned female voice. "Is everything all right?"

At the sound of that voice, Cal felt Lindsey pull back. Her hand slipped from his, her skin feeling impossibly smooth where it grazed the callouses at the base of his fingers. Then he saw her fingers curl into her palm, and the tension climbing up his back short-circuited in the vicinity of his chest. It almost seemed as if she'd trapped his touch so she could hold on to it a little longer—which didn't make much sense given that she'd looked as if she could cheerfully belt him.

"I'm fine, Essie" he heard her call to a pixie-faced woman wearing an apron as white as her hair. "I was just keeping Cal company while he took a break." Battling the breeze for her hair, she caught most of its length at her nape and looked back up at him. "Have you met Essie yet?"

He had the feeling she knew he hadn't. He also had the feeling he was about to. Lindsey's expression was one of benign innocence, along with a touch of the determination he'd encountered head-on the day he'd met her.

It was the steel beneath her softness that tended to catch him off guard. But he was learning. "You said you were trying to help me," he heard her whisper, her voice shimmering like silk over his suddenly raw nerves. "It's not going to get any easier if you don't try to get along."

She wanted him to give the good citizens of Leesburg a chance. Watching the woman who owned the bakery next door approach, seeing Lindsey start toward the woman herself, he was sorely tempted to turn on his heel and get back to work. That was where his efforts would yield the most results. He was certain of that. But Lindsey was glancing back, her smile encouraging, and it would have been too blatantly rude to pull a disappearing act now.

He wasn't going to be a jerk and embarrass her. After the way she'd defended him, he figured he owed her one anyway.

Cal vaguely remembered Essie. Her tight curls hadn't quite been the color of bleached flour back when he'd come into her bakery with a spare dime for a doughnut. But she did look familiar. He didn't tell her that, of course. He merely acknowledged Lindsey's introduction with a nod and a quiet "Ma'am," then excused himself to go pound boards until his arm ached and he was too tired to focus on another nail head. The restlessness he felt had nothing to do with the woman he'd met. Essie had been reserved, but he'd expected that. The restlessness had to do solely with Lindsey. It had been a mistake to touch her. It had been an even bigger mistake to let himself give in to the need he'd felt to be with her for a while.

It only made him want her more. Which was all he could seem to think about when, having called it quits a little after eight o'clock that night, he stood at the window of the tiny studio apartment and watched her disappear into the dark as she headed for home.

It didn't make any sense to him, but there were times when he would see her leaving—as she was now, with a stack of her shirts to work on, or hurrying off to a meeting of some committee or other—that he could almost swear she was pushing herself as hard as he was. He couldn't understand why she was doing it, though. She was a beautiful woman. Smart. Generous. Involved in everything. Yet when she went home late every night, she went alone.

He thought about following her, about jogging down the stairs after her to carry the overloaded bag she toted, then asking if he could sit with her on her porch for a while. But he didn't move from where he stood with one hand braced high against the window frame and the other clenching a glass of milk. Because that wasn't really what he wanted. What he really wanted was to bury his hands in all that beautiful hair and taste the fullness of her mouth; to strip away the restraints between them, then ease himself into her and put an end to the fire burning under his skin. But the fact that he would have settled for sitting with her on her porch kept him right where he was.

There was something dangerous about wanting to be with a woman that badly.

So he continued staring out the window—until he grew tired of looking out at the dark and sat down at the table to his sketch pad and another meal eaten alone.

The morning sun was higher than he wanted it to be when he found himself looking out the back window again. Someone was knocking—pounding, actually—on one of the doors below him.

"Lindsey? Yoo-hoo!" a female voice singsonged. "Are you in there?"

Snapping his jeans as he turned from the window, he grabbed a shirt from the back of the chair. He had the shirt on, but not buttoned, when he opened the door to see Essie, the bakery lady, peering in Lindsey's workroom window.

"She isn't here yet," Cal called down.

Essie's tight curls didn't budge by so much as a hair when her head snapped up. "Oh, my... I didn't... Good morning" she finally decided on, looking a little flustered as she stepped back so she didn't have to crane her neck so much to see him. "Lindsey plays her music so loud when she's alone sometimes that she can't always hear when someone is at the door. I thought maybe that was why she wasn't answering." She clasped her hands against her apron, her fairy-godmother features pleasant but cautious. "She isn't here?"

"I think she's picking up shirts from Camille's before she comes in." At least, that was what he'd overheard.

The angles of Essie's silvery eyebrows dipped in disappointment. "Well, in that case, would you mind asking her to stop over when she has a minute? My big fluorescent light burned out and she usually replaces it for me."

Of course she does, Cal mentally muttered, afraid to wonder what else Lindsey did for whom in this town. "Do you have a replacement tube?"

"Well, of course I do," she returned with a look that said she wouldn't have asked Lindsey's help in replacing a light if she hadn't had something for Lindsey to replace it with. "But I don't climb ladders very well anymore. That's why she does it for me."

It hadn't been his intention to offend the woman. Nor had he cared why she asked Lindsey for her help. Not bothering to explain himself, which he seldom did anyway, he reached around and closed the apartment door. "Show me where it is. I'll do it."

Surprise snapped her eyebrows back up. "That's very kind, but I don't want to impose on you. It doesn't need to be done right away and I know Lindsey doesn't mind."

I mind, he thought, the thud of his boots on the stairs echoing in the still morning air. "Do you have a stepladder?"

Essie's hands parted, one lifting to adjust the band of her nearly invisible hair net. Until now she hadn't subjected him to any particular scrutiny. But as her eyes narrowed on him, it wasn't skepticism he saw in her expression. It was speculation. Pure and simple.

"Yes, I do," she finally told him. Her twinkling eyes made a quick pass from his neck to his boots. "I hope it will hold you," she added, then turned, motioning him to follow her and the scent of baking bread across the graveled utility lot she shared with Lindsey. "You really don't need to do this, you know. But I do appreciate it. It's real neighborly of you."

Cal wasn't doing it to be "neighborly." His motives were purely self-serving.

At least he'd thought they were before, having made short work of the light problem, he returned from putting away the ladder in Essie's storage area and found the grandmotherly woman holding out a pink box. It contained doughnuts. A dozen maple glazed, she told him. His favorite, if she remembered correctly.

There was nothing wrong with her memory. They were indeed his favorite. Which was why Cal frowned at the box, until it occurred to him to ask why in the world she would have remembered something like that.

"I didn't remember it until just a bit ago," she told him, looking as if she were comparing the man with whatever memory she had of him. "Then it dawned on me what was nagging me about you. You were in grade school. Not much more than ten or eleven at the time. But you would come in here about once a week with your little brother and buy one doughnut. You were the only boy I ever knew who always gave his brother the bigger half.''

Though what he'd done had made an impression on Essie, Cal couldn't remember it himself. He didn't even want to try. Yet oddly, at that moment he wasn't thinking about how he tended to run into bits of the past at every turn. Or fighting off the feelings that were coming closer to the surface all the time. As he started to leave, he was wondering only if this was what Lindsey had meant about giving people a chance. All he said to Essie on his way out, though, after he'd thanked her, was that he'd fix her squeaky screen door for her. For a dozen doughnuts, it was the least he could do.

It was the distinctive screech of Essie's screen door that caught Lindsey's attention as she climbed out of her Bronco and started for her workroom door. She was far later than usual this morning, though she wouldn't have been if she hadn't stayed to have coffee with Camille. Something she'd had no business doing, except the woman had been starved for adult company. With only three hours before she was due at a Rotary luncheon, Lindsey had a treasurer's report for the local chapter of the Texas Wildflower Propagation Organization to finish and a mailing to stuff for her grand reopening sale. She also had what felt like a dozen things to do before evening—though she couldn't recall what a single one of them was when she saw Cal walk out the bakery's back door.

He was fifty feet away, yet she felt his presence as strongly as if he were merely inches from her. He moved with the grace of a cat, his long-legged stride at once easy and purposeful. Tall, powerful, he strode toward her, his denim shirt hanging over his jeans. His hair looked as if it might have been combed with only his fingers, and when he'd shaved he'd taken a nick out of the tender flesh beneath his lower lip.

It had only been in the last couple of days that the split at the far corner of his mouth had stopped looking so sore.

Her glance slipped down when he stopped in front of her, over the flare of dark chest hair exposed above the single button he'd fastened halfway down his shirt to focus on the pink box in his hand.

Looking lower had been a mistake. The box was in her view. But as he pushed back the tail of his shirt to fish his apartment key out of his pocket, so were his hard abdominal muscles and the soft swirl of hair that arrowed toward his navel and disappeared behind a snap and worn denim.

Her throat felt as dry as the thumbprint of powdered sugar next to the neatly tied string when she very calmly looked back up.

"What's going on?"

"Essie needed a light changed."

"She asked you to help her?"

"No. She asked for you. But I needed you to mark where you want your mirrors when you got here, and I didn't want you to get sidetracked. I want to hang them this morning."

"I don't get sidetracked," she insisted, even though she knew he thought she did. He smelled faintly of shaving lather, and the way he stood there, looking so utterly male, definitely tested her concentration. "I just reprioritize a lot. It looks like you had a problem, though. Late night?"

He usually started well before eight in the morning. It was now after nine, and he was barely dressed.

"I was working on something."

She was surprised, then puzzled. "I thought you had quit for the night when I'd left."

He'd gone upstairs just before eight. She knew that because she'd heard the stairs creak and the door close while she'd sat at her desk with her sketch pad, wondering what he would do if she went up after him. All she'd wanted was to ask if he'd be interested in sharing a can of whatever she had lurking in her pantry for dinner. But before she could consider that the thought might be prompted by more than her desire to make his stay here easier, she'd heard the shower go on. As hard as he worked, she figured all he'd be interested in was refueling and getting some sleep.

Obviously she'd been wrong.

"I didn't come back down here," he told her, not sure why she'd shied from his glance just then. "I was working on my own stuff. Here." He held the box out to her. "Hang on to these while I finish getting dressed, will you? I'll be down in a minute."

She stepped toward him, looking down as she took the box with a murmured "Sure."

Her fingers brushed his, the sensation compounding the jolt of heat spiking through him when he breathed in the clean scent of her hair. Gritting his teeth against the effect of her nearness, he reminded himself of the decision he'd made somewhere around one o'clock that morning.

Unless she made it clear she wanted him in her bed—something he regarded as highly unlikely considering, among a whole truckload of other things, that she didn't seem the affair type—he would keep his hands off her. He wasn't going to avoid her, though. He couldn't. Something about her made being in Leesburg a little easier. In a way, it seemed almost as if she was a friend. And heaven knew, since it would be at least a month before he finished here, he could certainly use one. Therefore he'd keep his mind on his work and his hands to himself.

It was a noble goal. Unfortunately, it was also a goal destined to go down in flames.

Chapter Six

"Who are you?"

The voice, small and shy, reached up to where Cal stood on the ladder, checking the fittings on the eight-foot mirror he'd just hung outside Lindsey's new dressing room. In the mirror's reflection of the empty, semipainted space, he could see the gap in the filmy-white plastic and a little girl with blond pigtails clutching a lace-covered bear. Another bear, one holding a bouquet of pink balloons, grinned at him from the front of her T-shirt.

"I'm Cal," he returned, wondering why the kid was frowning at him. "Who are you?"

"Amy. Lindsey is my aunt."

"She is?"

Amy nodded gravely. "She said I have an Uncle Cal. Are you married to her?"

The question was as unexpected as the revelation. Somewhere in the periphery of his mind, Cal had been aware that his brother had acquired children along with a wife. But, as he uneasily eyed the child staring at him, he'd never considered himself having gained any title in that acquisition.

He'd certainly never considered anyone mistaking him for somebody's husband, either.

He was saved from having to respond on either count by Lindsey. Appearing behind the child like a guardian angel, her smile landed atop the child's head and she settled her hands on the narrow little shoulders.

"You know I don't have a husband," he heard her say in a voice as gentle as spring rain. "Cal is your new daddy's brother. You know," she coaxed, "the way Annie and I are your mom's sisters, so we're your aunts? Logan has brothers who are your uncles."

Amy looked up, her little head tipping back so she could see Lindsey's face. "He's not like Uncle Rob?"

"No, honey," Lindsey replied, soothing the child's confusion between Annie's husband and Logan's brother. "Not like him."

"He can't divorce us?"

"Uncle Rob isn't divorcing *us,* Amy. Not exactly," she qualified, looking as if she might be considering the accuracy of her conclusion. "That's not something you need to worry about with Cal, though. He'll be your uncle forever. He can't stop being part of the family just because he's unhappy with someone in it."

"You mean I always have to have Michael for a brother?"

Understanding joined gentleness. "Is he still hiding bugs in your bed?"

"No," the child said, her nose wrinkling. "But yesterday he put one in my lunchbox. I screamed."

Lindsey was sure she had. Along with every other little girl who'd been at the table when the hapless critter had been exposed. Michael, bless him, was such a . . . boy.

"Yeah," Lindsey drawled sympathetically, drawing one of Amy's soft pigtails through her hand. "Like that," she agreed. "It's the pits being the littlest sometimes. But you'll be friends with him someday. Just as your mom and I are. And she used to do much worse things to me than put bugs in my lunch."

"She did?"

"Uh-huh." Mischief danced in Lindsey's eyes, bright like the sun holding her and the child in the beam shining through the window. "When I was about your age, she used to take me on *dates* with her."

"With boys?"

"With boys."

"Really?"

"Really."

From his perch on the ladder, Cal saw Amy's hand fly over her mouth, her eyes sparkling as if she were holding in some wonderful new secret. The kid was actually kind of cute. Sweet, he supposed, though it wasn't a word with which he was very familiar. Yet it was Lindsey who had his attention. And the need he'd felt to deny what she'd voiced with such ease.

He can't stop being part of the family just because he's unhappy with someone in it.

What if a person was never part of a "family" to begin with?

"Let's get out of here so Uncle Cal can get back to work," he heard her say as he banished the question. "Do you want to help me with the new window display?"

"Can I make paper dolls, instead?"

Lindsey told the child she could, adding that she should get one of the sketch pads from her desk. "Not the one with the blue cover," she called after the little girl had spun on the heel of her pink sneaker and taken off like a shot, bear in tow. "That's the one I'm working in."

"What was that all about?"

"Sounds like she just wants to draw." Turning, Lindsey gave a shrug—and promptly went still when she saw Cal descend from the third step of the ladder in one stride.

"Not that. Who's Rob?"

The quiet demand stole the ease from her expression. "My sister Annie's soon-to-be-ex. Sam told the kids a few days ago that he wouldn't be part of the family anymore," she explained, suddenly feeling the same guardedness she could sense in Cal. "Rob was the only uncle Amy knew before Sam married Logan, and when I said you weren't my husband, I think she got confused about how you could be her uncle."

He hadn't appreciated what she'd said to Amy. That was all Lindsey could tell from the steady way his eyes held hers. She knew he wanted nothing to do with his older brother. But she could hardly deny to a child who the man was. Especially after Amy had earlier said he looked just like her new daddy.

"You're not upset because I told her who you are, are you?"

Lindsey was prepared to defend what she'd said. But it wasn't necessary. Cal avoided the subject of anything concerning Logan like the proverbial plague. Already he'd backed off, but his eyes remained on hers. She never knew what he was thinking when he looked at her as he was now; his eyes intent on her face, unblinking, steady. She knew only that she could sense a certain determined restraint in him, in herself, and that she was deceiving herself about him in ways she didn't dare explore.

"Aunt Lindsey?" she heard Amy call. "Should I come in there with you and Uncle Cal?"

"Just sit down by the window, honey. I'll only be a minute."

The intensity gave way to incomprehension. "Uncle Cal," he repeated, sounding as if the words were as foreign to him as Sanskrit. "Just like that? The kid sees me once and I'm in?"

"Children can be pretty accepting."

"I thought kids were supposed to be afraid of strangers."

"You're not a stranger. You're family."

The woman was hopeless. She spoke as if that circumstance should make some sort of difference, as if being "family" forgave all manner of circumstance, along with common sense. But Cal didn't feel like telling her the child's acceptance of him undoubtedly had more to do with Lindsey's attitude toward him than anything familial. She had an entirely different view of family than he did. She saw them as friends. As allies. He didn't want to consider what he thought about the concept. And he most certainly didn't want to debate that concept with her.

He would tell her what he thought of her, though.

"You'd make a good mom," he said, thinking how patient she'd been with her explanations. Thinking, too, how gentle she'd seemed talking to Amy. "You should have kids of your own."

The observation was spoken as a matter of fact, his tone as unremarkable as it might have been had he told her she should hang the wall mirrors three feet to the left.

Completely unprepared for the change of subject, much less the subject itself, Lindsey felt her defenses make a distinct shift. "Oh, I don't think so," she muttered, forcing a lightness into her tone that didn't want to be there. "I'm a firm believer in the two-person method of parenting. Since I'm not interested in marriage, that pretty much eliminates the daddy part of it." She shot him a wry look. "I'll just spoil my nieces and nephew, instead."

Her admission surprised him. The certainty in it. The conviction.

"Why aren't you interested?" he wanted to know, not sure what difference it made, since he'd never entertained the idea of marriage himself. Heaven knew he'd never seen a good one.

The way Cal frowned made Lindsey smile, when she really didn't feel like smiling at all. There were times when he could be as blunt as the business end of a ball-peen hammer, but it wasn't often that she saw him confused. It made him more approachable somehow. Or maybe all it did was lower his guard enough for her to discover yet another link in the invisible chain that was somehow binding them. He was no more interested in the institution than she was. And that gave them a little more in common— though she doubted he had any idea how much in common they had already.

"I was interested. Once," she admitted, waiting to feel the hesitation that normally accompanied this particular topic. "I was engaged to a man I'd worked with at the design firm in New York. We came very close to getting married."

"How close?"

She lifted her shoulder in a slight shrug and saw something shift in his eyes. Something quick and indiscernible.

"How close?" he quietly repeated.

Lindsey had never said a word about her almost-marriage to anyone in this town. Only her sister knew. But

Lindsey had the feeling Cal understood what it felt like to be betrayed, and what it was like to deny an essential part of himself. Their circumstances were so very different. Yet in a way they were so very much the same. He was denying his need for his family. She had simply stopped dreaming of having one of her own.

"I made it to the church," she finally said. "John didn't. He decided he didn't like the idea of children and a house in the suburbs after all."

There wasn't much more to say. She'd been left standing at the altar. That was it in a nutshell. That was how she liked to think of that particular event, too. As being tightly contained. Over, dealt with and compartmentalized in a mental box that was gathering dust in the back of her mind. But as comprehensive as her response was, it grossly understated how devastated she'd been.

The mental box apparently hadn't become as dusty as she'd thought. Even now, with three years and two thousand miles separating her from that day, she could still remember how she'd felt when her mother had come back to the bride's room at the church half an hour after the ceremony was supposed to have started.

Lindsey crossed her arms over the hollow ache in the pit of her stomach. Unable to bear the intensity of Cal's quiet scrutiny, she shifted her eyes down, past the frayed hole in the sleeve of his workshirt, to rest on his muscular forearm. She'd felt protected in those arms once. Odd how she kept remembering that.

Finding that thought far too seductive, she turned her focus to the room. To its soft-peach walls. The beautifully polished moldings. The smell of fresh paint. She didn't want to remember that awful sense of not having been good enough, the confusion over what she'd done wrong to make her fiancé not want her anymore. The sense of abandonment. She did everything she could to avoid the feelings. But they wouldn't quite go away.

So she told Cal that John hadn't come. That he had left her alone to cope with two hundred and fifty friends and family members fidgeting in ribbon-bedecked pews, ten pounds of caviar on ice at the country club and a future that wasn't going to happen.

I'm sorry, Lindsey. I just can't do it. I just can't see myself as someone's husband. When things calm down, we'll talk.

That was what his note had said. Only she hadn't known what he'd meant by "things." Unless he'd meant when she herself had calmed down. But she never had been the hysterical type and there'd been nothing to talk about anyway. He hadn't wanted her, and he'd humiliated her in front of her friends and family. Enough said. So, with a calm that had felt suspiciously like numbness at the time, Lindsey had returned his ring, his gifts and all the wedding presents. The only thing she had left of that day was the knowledge that she would never put herself in that position again.

"Then you took off."

Cal's perception didn't strike her as particularly remarkable. As she trailed her finger over the door frame he'd sanded to satin smoothness, she thought only that he sounded as if he understood. She'd rather expected he would. After all, they had so much in common.

"Four days later." Feeling hurt, bewildered, lost, she had run from the dreams she'd honestly thought John had shared with her. Run from them, then buried them somewhere along the way. "I left New York to drive to the base in Albuquerque. That's where Annie and her husband were stationed at the time," she explained, thinking how much had changed since then. Thinking how much was changing even now. Poor Annie. "I wasn't in any hurry to get there, so I sort of took the scenic route . . . and passed through Leesburg on the way."

"And came back?"

"I never left."

The understanding with which she'd credited him was no longer in evidence. He couldn't fathom why she was so drawn to this place. She knew it and he didn't try to hide it. But she wanted him to understand. Why, she couldn't really say. She knew only that she wanted him to appreciate what she'd found in this place that he had felt so compelled to escape.

"I wanted a home more than anything in the world, Cal. I'd never spent more than two years in any one place in my whole life, and when I pulled in here . . ." She shook her head, trying for words to describe what, until now, had only been impressions. "It was just so different from anywhere I'd ever been," she concluded, her voice hushed.

She remembered how pretty it was with the flowers blooming in the square, and how peaceful. She told him that, describing the colors, the quiet. Then she told him how she'd walked along the tree-lined sidewalks and bought an ice-cream cone from the Sweet Shoppe, and how she'd gone back to the square and sat on a bench, watching the birds play in the fountain by the bandstand and the people come and go.

She spoke of sounds and scents and feelings. Of people who smiled and children who laughed. And as Cal watched her turn from him again to move about the room as she spoke, touching the new surfaces he'd created for her as if she couldn't believe they were really hers, he found himself thinking that the place she described was not a place he'd ever seen. He'd seen the town only as an escape from the ranch. She made it sound like a place where a person would like to belong.

"When I left that day," she continued before his defenses could kick in and make him deny the thought, "I got about three miles down the road and found myself turning around. I'd seen a sign in the window of May's Dress Shop for part-time help. The next thing I knew, I was living in the apartment upstairs."

She'd come to a stop by the ladder, only a few feet from where he stood. In the mirror's reflection he could see himself towering over her. He in work clothes and in need of a haircut. She in deep blue, immaculately groomed. What he watched, though, was her smile. It was as soft as her voice.

"What I found here, Cal, was...home."

She really believed that. She was as convinced of that as he was of the conclusion he drew in the long moments he studied her upturned face. But he didn't believe for a moment that she'd found what she was looking for. She had merely settled for what she had come across. Neither had she discovered anything here that he hadn't. This place offered her exactly what it had offered him. An escape from the hurt. From a life that wasn't what it should have been. But he wasn't about to scrape away the protective gloss she'd put on her reality. She'd built herself a life she could live with. He had no business tearing it down.

He had no business touching her, either. But before he realized he'd reached toward her, he was nudging her hair back from her cheek.

"John was a fool."

"It's nice of you to say so."

"I didn't say it to be 'nice.'"

He hadn't realized how badly he'd wanted to touch her. He wasn't going to worry about that, though. As he stood with his hand curved like a benediction at the side of her face, the tips of his fingers barely grazing her skin, his only thought was that she hadn't drawn back. Or looked away. If anything, her expression had only softened more.

That she accepted his touch so easily totally destroyed his resolve.

It seemed as if she was about to argue with something he'd said. All he knew for sure was that a smile had slipped into her eyes. Wondering if she had any idea what it did to him when she looked at him that way, he slid his hand into her hair.

An instant later, he pulled her toward him—and the smile faded. He couldn't tell precisely when it disappeared from her eyes. He just knew it was no longer there when he tipped her head up and bent his own toward her so he could do what he'd wanted to do ever since he'd had her in his arms outside Papa Joe's.

His mouth closed over hers, one hand gliding down her back to draw her closer. He felt her hesitate. Or maybe it was he who went still in the scattered instant before her hands curled at his waist and he felt her mouth soften beneath his. Then he wasn't thinking at all. The tip of his tongue nudged hers and he felt her open to him like a flower seeking sunlight.

She wants this.

The realization hit him like a fist.

Need, fierce and hot, slammed into him. He hadn't expected it. The hunger. The swiftness. There was no slow build. No gradual escalation of impressions and sensations. Just the need.

The effect stunned him. Then it forced him to take it slow. What he wanted to do was back her against the mirror while he drank from the sweetness of her mouth. To run his hands over her body and learn every nuance of her shape. What he did was ease back to search her face.

She hadn't been prepared for the impact, either.

With a groan, he lowered his head once more.

She should have stopped him. The thought occurred to Lindsey vaguely, but she ignored it. She wanted his kiss too badly. She didn't *want* to want it. But it was too late for mental debates. Wrapped in his steely strength, she felt his warmth seep into her, tightening some places, softening others. Making her forget. Making her yearn.

She leaned into him, seeking his body as he sought hers. He felt familiar, and that alone chased back the warning voices. Familiar because he'd imprinted himself upon her the first time he'd held her against him. She'd never been able to shake that feeling, or the thought that she'd never before experienced such a sensation. Later, she would deny its import. As she had done every day since she'd met him. Now, with the evidence of his arousal pressed against her stomach and his hand drifting over her hip to draw her closer, that feeling of being branded only intensified.

She whispered his name, feeling the tension snake through his body as he made little forays from one corner of her mouth to the other.

"Cal, please," she whispered again, struggling for sanity while warmth swirled down from where his lips touched hers.

"Aunt Lindsey? Mommy is here."

Neither of them had heard the chime. At least, Lindsey hadn't been aware of it until it sounded again when the front door closed. She felt Cal stiffen, and went rigid herself an instant before he lifted his head.

"Lindsey?" called a puzzled female voice.

Her composure in shreds, doing her best to pull it back together, Lindsey stepped back to see Sam frozen in the doorway. Amy stood at the gap.

Lindsey hadn't a clue how long Amy had been there. Long enough, she suspected, unconsciously touching her kiss-swollen mouth. The little girl was looking at her as if she didn't know whether to giggle or tiptoe away. As for Lindsey's sister, it was apparent that Sam had seen enough to explain the stunned look on her face. The gap was easily wide enough to give her a clear view of her and the man who'd just dropped his hand from her waist. Though Lindsey avoided Cal's eyes, she caught the quick clench of his jaw.

The store was suddenly as quiet as a church at midnight. The audio tape in the workroom had even run out. Not by a single note was the heavy silence interrupted when Sam, looking very much as though she'd rather leave, walked past Amy to the gap. The sheet of plastic crackled when she cautiously pushed it farther aside, the sound brittle in the ominous quiet.

"Hi," Lindsey said, determined to put that silence to an end. "How'd it go at the printer's?"

"It went fine." Questions furrowed Sam's brow. "We got a good price."

The printer was immediately forgotten. Aware of the deceptive casualness in Cal's stance, and the subtle agitation behind it, Lindsey abandoned small talk. Sam wasn't interested in it anyway. Her attention was on the man standing as still as a rock pillar an arm's length from Lindsey. In one quick glance, she'd taken in the bandanna holding his dark hair back from his rough-hewn features, the piercing blue eyes that met hers head-on and the powerful build that had hidden her sister only seconds ago.

Lindsey didn't need to see the strain behind Sam's smile to know she was truly torn about making this particular man's acquaintance. Wanting to ease that strain, for all their sakes, Lindsey started to make the introduction—only to find her sister taking care of it herself.

"I'm Samantha," she said, holding out her hand as she looked up at the man who bore more than a passing resemblance to her husband. "Lindsey's sister," she added, pausing as if to consider the wisdom of mentioning her other relationship. "And your brother's wife."

Taking her hand, he engulfed it in his calloused grip. "I've wondered if we'd meet."

He knew she had been avoiding him. That knowledge put honest chagrin in Sam's smile. She was not in an easy position, though she wouldn't apologize for where she stood. She merely stepped back to slip her arm around Amy's shoulder.

"You're doing a beautiful job on Lindsey's shop," she said, diplomatically seeking safe ground. "It looks as if it's almost finished."

"It is. I'll move her fixtures in in a day or two."

"When will you start on the bandstand?"

"As soon as I finish the outside of this building. Two, two and a half weeks. If the weather holds."

Sam's only response to that was to draw a forbearing breath.

"Well," she said, determined to find something positive to cling to, "it will be nice to have it done." Seeming to suddenly remember she was in a hurry, she glanced at her watch, the lights causing her wide diamond wedding band to flash.

"Basketball practice should be over by now, Lindsey. I've got to pick up Michael and get home. Do you mind if Amy comes here after school again tomorrow? Erin has another drama practice, so there won't be anyone at home. I need to run out to the herb farm and help Mrs. Sweeney decide which shots to take for her new publicity brochure. On second thought," she added, turning slightly from the man watching them both, "maybe you should come with me. You've got a great eye for that sort of thing."

That was not subtle. "I thought you wanted me to watch Amy."

"Mrs. Gunther might be available."

Amy, who had been playing with the bow around her lacy bear's neck, tipped her head up. "I could stay here with Uncle Cal," she said, ever so helpfully.

"Oh, I don't think so," Sam hurriedly replied, scarcely glancing at the man whose eyebrows had just darted up.

Lindsey stepped in. "She'll stay here with me. I can't go with you anyway, Sam. I have work to do."

Sam didn't seem terribly pleased with that response. Even if she did expect it. At least, that's how Cal saw the situation in the moments before the petite blonde looked up at him once more.

This time her discomfort wasn't quite so well masked. "I'm glad we met," she said in spite of it.

Cal responded with a tight nod, not so sure she didn't really mean that she was simply glad their meeting was finally over. He doubted she'd ever be so blunt with someone she didn't know, however. The woman was too much of a lady, too classy. Like Lindsey, in that respect. Only far more reserved.

That someone like her had married his brother would have given him pause had he not been so aware of her distress. As she turned away, sending her sister a glance that urged her toward the door with her, he could almost feel the woman's ambivalence toward him. He didn't doubt for a moment that she had major reservations about what she'd seen going on when she'd walked in.

It was Lindsey he was concerned about, though. He had no idea what to make of the way she'd refused to meet his eyes. He did know, however, that there was a problem between her and her sister. A problem created by his presence. Seeing the apprehensive look she'd sent in his direction just before she'd disappeared behind her niece, he couldn't avoid the feeling that she had defended him to more than just a few people in town.

As bad as he'd felt that he might have caused a problem for her with her friends, he felt worse knowing he might be responsible for a rift between her and her sister. Family didn't matter to him. But it did to her.

Just as the town mattered to her. But it didn't to him.

He didn't want her to matter. But she did.

He shut his eyes, whipping off the folded bandanna to push his fingers through his hair. Frustration shot through him as he turned, and found himself facing the mirror.

The man staring back at him looked a little rough around the edges. A little rough period. But the man in the mirror looked like he felt. Like the outsider he was.

Cal turned his back on his taunting reflection. Swiping up a hammer from the floor, he shoved those thoughts from his mind and jammed down all the conflicting feelings that had come with them. The only feeling he couldn't escape was the one that refused to be ignored. He'd had enough trouble keeping his hands off of Lindsey before. Now that he knew how she tasted, how she responded to him, he'd probably have to glue his hands into his pockets to keep them to himself.

"There is a resemblance."

"There sure is," Lindsey agreed, praying Sam was in too

big a hurry to pursue any other observations right now. "You know, you never said what kind of look Mrs. Sweeney is going for with her brochure."

"That wasn't subtle, Lindsey." Sam paused, tilting her head to get a better read on her sister. "Are you all right?"

"Sure. I'm fine."

"You don't look fine. What's going on?"

Sam's voice was as low as the sun setting behind the steeple of the community church. They had just come to a stop on the empty sidewalk outside the shop, beside Sam's boring-beige sedan. The town was shutting down for the night, most of the businesses already sporting Closed signs in their windows. Amy was inside the car, putting her bear in a seat belt.

"Nothing is going on. He's working and I'm working and sometimes we talk." She should have known her sister wouldn't let it go. "That's all."

"You weren't talking when I got here."

It was hard for Lindsey to tell where Sam was coming from just then. She appeared a little concerned. But, then, Lindsey felt concerned herself. Her sister also appeared confused. They shared a lot.

"I was just telling him about John…and he kissed me. He was just being . . . nice."

The quality of Sam's concern underwent a subtle but distinct change. "You told him about John?"

"Don't read anything into this that isn't there, Sam. Even if you overlook the fact that he and I hardly agree on anything, he's leaving as soon as his jobs are done. He hates it here."

For a moment, Lindsey thought her sister might mention that their failure to agree didn't mean anything, and that she was going to have to argue her point about how there really was nothing going on between her and Cal. But second thoughts made Lindsey realize that Sam would not be encouraging where Cal was concerned. For a number of very practical reasons.

Two doors down, Babs stepped out of her beauty shop. After locking up, she waved, keys in hand, to the two sisters visiting on the sidewalk.

Lindsey and Sam both waved back.

"This isn't a good place to talk."

"No, it's not," Lindsey agreed. "There's nothing to talk about anyway."

Sam didn't seem convinced.

"I have to go," she said, sounding as if there were a few other things she would have said, given more time and a different location. "But just one thing. Has he mentioned anything about Logan?"

"Not a word."

"Do you have any idea what he might do? If he'll come out?"

Lindsey shook her head. "Sorry, Sam. Not a clue. He doesn't confide in me."

For a moment, Sam just stood there looking very much as if she wanted to ask Lindsey to talk to him about his brother. Maybe even encourage him to see him. For Logan's sake, now that Logan knew he was here. But all her sister did was give her a resigned smile, a quick hug and tell her to "Be careful," as she headed for the driver's door. There was no way she would ask her to do anything where Cal and Logan were concerned now. Lindsey was absolutely certain of that. Not when she felt it might make Lindsey's situation more complicated than it already appeared to be.

As it turned out, Cal complicated it himself less than half an hour later.

Chapter Seven

"You're not working tonight?"

Cal's deep voice came from behind her. Near the open door of her workshop. Disturbed by that smoky sound, disturbed by him, Lindsey kept her focus on the yellow canvas bag she was filling with stencils and fabric.

"Not tonight. Between what Camille is working on at her house and what I've done myself, I'm caught up on my back orders." Summoning what she hoped would pass for an unaffected smile, Lindsey glanced in the direction of his dark-khaki work shirt. He was by the door, leaning against its frame. "I believe that's a personal first."

"We can all use a few of those."

Thread landed atop the fabric in the bag.

"Are you taking some more stuff out to Camille?"

"No."

"Do you have a meeting?"

"No."

"Meeting a friend for dinner?"

She shook her head.

"You're just planning to avoid me then?"

Lindsey's glance jerked to his, but her denial fell silent.

"You could just tell me to go to hell," he said in a voice as smooth as butter. "It might be easier."

The ribbon she'd picked up slid through her fingers. Cal hadn't moved from where he stood in the doorway, his left shoulder against the frame and his hands jammed into his pockets. The casualness of the stance didn't fool her. Like the ease in his voice, it was deceptive. Dangerously so.

"Easier than what?"

"Pretending. You're actually not very good at confrontations, are you?"

"I can hold my own."

"Then tell me why you're burning rubber to get out of here. That way I'll know what to apologize for first."

That he thought an apology necessary at all forced her to glance up from the sachet materials she gathered. That he thought himself guilty of multiple transgressions made her forget them completely.

"The only thing I can imagine you'd be sorry about is that you kissed me. But you hardly owe me an apology for that." She'd take her share of blame. He'd hardly acted alone. "If I remember correctly, I kissed you back."

"You did."

His unhesitating agreement was more than a little disconcerting. So was the way he slowly straightened, his big body all but blocking out the fading evening light.

"But I embarrassed you in front of your sister. It's easy enough to tell she'd prefer I disappear. But the two of you are close, and now she's upset with you. Because of me."

He didn't move. He simply remained where he was, a big man who suddenly seemed much bigger in her eyes be-

cause he was shouldering the blame for a situation that had
plenty of guilty participants to share the load. He didn't
mention why Sam would be prejudiced. Nor did he dis-
count Sam's opinion of him because of the loyalty she had
to her husband. He simply took responsibility for his actions and the consequences and... apologized.

Lindsey didn't know too many people who could do that
without also offering a half a dozen excuses.

"How much longer are you going to work?"

The question drew his heavy eyebrows together. "I'm
pretty much finished. Why?"

"There's something I'd like to explain to you."

"So, explain."

"Not here." It would take a while, and she couldn't help
but think they could both use some time away from this
place. Last night, while at her machine, she'd heard him
pacing the floor upstairs, the boards creaking as he'd
roamed the confining space. "Would you come for a walk
with me?"

Cal didn't answer. Not directly. After looking as if he
might have had to wrestle with the idea for a moment, he
simply said, "I'll meet you out back," and turned to the
other door to close up. Lindsey headed in to do the same,
leaving her carryall where it was and taking only her jacket
and house keys after she'd turned out all but the security
lights.

When she stepped outside a few minutes later, Cal was
coming down the steps, shrugging on his leather jacket.

The mercury tended to drop when the sun set. But it
wasn't the chill settling into the air that caused Lindsey to
hug her arms to herself when Cal stopped in front of her.
The posture was purely defensive. He had ripped a hole a
yard wide in the cloak of protection she'd so carefully wo-

ven around herself. When she'd felt his arms around her, she hadn't cared. She hadn't wanted that cloak at all. She just wanted him.

But wanting him made her want so very much more and, with Cal, that was impossible.

"Ready?" he asked, keenly aware of her hesitation.

She gave him a nod, outwardly calm, inwardly...not.

They headed through the graveled lot, Cal with his hands in his pockets and Lindsey with her arms crossed over her baggy purple jacket. A gentle twilight hovered over the streets, the only sounds those of birds settling in for the night and the bark of a dog somewhere down the road. They left the businesses and darkened eyes of building windows behind them, moving past the pecan grove that was beginning to bud and the field that had gone fallow.

Lindsey scarcely noticed any of it. She was aware only of the man beside her—and that she needed to relieve the blame he had placed on himself.

"What you said—about apologizing," she began, keeping her eyes on the tree roots poking through the buckled sidewalk. "You don't need to apologize for anything concerning me. I admit Sam and I have a difference of opinion where you're concerned. I'm afraid that was obvious. But you're not responsible for it."

"You don't believe that any more than I do."

She hugged her arms tighter. "I wouldn't have said it if I didn't." She didn't want to argue with him. She just wanted him to listen. "You're not responsible for how I act or react and it's my actions she has the problem with. But that's not what I wanted to talk to you about," she added before he could point out his role in turning her knees to wax less than twenty minutes ago. "I want you to understand that Sam is really a very nice person. She's just concerned right now, so she wasn't quite as friendly as she could have been. You're going to run into each other again, so give her another chance. Okay?''

Without breaking stride, Cal cut her a sideways glance. Amazing, he thought, studying her profile while she studied the cracked cement. Her sister was upset because he was in town, yet Lindsey didn't want him thinking ill of the woman. More incredible still, her sister was upset with her, yet Lindsey readily offered excuses on Sam's behalf.

''What's she so concerned for? I'm just doing what I was hired to do. Once it's done, I'm out of here. It's not like anything is going to happen.''

''She's concerned for the people she cares about,'' she returned, her voice hushed. ''She doesn't want anyone to get hurt.''

Cal shook his head, at a loss. It was obvious enough that the people Sam cared about—where he was concerned, anyway—were her husband and her sister. But he wanted nothing to do with Logan. As for Lindsey...

As for Lindsey, he had to admit that he'd already considered the damage she could do to her reputation by associating with him. Having acknowledged that possibility himself, he could hardly fault her sister for sharing the concern. He was sure she did, too. Sam looked like the type to worry about that sort of thing. But there was another kind of hurt he hadn't thought about. Until now.

It was in his power to make Lindsey care about him. In some ways, she obviously already did. He found the thought—and the realization—as compelling as it was humbling. More than anything else, it simply yanked Sam's concern for Lindsey into perspective. Along with the power to make her care came the power to hurt. He'd be willing to bet his best chisels that was why Sam had looked like a mother cat searching for her kitten when she'd first seen him.

The sidewalk ended halfway down the block. The block itself ended at a stand of gnarled live oak. Instead of turning as Lindsey normally would have to go home, she kept going straight on the dirt path that led to the meandering creek. She needed to keep moving, to keep away from confining spaces so she wouldn't be so acutely aware of the man beside her.

Twilight grew fainter beneath the umbrella of tree branches. Farther ahead, Lindsey could hear the gurgle of water flowing over rock. The sound calmed, soothed, beckoning her closer. Beside her Cal's smoky voice sounded quieter than it had only moments ago.

"You must think a great deal of your sister."

"I do."

"Even though she took you on her dates?"

A tenuous smile wrinkled her nose. "She must have hated having to do that."

Cal didn't have a clue how a person would feel having to drag along a younger sibling on a date. After Logan had left for college, he'd kept his younger brother with him simply to keep him safe from their father.

He knew what it was like to be the younger one himself, though. He'd spent plenty of time trying to keep up with Logan.

"So you think things will be okay with you and Sam?"

It wasn't only his concern that touched her, though she never would have expected him to care. It was the distance in his voice. The hint of distraction. He sounded as if perhaps he was thinking of someone else.

"Sam and I have our disagreements, Cal. So do Annie and I. And Annie and Sam. Certainly not as many as we did when we were growing up, but we're three different people. We're bound to have different opinions at times. That doesn't affect the way we basically feel about one another. We're sisters." She skimmed a smile past his chest. "We'll be fine."

She'd wanted to reassure him. To let him know that there was no danger of a rift developing between her and Sam the way there had with him and Logan. Or perhaps what she hoped he might see was how important it was not to let a difference of opinion get in the way of what really mattered.

She might have told him that, too. Was planning on it, in fact, when they moved beyond the arms of live oaks and came out beside the narrow creek. But he spoke before she could find the courage to broach the subject he always so carefully avoided. When he did, she completely forgot what she was about to say.

"What about us, Lindsey. How will we be?"

The gentle sound of water rushing over rock wasn't as peaceful as she usually found it. Her nerves hummed like a swarm of mosquitoes. "I'm not sure what you mean."

"You haven't looked me in the eye since your sister showed up."

She gave a little laugh. "Sure I have." Just to prove it, she glanced up at him, at the beautiful angle of his jaw, at the faint redness that was all that remained of the cut at the corner of his mouth—and saw the confusion in his eyes.

An instant later, she'd turned back to the path, prepared to continue on to her house. But his hand curled around her arm and he was turning her to face him.

"That's exactly what I mean. What's going on? You didn't seem to have a problem with me kissing you. At least you said you didn't. But that's not the way you're acting now."

He wouldn't have pushed if she hadn't responded to him the way she had. Had she reacted any other way in his arms, he would have cut his losses by telling her it was just something he'd needed to get out of his system, that it wouldn't happen again, and chalked the whole thing up to experience. But he'd felt the unmistakable softening in her, the way she'd leaned into him, holding on, encouraging him. She'd kissed him just as hungrily as he had her.

"Wait a minute," he muttered, suspicion suddenly rapier sharp. With the tips of his fingers he nudged her chin up, refusing to let her avoid him any longer. "That scared you, didn't it?"

It wasn't a question.

Since she couldn't deny his conclusion with any conviction, Lindsey opted for challenge.

"So?"

His hand skimmed her cheek. She wasn't fooling him with that chin-up attitude of hers. Her reaction to him had truly frightened her. Why, he wasn't sure. Unless she had been as unprepared for it as he. He'd never forget the hard jolt of urgency he'd felt the moment she'd opened to him. The incredible need.

Sweet heaven, he thought, slipping his hand up her arm. If that was what she'd felt, too, they could set the sky on fire.

The muscle in his jaw clenched. "You aren't the only one."

His voice was quiet, his tone almost grudging. To Lindsey, he didn't sound any more pleased with the situation than she did. She didn't know why that disarmed her. Maybe because it meant he understood. Or maybe it was just the feel of his hand stroking over her shoulder that soothed her. As she searched his eyes, saw the heat in the shadows, the knot in her stomach slowly started to unwind. Other sensations replaced it. Heavy, liquid.

"So," he whispered, tracing his thumb along her lower lip. "How afraid are you?"

"Very."

"Do you know exactly what it is you're afraid of?"

She didn't hesitate. "You. Me."

"Yeah. Me, too."

His thumb brushed her lip again, his eyes glittering hard on her face. "So what do we do?"

She couldn't picture him afraid of anything. Ever. Especially her. "Nothing. We just leave things as they are. Or were," she corrected, because the present circumstance was creating havoc with her sense of self-preservation.

"I have a feeling that might not work."

Something in his eyes softened, drawing her in. Pushing his fingers through her hair, he tilted her lips to his. "Maybe you should think of something else." His breath felt hot against her skin, his lips incredibly tender when he brushed them over hers. "But don't worry about it right now," he whispered, carrying his kiss to the corner of her mouth. "There's something else you need to think about."

She couldn't imagine what that something could be. Not when he was being so incredibly gentle. His lips touched hers again, nipping, teasing.

Then he was pulling back and she was scrambling to make sense of what he'd just done. "What else do I need to think about?" she asked, wishing he hadn't stopped, grateful that he had.

"Food."

"Food?"

His own breathing suspiciously uneven, Cal skimmed his hands down her arms and stepped back. A single erratic heartbeat later, he shoved his hands in his pockets. "You said you didn't have any plans, and I'm tired of eating alone. You've got your choice. Your place or mine. All I have is canned stew.''

It took every ounce of fortitude Cal possessed to deny the need clawing inside him. He wanted her. In bed. Now. But he'd tasted her hesitation and he wouldn't risk the relationship that had somehow formed over the past week by pushing too fast. He needed it. It was the only thing that made being in Leesburg bearable. He was getting used to cold showers anyway. Not that they ever did any good.

''Meaning you'd rather come to my house,'' she concluded.

''Is that unreasonable?''

''No. It's just dangerous. I'm a lousy cook.''

The admission wasn't intended to make him change his mind. Not that she didn't question the wisdom of being with him any more than she had to. She really was a terrible cook. Nearly everyone in town knew it. Between the brownies she'd once made for a church tea and the casserole she'd concocted for a luncheon shortly thereafter, there wasn't an organization in town desperate enough to ask for her donation of a food dish for whatever cause it was sponsoring, hosting or celebrating that week. She told him that, too, as, knowing she couldn't leave him to eat alone, she followed the path to where it came out in the field across from her house.

Cal didn't seem worried, even if he did seem a little surprised that she wasn't more accomplished than she claimed to be in the kitchen. He merely told her he'd survived his own cooking this long, so he was probably immune to whatever she could come up with, then turned his attention to the white clapboard house with the gray shutters when she started toward its porch.

A football was stuck between the porch slats.

Seeing it, Cal raised an eyebrow.

"That's Jeremy's," Lindsey explained opening the front door.

"Jeremy?"

"The little boy next door."

The image of her tossing that ball to some chubby-cheeked little kid stuck in Cal's head as he followed her in. For some inexplicable reason, he had the feeling she'd mastered a perfect spiral pass. As he stepped into the house, the subtle scent of gardenia greeting him like an old friend, he didn't think that anything about Lindsey should surprise him anymore. The woman was nothing but a walking, talking collection of contradictions.

She could sew, but she couldn't cook.

She adored kids, and family meant the world to her, but she didn't want to get married and have a family of her own.

Her boutique was mostly soft pastels and lace. Her own clothes tended toward bold purples, corals, deep pinks and denim.

And her home was...well, contemporary, he supposed, with a few antiques thrown in just to keep things from being boring.

One old piece in particular caught his attention.

"Mind if I take a look at that?"

Lindsey's hand was on the knob of the closet door and her mind on the meager contents of her pantry, when she turned to see that Cal had stopped halfway into the room. He was frowning at the delicate side chair next to her beige modular sofa.

Knees creaking, he crouched beside the eighteenth-century Hepplewhite that had traveled in the passenger seat of her car, wrapped in a blanket, all the way from New York.

"It looks like an original," he said, the words almost reverent as he ran his hand along the elegantly curved arm.

"How did you know?"

He didn't just touch the wood, she noticed. He caressed it. Gently, like a lover. Strong, sensual, his fingers drifted over the grooves and curves, seeming to take pleasure in the texture of the grain, the richness of the finish.

"I just recognized it. This is one of his later designs," he said, his dark head disappearing behind the oval back. He tipped the chair up, checking out the underside of the seat and leg joints, then eased it back down. "Where did you get it?"

"At an auction."

Drawn by the concentration in his expression, she moved closer. He didn't seem to think it was at all unusual for someone to walk into a room and spot the only truly valuable antique in the place. Lindsey did. Yet what impressed her more just then was that his interest removed the somberness from his expression, taking years from his rugged face.

"I'd always wanted something old and venerable," she told him. "Something with a real history to it."

Incredibly, the corners of his mouth lifted. It wasn't quite a smile, but the effect was devastating. "Furniture with a past?"

She'd never thought of it that way. But, then, she'd never thought that a chair could make so much difference in a person's mood. Except it wasn't just the chair, she realized, watching him trail his fingers over the arm once more. It was the wood. The contact with it.

Watching his hand, seeing how carefully he stroked the chair, she found it truly pathetic that she actually envied a dead tree.

"When did you study antiques?"

She wished she hadn't asked. In the instant it took for him to turn to her, the somberness returned.

"I never studied them. Not formally," he admitted, shoving his hands into his pockets as if to keep them to himself. "I just apprenticed for a guy who specialized in replicas and restorations. I read everything he had. And I picked up things from pieces we worked on."

"If you read everything a specialist had, you studied them," she informed him, wondering why he minimized his knowledge. Her glance narrowed on the beautifully crafted chair. "You made pieces like that?"

His quiet "Yeah" had a distinctly dismissive sound to it when he turned.

Without another glance at what had first snagged his attention, he crossed to where she stood by the dining table. The thing was covered with invoices, files and adding-machine tape. Obviously that was where she did her books. "Where's the kitchen?"

"In there," she muttered vaguely, still studying the chair. She'd looked at it hundreds of times, but she'd never before noticed what she saw when she considered that Cal had made something just like it. What had gone into it. The patience. The skill. The time.

It wasn't just furniture. It was a form of art. And if the appreciation she had seen in his eyes was any indication, Cal wasn't just a carpenter. He was a craftsman.

Suddenly, an image of the small inserts on her new dressing-room doors flashed in her mind, an image of exquisitely formed vines and leaves embellishing satin-smooth wood.

Suspicion hushed her voice. "Did you carve the panels on the dressing-room doors you built for me?"

"Yeah," he mumbled, as if the matter were insignificant. "I did."

She thought he'd bought them. "When did you have time to do that?"

"At night." When he couldn't sleep.

"They're beautiful," she told him, though all he did was look a little uncomfortable at the compliment. "But Jett told me you built . . . buildings."

"I do. When there's work. What's that got to do with dinner?"

"It has nothing to do with dinner." She frowned up at him, refusing to let him change the subject. "I was just wondering why you're working on houses or offices or whatever, when you have that kind of a skill."

"Because there aren't many places where that kind of work is done, and I don't want to work in a shop that turns out nothing but cabinets for tract houses. Unless I can have my own shop, I'd rather follow the trade."

Inquiry sharpened her glance, her head tilting slightly as she studied his unremarkable expression. "Do you want your own shop?"

He was an arm's length from her. Close enough to see the tiny chips of gold in her deep-brown eyes and the smooth texture of her full, inviting mouth. Behind her, he could see a doorway and the side of a refrigerator. As edgy as he was feeling, he had to satisfy one kind of hunger or the other. Soon.

"That's why I took this job," he told her, not sure what to make of how often her questions hit their mark. "So I could buy a building and more tools." He settled his hands on her shoulders and promptly turned her around. "Get a can opener, will you? I'm starving."

* * *

He wanted his own woodcrafting shop. A place where he could build custom pieces. Of his own design, preferably. Of someone else's, if necessary. He just wanted to be in one place. Working with wood. That was what he'd always wanted to do.

That was what Lindsey learned from Cal that evening while they sat in the small bay of her little country kitchen and ate salad and frozen chicken pies hot from the microwave.

He allowed her no insight beyond that, however, stopping short of mentioning just how long "always" had been while he finished his meal and polished off the rest of what she couldn't eat. Since Lindsey didn't want to risk having him clam up on her, she let that question go. It wasn't necessary anyway. Remembering what Louella had said about Cal having helped her brother with a high-school woodworking project, and the woman's offhand comment about the quality of the work, Lindsey had the feeling his desire went back further than he cared to remember.

Instead she asked where he wanted his shop to be, and he told her he figured he'd buy a place somewhere in Austin. Then she asked if that was where he'd apprenticed, and the conversation seemed to stall.

"I just thought that was where you'd learned about antiques," she explained, not sure why the question had caused him to hesitate.

"I learned about them in Georgia," he finally said, looking as if he knew answering her question would only lead to another.

Resigned, he lowered his fork to his plate, studying the curve of the tines. "My shop teacher in high school had a friend who was restoring an old house in Atlanta. The guy needed somebody with more muscle than skill, who was willing to work for food and a roof over his head. Teach knew I wanted to leave, so he told me about him. I worked for Stan for six years and three restorations, then he took a teaching position and I headed for the union hall to sign up and find work.''

His expression devoid of emotion, he picked up his plate and headed for the sink. His response had been little more than a recitation of facts. Quickly stated and with no indication that another question would be welcome, much less answered.

Coming up beside him at the Wedgwood-blue counter, Lindsey ventured one anyway.

''How did you wind up in Austin?'' she asked, when what she really wanted to know was why he'd wanted to leave the ranch so long ago.

His answer came with a tight shrug. ''Just drifted back.''

He had closed up in front of her. He'd been fine while they'd spoken of his shop and what he wanted to do with it. But her innocent inquiry had brought him too close to the invisible borders he'd set for himself, the borders that separated his life now from whatever it was he'd left here. She'd seen the wall come up just before he'd mentioned high school.

Hating the way that made her feel, she pulled back from what she desperately wanted to pursue.

''You'd better make it a big shop,'' she told him, willing the muscle in his jaw to relax as she took his plate from him. ''If the rest of your work is anywhere near as good as what you've done for me, you'll have more to do than you can handle.'' He didn't skimp. He didn't take shortcuts. That sort of pride in a person's work was rare. ''Speaking as someone who has worked with too little space for too long, find someplace huge. You'll practically be living there.''

He finally met her eyes, his dark head towering above hers. She didn't know if it was the change of subject or her very intentional compliment on what he'd done for her so far, but some of the distance receded. In its place was something that looked like curiosity. Or maybe disbelief. There was a faint pinch to his brow as he studied her face, but he said nothing. He just stared at her as if he found it difficult to believe she had that much faith in him, then lifted his hand to caress the side of her neck.

"I'll make sure it's big enough," he said, then slipped his fingers up the back of her head and drew her forward. His kiss tasted faintly of thanks, but mostly of need. Need for things she couldn't fathom. Need for things he probably couldn't fathom himself. But when he took her hand and led her to the front door long moments later, he said only that he would see her in the morning, then left her watching him from the threshold.

For a long time after he'd gone, Lindsey stood in the doorway with her fingers pressed to her lips, reluctant to close the door and, once again, be alone. She wasn't like her sisters. They were both nesters, very much in need of the security they found in their homes. Lindsey wasn't like that. It wasn't physical surroundings that gave her security, which was probably why she was rarely ever home. It was being in motion. In doing. She hadn't always been that way. But it was how she was now. And a person was happiest when she learned to be content with what she had.

Yet as she stood there, looking from the warm lights glowing from the house of the family next door, she didn't feel any of the contentment she'd worked so hard to achieve.

Cal would be leaving. Not tomorrow or next week. But he would be leaving. It didn't matter that the more she learned about him, the more she needed to know. Or that a part of her was beginning to ache for things she'd made herself stop wanting. What mattered was that he wanted no part of everything that mattered to her—and that whatever need he felt for her was only temporary. Soon he would be gone. He'd made that clear more times than she could count.

Chapter Eight

"You look like you could use this whole pot this morning." Essie hefted the globe-shaped carafe, preparing to pour the cup of coffee-to-go Lindsey had just ordered. From beneath her crown of snowy curls, blue eyes twinkled. "Had someone in here not long ago who looked like he hadn't had much sleep, either," she said mysteriously. "Must have been something in the air last night preventing folks from getting a decent night's rest."

Stifling yet another yawn, Lindsey shook her head at the speculation in the cherub-faced woman's eyes. "I have no idea what you're talking about, Essie. Or who. All I know is that I was up until four a.m. making sachets shaped like Texas. I got them done, too," she added, omitting the fact that she hadn't started the project until midnight because thoughts of Cal had kept her tossing and turning in bed until then. "All two dozen of them."

CHRISTINE FLYNN 149

Essie's speculation faded. Disappointed that her hinting hadn't turned up anything promising, she plucked a foam cup from the stack by the coffee maker and dutifully latched onto the new subject. "Those sachets for the craft fair over at the church? The ones Mary Johnston was supposed to have donated?"

Lindsey told her that they were, far more interested in the dark, steaming liquid the woman poured into the cup than she was Essie's commentary about how hard it made things for others when someone didn't keep a commitment. Running on three hours of sleep and needing coffee before she encountered Cal, Lindsey was hard-pressed to concentrate on much of anything else at the moment. She really hadn't minded the project anyway. It had given her something to do last night other than pace.

"About an hour ago," Essie was saying, sounding as if she'd changed the subject somewhere along the line, "and he asked me to give you a message."

The woman's words accomplished what even caffeine would not. The instant they registered, surprise, hesitation and something that felt suspiciously like loss vaporized Lindsey's fatigue.

"Cal's gone?"

"He left about an hour ago," Essie repeated, her thin, white eyebrows lowering at the disquiet in Lindsey's expression. "He said to tell you that he didn't move those big dressers of yours because they go in the middle of the room. He thought it would be easier for you to set up the rest of your merchandise with some free space to work in." A white, plastic lid was pressed into place with a quiet little snap. "He moved everything else to where you had it on your floor plan and he'll take care of the dressers when he gets back."

"From where?"

"Austin," Essie said.

Her puzzled look made Lindsey think the woman had either already mentioned that or that she would have, had Lindsey been a little more patient.

"He needs some kind of sealer or scaler or something that Gil didn't have over at the Feed and Hardware and he didn't want to wait for him to order it. Said that as long as he was there, he'd run by his place to take care of a few things, and that he'd be back by one o'clock or so," Essie added.

Relief washed over Lindsey, unexpectedly, like the reaction that had preceded it. Refusing to consider why that reaction had been there, she allowed herself only to wonder why he hadn't mentioned his plans last night. She was curious, too, about why he'd had Essie convey them instead of leaving her a note.

"I take it he came over to get coffee this morning," she said, certain that would explain Essie's involvement.

"Actually, he came over to fix my screen. He noticed that it needed new hinges when he changed my light the other day," she explained, wiping her hands on her apron. "You want a muffin with this?"

Shaking her head to indicate that she'd pass this morning, Lindsey slid two quarters over the pastry case in exchange for the coffee. "He fixed your door this morning?"

"Sure did. Right before he left. Took some of my maple-frosted doughnuts with him, too."

Lindsey didn't mean to stare at Essie as if she seriously questioned the woman's grasp on reality. But what Essie had said didn't make sense, given the amount of work involved. It would have taken Cal hours to move his power tools from where he'd been working, to sweep up and to move in the display fixtures. To have had time on top of that to change the hinges on Essie's door he must have been up half the night.

As she had been. Not that her inability to sleep had anything to do with his. It just surprised her. So did what he'd done for Essie. For whatever reason, he'd actually allowed himself to step beyond the boundaries he'd set for himself in this town.

"He's an interesting man," Essie observed, her tone deliberately bland. "Not at all what a person would expect. Once you get past that standoffishness of his, he's really rather nice." She cocked her head, the speculation behind her silver-rimmed glasses running rampant. "Don't you think?"

Essie was usually much better at hinting for information. At the moment, the woman was as transparent as the glaze on her fruit tarts. She was clearly hunting for some clue to what, if anything, was going on with her and Cal. She had been since the moment Lindsey walked in. Realizing that, Lindsey also now understood that it had been Cal who had come in before her looking so tired.

Fortunately, Essie's not-so-subtle attempt to ease information out of Lindsey was interrupted by the arrival of Sue Albrecht when she stopped in to pick up a coffee cake for a before-school teachers' meeting. Sue, the enormously patient woman in charge of the home-ec department, promptly reminded Lindsey that she was due in the home-ec room for the prom dress project at one-thirty that afternoon, then asked if she could peek at the improvements to the boutique. The request afforded Lindsey a perfectly legitimate opportunity to avoid any further discussion about her carpenter, since Essie couldn't leave her bakery and Sue, unlike nearly everyone else in town, was far too polite to pry.

That didn't mean Lindsey didn't think about Cal, though. For his sake, she was glad Essie had discovered how much more there was to him than the old rumors allowed most people to believe. But getting past his protective facade wasn't all a person had to do to get to know the man. That unapproachable mien of his was only the surface. It was the layers beneath that were so daunting.

Not that she was interested in chipping away at them. Not for herself. Or so she silently insisted when she left him a note telling him she was at the high school if he hadn't returned by the time she had to leave.

Cal would have been on time had he not added another errand to his list. After he picked up the supplies he needed, he stopped by his apartment to check his mail and pay his rent. While he was there, he thought he'd check the classifieds in the paper for a lathe, now that he could get serious about opening his own shop. But something about encountering the scattered newspapers in front of his door and the collection of fliers hanging on the knob robbed him of the little enthusiasm his fatigue allowed for his new venture. He'd forgotten to cancel the paper, so it was his fault they'd piled up. Had the same thing happened to Lindsey, a neighbor would have picked them up so the place wouldn't have looked quite so abandoned.

Not sure where that thought had come from, not liking the way it made him feel, Cal stayed only long enough to remember why he spent so little time in the place he loosely referred to as "home," and headed out of town. On the way, driven by the need to do something positive, he stopped at a real-estate office to see what sort of buildings were available for a woodworking shop. The agent, a nervous little guy who practically backed himself into the wall when Cal walked in, actually came up with a few possibilities—once he'd realized that the big man in the black T-shirt and ponytail hadn't come in looking for trouble. But the man's alarmed reaction stuck with Cal long after he was back on the road and the last of the three buildings he'd looked at was fast fading behind him.

He didn't like the feeling it left him with, either.

More than once he'd been told he could intimidate any woman—and most men. To be honest, he supposed he'd made use of that ability more than once over the years, too. He wasn't particularly proud of being able to stare a man down. But it beat the hell out of having the hell beat out of him, which was why he'd honed the ability in the first place.

Not that he'd been in a position in the past fifteen or so years where he'd had to physically defend himself. Or anyone else, for that matter. Other than the few scuffles he hadn't managed to avert at Papa Joe's, he hadn't been in a fight since he was seventeen. And that had been with his father. His old man had been on one of his binges again, staggering and swearing and taking it out on Jett, because by then Jett had been the only one around not big enough to defend himself. That had been the night Cal had laid his dad out cold on the living-room floor. It had also been the night Jett had run away from home. Jett had been fifteen years old at the time. Cal had helped him pack.

Logan had been gone three years by then.

Cal forced his grip on the steering wheel to ease. He had no idea why he was letting himself think about such things. Unless it was simply because he couldn't avoid them any longer. Everywhere he looked, he found another reminder. Then there was Lindsey and that incomprehensible loyalty she had to her own family.

Someone like her could never understand how it had felt to grow up with a constant knot of fear in his gut—the constant apprehension of never knowing when his father was going to backhand him for some transgression, real or imagined. Of never knowing what was the right thing to do, because the person he wanted to please couldn't be pleased no matter how hard he tried. So he had stopped trying, and had concentrated only on protecting himself until he could escape.

And he had.

So why, he wondered, when he realized he'd taken the old highway rather than turning off at the freeway back in Austin, was he driving along the only public road in the entire state of Texas that would take him past the turnoff to the RW Ranch?

To prove you can drive right past where you grew up without giving it a second thought, he told himself, refusing to consider any other possibility.

An hour later, that was exactly what he did, blowing by the turnoff at a steady sixty miles an hour. Thirty minutes after that, feeling as restless as a caged bear, he was in Leesburg, reading the note Lindsey had tacked on her back door.

She was at the high school. According to the note, when she left there she had to carpool five members of the basketball team over to Fredricksburg for a game, so she would see him tomorrow. She hoped all went well for him in Austin.

Not wanting to believe her absence made any difference, he jammed the note in his pocket and proceeded to haul a ladder, scrapers and masking tape out to the sidewalk. During the day, while he had light, he would prepare and paint the outside of the building. At night, when he couldn't do anything else, he'd cut out and build the cornices and architectural gingerbread he would attach later.

Two weeks was the time he'd allotted himself for the task. One more to restore the bandstand. It would be a push to get that much work done so quickly. Especially working alone. And if the weather turned, his schedule would go right out the window. But he needed to know there was an end in sight.

He'd learned long ago that by focusing on his escape, he could put up with anything for a while.

The man was obsessed.

Or so it seemed to Lindsey when she turned the corner from her house the next morning and saw a long, aluminum ladder propped against the side of her building half a block up the street. Cal was on it, scraping old paint from the eaves. From the paint chips and curls littering the ground, he'd been at it for quite a while, too. When she asked how long, though, after what she'd thought was a pleasant "Good morning," his response was something less than congenial.

"Awhile," he muttered, then added that he would move the display dressers whenever she was ready, and returned to his task without so much as a glance.

From where she stood a few feet from the ladder to avoid the shower of falling paint flakes, she saw the muscle in his jaw jerk. Not knowing what was wrong, wishing it didn't matter, she simply said, "Whenever it's convenient for you." Then, turning, she saw Louella standing up the street, watching him.

As attuned to him as Lindsey was becoming, she suddenly realized his mood made sense. Lindsey could well imagine how he felt about this part of his job. Inside her shop, he'd been able to do his work in relative peace. Exposed to the entire square, he'd probably get nothing but grief.

"Do you want some help?" she asked, thinking it might be easier for him out here if he had company as a buffer.

From his perch ten feet above the sidewalk, Cal glanced down to where Lindsey stood with her hands on her hips. The morning sun caught the hair tumbling around her shoulders, creating a halo of silver and gold out of deep wheat. That same bright light illuminated the fine grain of her skin, revealing a flush of pink in her cheeks. She looked as fresh as the early-spring air, and far less wary than he feared she might be, given the direction their relationship had taken the other night.

But, then, Lindsey wouldn't consciously let her apprehension show anyway. She was as protective of herself as he was of himself.

Though he'd never considered it before, the trait wasn't always an asset.

"Do you know anyone who has a longer ladder?" he asked, sounding as if he were truly trying to ease up. "This one won't reach the pitch."

"Logan might." She squinted up at the high peak of her roof. "I'll ask Sam if she knows."

"Don't bother your sister."

"It's not a bother. She won't mind."

"*I* mind. Forget it."

The look he sent her would have toasted ice.

Not appreciating his reaction, appreciating even less that his moods could so easily affect hers, she sent it right back.

"For Pete's sake, Cal. It's just a ladder. Who it belongs to doesn't make any difference. Do you need it or not?"

He hesitated, though she couldn't tell if he was weighing how badly he required the piece of equipment or considering whether he wanted to venture even vicarious contact with Logan. His reactions where his brother was concerned were still dishearteningly negative, but at least they were losing that knee-jerk immediacy.

At least, it appeared that way to Lindsey as she watched him drag his hand over his face and blow out a deep breath. It also appeared that she frustrated him as much as he did her.

"Can you think of anyone else?" he asked, ever so patiently.

"Not offhand."

"Then I'll find somewhere to rent one. Thanks anyway," he muttered, and turned back to his task.

Lindsey hiked her bag higher on her shoulder and started toward the café, thinking the man's head as thick as the board he was stripping.

"If you're going for coffee," she heard him call down, "don't get any for me." The metal scraper sent a mist of paint dust floating to the cement. "Essie brought me some a while ago."

Essie delivered? That was a first.

"That was nice," Lindsey told him, wondering if maple-glazed doughnuts had come with what was undoubtedly exclusive service. "So was what you did for her yesterday."

"It was nothing," he muttered, not seeming at all surprised that she would know about it.

"It wasn't 'nothing' to Essie. I'm going to find a ladder."

Seeing exasperation darken his features, she felt sure he was about to repeat his intention to rent one, when she turned on her heel and headed to where Louella stood outside the diner's front window. She could feel Cal's eyes on her back as she approached the chatty waitress, but she wasn't going to risk turning around and meeting his glare head-on. There was no sense in letting the whole town know she thought he was as stubborn as sin.

"Everything still going okay over there?" Louella asked, opening the door to lead Lindsey inside.

"Sure is. The man practically works himself into the ground."

"Guess some people can change." Bright plastic bracelets clicking, Louella slipped behind the counter and reached for the stack of take-out cups. "One or two this morning?"

"Just one," Lindsey told her, then asked if she knew where she could get a ladder, since the woman was acquainted with just about everyone in town.

Offhand, Louella didn't know who had a long enough one, either. So while she fixed Lindsey's coffee, Lindsey headed up the block to ask Sandy over at the newspaper office if he had one. She got as far as the barbershop and the trio of elderly gentlemen parked on the bench in front of it, before she remembered that the newspaper office didn't open for another hour.

Rats, she muttered. "'Morning," she said to the two rheumy-eyed men watching her. The third man, old Mr. Josephson, sat with his chins tucked to his chest, the rhythmic rise and fall of his rounded shoulders seeming to indicate he was in the midst of his morning nap.

"Whatcha after?" Gramps asked.

Whenever the weather was sunny and warm, as it was today, that bench was regularly occupied by members of the retired set. In full view of the square and the shops surrounding it, it afforded an excellent view of everyone's comings and goings. Because of that, Lindsey didn't have to explain why she wanted a longer ladder when she answered Gramps's question. They could clearly see why Cal needed it. She only had to explain why he didn't already have one of an appropriate size.

"I thought he was supposed to know what he's doing," Hugh muttered around the stem of his pipe. "What sort of carpenter goes looking for work without the proper equipment?" With his arms crossed over his barrel chest and his outstretched legs crossed at the ankles, he transferred his frown from the man reducing the eaves to bare wood on the building down the street to the young woman in front of them.

"He didn't come looking for the work," Lindsey explained, forcing patience past the quick surge of irritation she'd felt at the criticism. "I found him and asked him to do it. And he's not just a carpenter," she had to add, thinking of the beautiful detail work he'd done on her dressing-room doors. She could only imagine the effort that had gone into carving those panels. "You should see the work he's done inside my shop."

"You saying he's good?"

"Come see for yourself."

Herb looked dubious. "You still got all them frilly things sitting around all over the place?"

"I'm afraid so. But you're welcome anytime."

Herb snorted. "I ain't going in no lady's fancy shop."

Mr. Josephson continued to snooze.

Gramps simply rubbed his bushy gray beard, looking as if he might actually be considering her offer.

"Seems to know what he's doing over there," he observed, ignoring the way Herb squinted at him. "He's not taking any shortcuts, anyway. Tell you what. Have him try Gil over at the Feed and Hardware. He's got an extension ladder I expect he wouldn't mind lending out for a while. Not with all the business you've been giving him. It might not be any longer than the one the boy's using there, but it's worth a try, I'd say."

Lindsey's smiling "Thank you" was met with the nudge of his thumb to the brim of his seed cap. Herb just gave another grunt.

Mr. Josephson slept on.

Lindsey's coffee was waiting for her when she pushed open the café's swinging door.

"I called my brother," Louella said from where she slid a plate of eggs in front of a customer at the opposite end of the counter. "He said he has an eighteen-foot extension type you're welcome to use. He's taking a load of hay out to the Rocking J tomorrow, so he'll be coming through town. He can drop it off in the morning."

Change jingled as Lindsey set it near the register. "Thanks, Louella. I really appreciate it. And thank Jack, too," she called back, thinking this was one of the things she loved best about this place. When a person needed something, all she had to do was ask. Invariably, someone came through.

Cal wasn't on the ten-foot ladder when she got back to him. He'd climbed down to move it over. Biceps flexing against the short sleeves of his paint-spattered navy T-shirt, he picked it up, moved it over eight feet and planted the thing back on the sidewalk as if it weighed no more than a handful of feathers.

Ignoring the memories of how it felt to be wrapped in those strong arms was impossible.

"Gramps said to try Gil. He thinks Gil's ladder is about the same size as yours, though."

"It is."

He'd obviously already checked there. "Well, Louella's brother has a bigger one. He'll bring it tomorrow. Is that soon enough, or do you need it now?"

"I don't like to borrow, Lindsey."

"You didn't. I borrowed it."

"That's semantics."

That was true. "People like to help, Cal. Didn't you like helping Essie?"

It was impossible for Lindsey to tell what thoughts were lurking behind Cal's piercing blue eyes. He simply stood there, one hand on the side of the ladder and the other planted on his hip, while his glance moved over her face, his expression a blend of exasperation and indulgence. When his eyes eventually drifted to her mouth, they lingered long enough to change from exasperation to expectation and indulgence to heat.

A moment later, seeming to remember their audience on the bench, he cleared his throat. "Yeah. I did," he finally, reluctantly, admitted, and turned back to his task.

Aware of that same audience, but more aware how the small smile he gave her made her heart feel full inside her chest, Lindsey headed inside to tackle her own project. It seemed so much safer than letting herself consider why his finding something to feel good about in this town should make her feel good, too. So, because it was safer, Lindsey threw herself into work the way Cal did, determined to have her shop open for business tomorrow. She had to leave early to take Mildred Gunther over to the retirement center in Adele to visit her mother since Mildred didn't drive, but she had plenty of time to get things finished up before then.

At least, she would have if Gramps hadn't decided to take her up on her offer to look at Cal's work. And if Sam hadn't called wanting to go to lunch. And if the postperson hadn't delivered an order for forty shirts. But falling behind again on her orders was the furthest thought from

Lindsey's mind when she arrived home that night and found Cal turning from her door.

The beam of her headlights caught him with his hands in his pockets as he started down her steps.

It was nearly nine o'clock. When Lindsey had taken Mildred home at eight, he'd still been working. Not outside, for it had been dark by then. He'd been working inside, in the large room she would use for storage. Lindsey had noticed the lights on. Just as she'd noticed that those same lights were out when she'd driven past moments earlier.

Not sure if it was anxiety or anticipation knotting her stomach, she climbed out of the Bronco and headed for the porch. Cal had remained right where he'd stopped when the headlights had hit him, his feet planted firmly on her top step and his hands jammed in his pockets.

"Hungry again?" she asked, thinking he might have shown up so he wouldn't have to eat alone.

She'd forgotten to leave on the porch light. With only a pale half-moon for illumination, she barely caught the negative movement of his head. She didn't need to see his expression to feel his agitation, though. Like the vibration of a tightly strung piano wire, it hummed through her body, fading her smile and tightening the knot in her midsection.

Needing to escape the shadows, she slipped past him, using the penlight on her key chain to find the lock while he held the screen door. He walked in behind her, waiting until she'd turned on the rose-shaded lamp by the sofa before he closed the door.

"I just came by to see if you needed anything from Austin. I've got to run back up in the morning. It's a personal errand," he added, not wanting her to think he was having to make the trip again for materials.

The lamp cast the room in a gentle pink glow. As the shadows outside had sharpened Cal's expression, that soft light now stole that hardness from his rugged features.

"Is everything all right?"

Her quick concern removed the unease he'd sensed in her only a moment ago. That concern was immediate, completely without reserve. And it went a long way to ease the restlessness that had plagued him ever since he'd called it quits for the night.

"Everything is fine," he told her, amazed that he suddenly felt as if everything actually was. He didn't know if he trusted the feeling. Certainly it wasn't one with which he was all that familiar. But he didn't care. All he cared about was that, right now, he felt better than he had since he'd seen her frown up at him from the sidewalk this morning. "I just want to have another look at a building I saw yesterday. If it's what I want, I don't intend to risk losing it by putting it off."

He wasn't sure why, but he'd thought she'd be pleased for him. Or maybe it was just that he wanted her to be, though he couldn't identify a reason for that, either. Maybe it was that, when he'd told her of his plans the other night, she'd seemed to believe in his idea. More important, she'd seemed to believe in him, something no one else had ever done. But the curve at the corner of her lovely mouth was a weak imitation of the smile he only now realized he'd hoped to see, and the look that darted through her eyes just before she glanced away struck him as strangely dispirited.

"I hope it's what you're looking for. That it's big enough," she added, as if to show her faith in him.

He moved closer, thinking she'd lift her gaze again. When she didn't he reached out, curving his hand at the side of her neck to nudge her chin up with his thumb. Searching her eyes, he could find no trace of what he'd seen before. It was almost as if she'd looked hurt, though that made no sense to him at all.

"Me, too. I don't want to waste a lot of time hunting around."

Finally, the smile formed. "So, you're the impatient sort," she said, as if she'd been trying to find some neat little pigeonhole to stuff him into. "Once you make up your mind you're going to do something, that's it?"

"Always."

The smile faltered. Beneath his fingers her pulse leaped.

"But I don't think I'm particularly impatient," he continued, marveling at how easily she accepted his touch. "I know some things can't be rushed, no matter how badly you want them. They just take a while to accomplish."

He was speaking from experience. There was no doubt about that in Lindsey's mind when she heard the edge slip into his voice. But she was far more aware of the heat of his hand where it rested against her neck, and the light in his eyes as they dropped to her mouth. She had the feeling he could be an extraordinarily patient man when he wanted to—and thoughts of what he could do with that patience were as provocative as they were threatening.

It was the threat that forced the question. "Do you ever change your mind about what you want?"

"I've never wanted that much." With a touch as light as air, he stroked the pulse at the base of her neck with his thumb. "I guess I never knew what I was supposed to want."

The admission, spoken so simply, tore right through her.

"You're supposed to want what makes you happy," she told him, wondering if there had ever been a time when he truly had been happy. "Or what fulfills you."

"What if you aren't sure what that is?"

He watched his thumb, seeming to draw some sort of comfort from the rhythmic motion. Or possibly, the comfort was simply in touching her.

Understanding the need for that contact all too well, she offered the only advice she could. "If you don't know, it's probably because there are things that make you unhappy standing in the way. If you can eliminate them, it might not be so hard to find the other."

"You make it sound so simple."

"No," she said, her voice hushed, despite the disquiet filling her. "Facing what hurts us is never simple. But maybe it's not as difficult as you think."

His brow lowered at that, but she felt his thumb brush the vulnerable hollow once more before he slowly raised his eyes to hers. A moment later, the motion stopped, and the contemplative quality ebbed from his expression. Defensiveness had taken its place.

"You're talking about Logan, aren't you?"

Chapter Nine

The flatness in Cal's deep voice had removed any trace of inquiry from his question. All Lindsey heard was accusation. She could still hear it. Though he'd spoken quietly, too quietly, his words seemed to echo between them in the small, silent house.

"Yes," she murmured, to keep that silence from magnifying itself. "I am."

His hand fell from her neck, threatening to take her courage with it. This wasn't her battle, but what was at stake had somehow begun to feel very personal.

"Why don't you just go see him and get it over with?" she urged, grabbing his forearm to stall his retreat from her. "Instead of fighting it, just do it. He wants to see you, Cal. Sam said he's wanted to see you since you got here. If you don't want to go to the ranch, he'll come here. But the decision has to be yours. He won't crowd you. It would just be so much easier on both of you if you'd just give yourselves a chance...."

"Don't, Lindsey."

He pulled back, the break in physical contact effectively shortcircuiting the less tangible connection they'd had only seconds ago. For a moment, she fell silent, quieted more by the need to protect herself than by his terse demand. But this was the man who had understood the need she'd felt to run when her life had fallen apart, and she wanted desperately to understand why he had.

He'd moved to the center of the room, the only place with enough space for him to pace. Not that he was. He stood as still and immovable as an oak, in the middle of the braided mauve rug, one hand clamped over the back of his neck and his shoulders rigid.

Lindsey remained rooted by the end table, guardedly watching him from the circle of pale light. "Can you tell me what happened?"

He could. But he wouldn't. She knew that the moment she caught his shuttered expression. "Let it go, will you? What's happened between Logan and me isn't something you can fix, so you can just stop trying. I'm not one of your projects."

"My projects?" She'd expected the dismissal, the irritation. They were his best defenses. It was where he chose to direct his irritation that she hadn't been prepared for. "What are you talking about?"

"Come on," he muttered, not impressed with her bewilderment. "Fixing things is what you do, Lindsey. That's *all* you do. If someone has a problem, you're the first one there to bail him out, or take over, or mediate. It doesn't matter that you're already so overloaded with commitments that you're never on time for anything. You're always looking for another project to take on."

Lindsey opened her mouth in protest, only she wasn't sure how to refute what was, basically, the truth. Instead, not sure what he found so wrong with what she did, she latched onto the only defense she could find. "How could you possibly know what I do, much less know what matters to me?"

He took a step closer. Without thinking, she took a step back and felt her shoulder bump the wall.

"I know what matters to you," he assured her, his voice low and certain. "But I really don't think you want to hear my theory about why you've locked yourself away in this place. As for how I know what you do," he went on, seeking even more distance from the subject she'd first raised, "I've spent at least half of every day since I got here less than a hundred yards away from you. I don't know what I've missed since I started working outside, but just a couple days ago you were taking on everything from a project for a church you don't even belong to because some lady didn't get her stuff made in time, to working out a car loan... which you cosigned," he stressed, as if that point was of significance to his argument, "for the woman who makes shirts for you."

"What's wrong with helping Camille get a new car?"

"There's nothing *wrong* with it." Exasperation flashed across his features. "But it was just another situation you wanted to fix. Just as you've wanted to fix what's wrong between me and my brother by dropping more hints than I can count about Logan and his family."

A faint roiling sensation knotted her stomach. She couldn't deny that she had wanted to get the brothers together. She would not, however, allow him to believe she had done anything intentional to push him toward Logan. She hadn't yet found an opportunity.

"You must have been looking for hints."

"Not hardly."

"You must have been," she insisted. "I haven't deliberately brought up Logan's name in any conversation with you . . . except when we were trying to find a ladder," she had to add, but that hardly counted. "If anything, I've gone out of my way to avoid it."

He didn't believe her. He also didn't care to belabor the point. "Then keep avoiding it."

Any sane person would have done just that. The man stood six feet away, his big body looming like a shadow and his expression just as forbidding. Between the daunting stance and the way his jaw was working, there was absolutely nothing about him that would invite anyone to pursue the subject any further.

Lindsey never had been one to settle for the obvious. To her, the fact that Cal hadn't clammed up at the mention of Logan's name meant that somewhere a door had opened. Just a crack, probably. But it was a start.

"I won't mention it again, if you'll agree to consider something."

Cal released a breath of pure frustration.

"You're as tenacious as a pitbull with a bone. You know that? No, Lindsey. I will not consider going out to the ranch."

"That isn't what I was going to suggest," she calmly stated. "I just wanted you to consider a possibility."

"What possibility?" he muttered, his voice utterly flat.

"That as much as you hate this place, you wouldn't have come back had you not really wanted to see him."

Her theory, so quietly spoken, had every protective instinct Cal possessed slamming into place. Backing her to the wall, he very deliberately planted a hand on either side of her head.

His breath was warm, his voice low, and every word he spoke bore a finely honed edge. "You really should get a life for yourself. You know that? The people around here might not mind you living vicariously through them, but you don't have any idea what you're talking about where I'm concerned. The only reason I came here is that I need the money you're paying me. That's the only reason. Got that?"

Her eyes were huge in her face, the vulnerability there as obvious as the confusion. And the hurt. Slowly she nodded, the acquiescent motion so unlike her that Cal couldn't avoid the swift pang of guilt that sliced through him. But years of protecting himself surged over any regret he might have suffered at his harshness. He had let her weaken his defenses. He would not let it happen again.

His hands slid past her head as he shoved himself away.

"I'm not sure what time I'll be back tomorrow," he said on his way to the door.

A moment later, he'd walked out.

Lindsey's knees held out until she reached the sofa. The slam of the door still echoing in her ears, she stared at the lace curtains swinging over the window on the door and sank to the edge of the cushion.

She wasn't sure what she felt at the moment, other than a little numb. She couldn't fault Cal's reaction, which she wanted very much to do. She couldn't even rustle up any anger at him, though she wanted to do that, too.

He'd told her to drop it and she hadn't listened.

He'd told her again, and she'd pushed anyway.

Then he'd pushed back.

You don't want to hear my theory about why you've locked yourself away in this place.

It had been a long time since Lindsey had felt as lost as she did at that moment. Not since she'd left New York. But then she had been able to focus on getting away, on putting it all behind her. Now there was no place to go.

Sinking back into the corner of the sofa, she dragged a throw pillow over to hug against her stomach. It was one Annie had made for her years ago, a needlepoint square that simply said Home.

This was her home. The only place she'd ever lived for longer than two years. But it didn't feel anywhere near as secure as it had not so very long ago.

Cal was right about her. She did tend to live through other people. But it wasn't something she'd deliberately set out to do, and she'd never meant to interfere. Most of the time, people came to her when something needed to be done. Even when she offered first, her intentions were always the best. But until she'd found herself with her back to the wall, she hadn't had to face what she'd done when she'd holed up in this place.

Cal had recognized it, though. And now that she'd pushed him into tearing away the facade, there was no escaping it. By becoming so involved in everything that took place in this town, she had created a life for herself that made it hard to notice what was missing from it—the husband and the children she'd once dreamed of. But she needed her life the way it was. She needed to have so much to do that she had no time for herself. It was her security; she had nothing else without it.

At least, her life had felt secure before Cal Whitaker had unearthed its foundations.

Drawing a shaky breath, she glanced at the antique chair he'd been drawn to just a few short nights ago. She wasn't the only one whose security had been tampered with. She had done the same thing to Cal when she'd all but insisted that he face what he'd sought for years to avoid. It was no wonder he'd lashed out as he had. He'd had to protect himself.

At the very least, she owed him an apology.

It was midafternoon before Lindsey heard Cal return from Austin. He didn't come inside the boutique, though she all but held her breath waiting to see if he would. He went right to work on the exterior of the building—which was where she found him after the twenty minutes it took her to screw up her courage to ask if he would come in to talk to her for a moment.

Unfortunately, he wasn't alone. Gramps and Herb had abandoned their bench to get a closer look at what he was doing. Standing on either side of the ladder, they were watching Cal pry off a piece of trim he intended to replace above one of the long windows.

All three men looked over when she rounded the corner. But only Gramps and Herb acknowledged her when, some of the sureness fading from her stride, she continued toward them. After holding her glance for all of three seconds, Cal went right back to scraping.

Though the day had warmed to a pleasant seventy degrees, Lindsey felt a definite chill.

"Just telling Whitaker here that I can't recall the last time this building got a coat of paint," Gramps said to her, oblivious to the sudden drop in temperature. "Won't hardly recognize it once it's done, I imagine."

The conversation she'd interrupted sounded purely social, the sort of idle chat that occupied most of the day for many of the folks in town. Had Lindsey not been so aware of how deliberately Cal was ignoring her, she might have found it curious that such a conversation was taking place between these particular men.

After acknowledging Gramps's comment and Herb's desultory nod with a friendly smile, she glanced up. Sweat already stained Cal's T-shirt where it pulled against his broad back, and the set of his shoulders looked just as rigid as it had last night when he'd walked out her door. "I just wanted to see how everything is going."

"Looks like it's going fine," Gramps responded, failing to notice that the comment might not have been directed at him. "With the weather warming up the way it is, no reason he can't get this done by the middle of next week, like he says he wants to."

"That soon?" Lindsey's head swung back to Cal. "I thought you said it would take two weeks. Even then, that was pushing it."

The claw end of a hammer was jammed under a strip of weathered wood. "I changed my mind."

Squinting through his spectacles, Herb pulled his pipe from his mouth, his expression one of disbelief. "I still can't see how you're going to do that," he said, also speaking to Cal's back. "This here's a lot of work for one man to do."

Gramps was prepared to answer that, too. "I'd have been inclined to agree, if I hadn't seen what he did inside there. He finished that by himself in no time at all."

Looking as if he might have been more impressed with what he'd seen than he'd wanted to be, Gramps scratched at his mop of gray beard. But the reputation of the boy was being overshadowed by the man. And Gramps had always called 'em like he saw 'em.

"Got to tell you, Whitaker," he finally added. "You did a right nice job in there. That woodwork is something to be proud of."

From where Lindsey stood, she couldn't see what effect the compliment had on Cal. All she caught was his modest and muttered "Thank you." She had no trouble, however, catching his hard frown when, still intent on his task, he shifted his position to get a better angle on the board he was attempting to remove.

The squeak of nails being pulled from old wood preceded the snap of the board when it splintered. Cal swore. Under his breath mostly. But the word was audible enough for Gramps to cast a quick, embarrassed glance toward the lady in their presence. Herb, apparently running on low batteries again, hadn't heard a thing.

"You might need some help with that," Gramps suggested, stepping forward himself. "Give me that chunk you just broke off before you put a nail through your hand."

Though he appeared to hesitate, Cal lowered the four-foot strip down to him, telling Gramps to be careful himself, then stepped from the ladder to retrieve the board. His heavy boots had barely hit the cement, when Gramps told him he'd take care of it and dragged it behind him to the discard pile around back.

Taking advantage of the older man's temporary absence, mindful of Herb, who often managed to hear far more than one would expect despite his temperamental hearing, Lindsey dared a step closer to Cal.

"What time do you think you'll finish up tonight?" she asked, her tone deliberately conversational.

"Hard to tell. After the light has gone out here, I'm starting on the shutters."

"How about a break for dinner?"

The look he gave her was brief, and totally impersonal. "I don't think so."

He needed to eat, but Lindsey refrained from pointing that out. Partly because his refusal of her subtle invitation had been so blunt, but mostly because a yellow

Sharkey's feed truck had just turned the corner and the rumble of it being downshifted drowned conversation completely.

As it was, she said nothing else to Cal. He wasn't co-operating with her and the truck was now pulling up to the curb, its engine choking a bit before grinding to silence. A man in his early thirties, thin as a blade and with a brown cowboy hat on his head and western-cut shirt shoved into his denims, slid from the driver's seat and went to work on something roped to the far side of the truck. A moment later a metal ladder, half again as long as the one Cal was using, popped skyward and started moving along the high sides of the box-bed truck.

"Hey, Herb," Jack Perkins said by way of greeting to the man when he appeared near the bumper.

"Lindsey," he added, acknowledging her with the lift of his hat brim while his glance skimmed to the big man behind her. Giving him a nod, too, he looked back to her, preferring her friendly brown eyes to the cool blue ones narrowing on him. "Sorry I couldn't get this here before. I know I told Louella to tell you I'd have it here this morning, but this dang truck keeps breaking down on me."

"Don't worry about it," Lindsey urged, aware of the frown flitting over his freckles as he propped the ladder against the side of the building and ventured another look at the man behind her. "I just appreciate you letting us borrow it."

"Anytime, ma'am. Say." The frown turned inquisitive. Pushing his hat back, he revealed his pleasant features to the man beyond her. "You Caleb Whitaker?"

Cal's eyes had narrowed, too, as if he were trying to determine what it was about the man that he found familiar—and whether that familiarity was good or bad.

"I am."

"Well, I'll be," the smaller man muttered, thrusting out his freckled hand. "I thought it was. I'm Jack. Perkins," he added. "That sister of mine said you was working over here, but, half the time I don't pay her no never mind at all. Guess this time she was right."

From the way Cal's hesitation slipped, it seemed he remembered Jack. But he didn't appear to have any idea who Jack's sister was. He didn't know Louella. Not that it mattered. Though he easily accepted the handshake of the man grinning at him, his manner was far more reserved than Jack's, far more cautious. But that was just Cal. By the time Gramps sauntered back from the discard pile to see what he was missing, Cal had already returned to work, though he did seem interested in what Jack was telling him about how he'd gone to work driving a feed truck for Sharkey's right out of high school and had been doing it ever since.

It was guy talk. And since Lindsey already knew that one member of the little party wished she'd disappear, she didn't stick around to cramp the conversation. Excusing herself, wondering if anyone else noticed that Cal was the only one who didn't acknowledge her, she decided she'd just have to wait until he called it quits outside to get him alone.

The only problem with that idea was that when he went in just before dark, he didn't go by himself. Jack was still with him.

She could hear the rumble of male voices through the wall that separated her workroom from his, catching only bits and pieces of their conversation between bursts from the table saw. Mostly she heard Jack, who, like his sister, had a real talent for bending an ear. A genetic thing, apparently. Even then, cutting out appliqués at her worktable so she could get a headstart on her order, Lindsey heard only the drone of words and not what was being said. It was only when Jack was leaving a couple of hours later and the men were at the back door next to hers that the drone became intelligible. Then she heard Cal decline Jack's offer to buy him a beer over at the Lone Star.

"But thanks for the offer," Cal was saying.

"Anytime. Holler when you need a hand hanging that trim. I still can't hammer a nail straight to save my soul, but I can certainly hold it up so you can do it."

Cal must have turned, because Lindsey couldn't make out what he said. She caught only the sound of a deep chuckle, followed by Jack's comment that he'd see him later.

Several very long seconds passed before she heard the door close. Several more before she heard heavy footfalls on the stairs and the thud of the apartment door above her when it closed.

Cal would have seen her light on. Obviously he'd chosen to ignore the fact that she was there.

She set aside the lace heart she'd cut out, her interest in work flagging completely. As hard as it was to have him upset with her, it was harder still to be denied the opportunity to say she was sorry. Just because he didn't know that was what she wanted was only marginally relevant. At the moment, refusing to consider that he might have somehow become more important to her than she'd realized, she concentrated only on the fact that it was totally unfair of him not to hear her out—a realization that had the advantage of adding irritation to the regret she felt as she folded fabric and turned off lights. Though the phenomenon didn't make a whole lot of sense to Lindsey, being irritated somehow made it easier for her to face him once she knocked on his door.

At least, it did until he opened it.

He'd taken his shirt off.

That was the first thing she noticed when she found herself staring at his beautifully sculpted chest. The second thing she noticed, after her eyes encountered his, was that he was not happy to see her.

Not all that pleased with him at the moment, she lifted her chin. "I know you're upset with me, but you can at least let me apologize."

That he had to consider her conclusion didn't bode well for its reception. Seconds ticked by while he stood with one hand braced on the door frame, the muscle and sinew in his bare arm looking as hard as his expression as he blocked her entry. Without a word, he abruptly turned and walked into the room behind him, leaving the door open and her standing at the threshold.

The stark little apartment was nothing more than one room and a bath. The green plaid sofa bed was straight ahead, unmade from the previous night. The overstuffed chair beside the one end table had the shirt he'd stripped off dangling haphazardly from the arm. To the right was the kitchen, a strictly utilitarian affair that consisted of little more than a white counter and sink, an old refrigerator and a stove, to which Cal had headed.

He was removing a pan from it, when Lindsey closed the door and stopped by the pea green Formica table just inside. The obnoxious color was nearly obliterated by old photos of the bandstand that he would use for its restoration, sketches of what appeared like furniture designs and a single, empty coffee cup. He obviously spent his evenings as she sometimes did, drawing pictures of future work.

The snap of the burner control flicking off sounded awfully loud in the silence.

"Why didn't you let Jack buy you a beer?" she asked, noticing the milk and the carton of eggs on the counter. "You could have had a sandwich at the tavern. Then you wouldn't have had to cook."

"I don't drink. Look," he said, canning the small talk. "I thought you came to apologize."

"I did."

"Then say whatever it is you have to say, Lindsey. I'm tired. I want something to eat, a shower and a bed. Unless you're planning to come to bed with me, I suggest you get on with it, then leave."

The breath Lindsey had just drawn caught in her throat.

His deliberately spoken words were unnerving enough. The expression in his eyes was even more so. There was nothing there but the same coolness she'd heard in his voice. He was shutting her out the only way he knew how, and doing a splendid job of it. He was a hard man, made that way by nature as well as circumstance. But Lindsey knew that, hard or not, he didn't like to fight, that it was something he did only when he could find no other way out.

That he'd found it necessary to hit so hard made it abundantly clear she wasn't the only one who'd found her back to the wall.

Lindsey groped for the door handle, intent only on making a dignified retreat. "It obviously doesn't matter what I say now," she said, the color draining from her face. "Good night, Cal."

Cal said nothing as she slipped out the door. He simply watched her go, jamming down his need for the peace he sometimes felt with her, along with the need to take away the hurt he had so deliberately put in her eyes. A greater need overrode both. The need to avoid the chaos she resurrected. Pushing her away had been the only way to do that. The only way, he repeated to himself, and turned to put back the food for which he'd lost his appetite.

Moments later, the slam of the refrigerator door caused the glass on the counter to vibrate. Instead of feeling relieved that she'd gone, instead of feeling he'd regained control, all he felt was angry. And...empty.

He knew only one way to deal with those feelings.

Work.

"I can't believe he's almost finished with your store, Lindsey. It looks just like your drawings. A perfect Alpine chalet. If the rest of the merchants do even half as much to their storefronts, this theme has simply got to bring in tourists." A satisfied smile glowed in Sam's eyes. "Ever since the mayor started talking about having someone do his grocery store this way, word is that everybody is getting excited about the idea."

Sam sat on the wooden bench near the bandstand, a carton of yogurt in her hand and her attention on Lindsey's store across the street. Lindsey sat next to her, sinking the pieces of fruit in her container with a plastic spoon. It was one of those beautiful days that heralded an early spring. Perfect for being outside, enjoying lunch in the balmy air. At least, Sam had seemed to think so. Lindsey would have preferred to have lunch just about anywhere other than in full view of the man finishing up her store.

Her sister, however, had been privy to Essie's praises of Cal and had herself become reluctantly impressed with his abilities. Pleased with what he was doing, she seemed perfectly content to spend her lunch hour admiring the transformation he was effecting on the building.

The old, green awnings were now gone, and the exterior had been painted white. A border of pale-blue gingerbread hung like icicles below the eaves, and window boxes with hearts and leaves stenciled below their scalloped edges hung under the waist-high windows.

Today, with Gramps, Hugh and a couple of their cronies "supervising," Cal was hanging the pale-blue shutters. Yesterday Jack had come by again to help out. Though Lindsey hadn't felt too sure about the older men's presence the first time she'd seen them with Cal, it had soon become apparent that Cal had grown accustomed to their company. According to Louella, who still served Gramps and Hugh their breakfast several mornings a week, Gramps enjoyed having someone new to bore with his tales of how things had been when he was a young man—not that anything had changed much in the past fifty or so years—and Cal provided a remarkably patient ear. In fact, he was slowly proving himself extraordinarily patient with another unlikely audience: the kids who stopped by on their way home from school, asking a zillion questions about what he was doing and why.

It was only when he caught sight of her that his wall went up so readily. Knowing when she wasn't wanted, she'd avoided him as much as he had her.

"Aren't you excited about it?" Sam asked, since Lindsey had yet to respond.

Lindsey submerged a sliver of peach. "Sure."

At the minimal reply, not to mention its lack of enthusiasm, Sam reversed her smile. "All right," she muttered, sounding tired of having carried most of the conversational ball today. "What's going on? This isn't like you."

"What isn't?"

"*This,*" Sam said, waving her hand from Lindsey's casual topknot to the toes of her sandals. "You're not acting like yourself. You're usually running on 'harried' and loving it, but you sound more in the dumps than Annie."

At the mention of their sister, Lindsey lifted her head, her concerns shifting priority. "Have you heard from her in the past few days? I tried calling her at Mom and Dad's last night, but there was no answer."

Pale-blond hair shimmered in the dappled sunlight when Sam shook her head. After Rob had filed for divorce, their mother had talked Annie into house-sitting for them in Florida while they were in Europe—mostly to give Annie a chance to regroup. "I haven't talked to her since last week. Maybe she's just staying busy."

Lindsey could appreciate that.

The yogurt again claimed her attention. It was either look there or across the street. She preferred staring at fruit flecks. "I asked her if she'd like to come here, but she said she really didn't know what she wanted to do."

"Is that why you've been so quiet lately, Linds? Because you're worried about Annie?"

Annie had definitely been on Lindsey's mind. What their sister was going through had to be hard, so much harder than what Lindsey had experienced herself. Annie had miscarried a couple of months ago. Then, last month, her husband had walked out.

"I just feel so bad for her," she admitted, though she was sure Sam could relate more to Annie's loss than she could. Lindsey had merely been rejected; Sam had lost her first husband. The women were always left alone. Even their mother had spent most of her life without her mate. With their father gone on various assignments most of the time, she might as well have been a widow herself.

"And I guess I'm worried about Logan," she added, shaking off her disquieting thoughts. "I know I swore I'd never worry the way Mom and you do, but I seem to be developing a real knack for it." A hazard of aging, she supposed. "I know he really wanted to see his brother."

Sam hesitated. The wait-and-see attitude she had adopted toward Cal had removed the strain from her conversations with Lindsey. It hadn't removed her concern.

"You say that as though you know for a fact that he won't. Did you talk to him about it?"

"In a manner of speaking."

"Any chance you can change his mind?"

"Not in this lifetime. He hasn't said a half-dozen words to me since the middle of last week."

"So that's it." The honk of a car horn drifted on the warm breeze, making Sam's soft words even quieter than they were.

Angling herself on the bench, Sam turned her full attention to her sister. "Do you want to tell me about it?"

Lindsey shrugged. "There's nothing to tell." Other than that she missed him. Missed talking to him. Missed being with him. She'd wanted to tell him about the compliments she'd received on her shop, and about the picture Amy had drawn of him on his ladder. She wanted to ask if he'd bought his shop, and about Jack, and see how he was really doing with so many people around all the time.

"He just accused me of trying to fix things between him and his brother the way I try to fix things for everyone because, according to him, I don't have a life of my own," she said all in one breath. "And I told him I really hadn't been trying to fix anything, even though I had wanted to talk to him about Logan. I'd just never found the right time to do it because I knew thinking about his brother hurt him too much.

"Well, I didn't tell him that part," she had to admit, rushing on after she'd paused for another lungful of air. "But it doesn't make any difference anyway."

The steady pounding of a hammer drifted across the square, the sound echoing slightly in the otherwise quiet afternoon.

"It sounds as if he knows you rather well." Sam made the observation quietly, something that looked strangely like suspicion lurking in her expression. "It sounds as if you know him rather well, too."

Lindsey had hoped her sister would overlook all that.

"You said it hurts him to think of Logan," Sam continued, as if the thought had just canted her perspective. "But it sounds as if your argument was about more than his brother. Is it possible the two of you got too close?"

Lindsey glanced over to meet the speculation in her sister's eyes. "That's ridiculous, Sam. No woman could get close to that man."

For a moment, Sam said nothing. She just looked at Lindsey as if she suddenly understood far more than she had only moments ago. "I think I may have said something similar once myself," she murmured. The caution in her voice grew almost palpable. "Are you in love with him?"

From where Cal stood on the opposite side of the street, he saw the sun catch the gold clip at the back of Lindsey's head, causing it to flash as she gave her head a hesitant, negative shake. He didn't know what the two sisters had been talking about for the past half an hour, but it looked as if the conversation had just come to an end. Lindsey was reaching to take something from her sister. Watching her dump whatever it was into the trash barrel by the walkway, he saw Sam follow to give her a hug, then turn to go back to her office when Lindsey headed toward her store.

Turning himself, he started picking up tools. This was the most he had seen of her in over a week. She hadn't stayed late a single night since she'd walked out of the apartment. Other than a couple of days ago, when he'd had to tell her he couldn't get the shade of red she'd wanted for the hearts on her window boxes, they hadn't spoken a half a dozen phrases that didn't consist of "Good morning," or "Hi," and both of those uttered only when someone else was within earshot and it would have appeared odd for them to not speak to each other.

That he even cared what strangers might think would have had him baffled had he not already been so confused. Always before, he'd been able to close out whatever threatened to hurt or harm him. But with Lindsey, his attempt to shut her out of his life hadn't worked. She was in his thoughts constantly.

Apparently he watched her a little more than he thought he did, too. Jack had caught him staring after her on her way to the café a couple of days ago and practically parted his ribs with his bony little elbow. The wily truck driver had promptly started in on him about having a thing for her, saying there wasn't anyone in town who'd ever gotten her to go out on a date. But, then, Jack said a lot of things.

One thing in particular had left an impression. Recalling it now, he realized how badly he'd treated Lindsey.

I've never forgotten what you did for me, Jack had told him the night he'd recalled how Cal had kept him from flunking out of shop class. Jack had been all thumbs when it had come to carpentry, something Cal wouldn't have cared about at all had the other kids not made so much fun of the scrawny little freshman. Cal had never been able to handle people picking on someone weaker than themselves. *You stood up for me when no one else would. And you know, man, my mom still has that box you helped me make.*

That Jack remembered something Cal had all but forgotten had not so subtly reminded Cal of something else he'd overlooked.

He had forgotten what Lindsey had done for him; how she had defended him, championed his work.

She'd been his friend. And he'd hurt her. As much as he missed her, he could only hope she'd be more willing to listen to him when he showed up at her house than he had been when she'd come to the apartment.

Chapter Ten

Lindsey's street was always quiet. With the sun sitting like a huge orange ball on the horizon, Cal thought everything seemed to grow quieter still. The pecan trees in the orchard on the corner were now in full leaf, the thick canopy of vegetation muffling the chatter of squirrels chasing each other up and down the thick trunks. On the other side of the narrow road, the grasses and wildflowers in the field seemed to whisper as the breeze nudged them toward the meandering line of trees lining the banks of the creek.

He had been there less than a month, but he'd seen the season change from winter to spring. Somewhere inside him, it felt as if something was changing, too; as if something was trying to break free of its protective covering. Having spent most of his life living in an emotional winter, he found the change threatening. Winter was dormant, protective. Spring was growth, transformation. One was safe. The other was . . . hope.

Cal wasn't a man who'd ever allowed himself to hope for much of anything that didn't involve simply getting from one day to the next. As he walked toward Lindsey's house, his footsteps heavy in the stillness, all he considered was that there was nothing more vulnerable than a newly formed bud.

He passed the only other house on the street, the sounds of dinner dishes being washed coming through an open window. All he hoped for now was that she was home. She hadn't been when he'd come by last night.

Somebody up there showed a little mercy. The door was answered on his second knock.

He figured she must have recognized him through the lace curtain on the window. When she opened the door, her wariness was already in place.

She didn't offer a smile. All he got was a guarded "Hi" that made it apparent she had no idea what to expect from him.

"Do you have a minute?"

"Sure," she replied, gracious despite her caution. "Do you want to come in?"

"Actually..." He glanced over his shoulder, toward the field and the glow of the sunset. "I'd just as soon stay outside. Would you mind coming out?"

The screen door seemed to balk a little when she pushed on it. Or maybe it was only her own hesitation Lindsey felt as she nudged it open. Cal's hair looked damp, as if he'd just come from a shower, and the shadow on his jaw wasn't as dark as it usually was this time of day. He'd obviously just cleaned up from work. From the reluctance in his expression, it was also obvious that he didn't want to be there. Or to be alone with her. Not that they would have much company on her porch. Her only neighbors seldom ventured out after suppertime, and except for whatever critters happened to be running around in the field across the street and the open lot next door there wasn't anyone else around.

"You're leaving, aren't you?"

The certainty in her voice made her words a statement. One that lowered Cal's brow as he stepped toward the rail to give her more space. "What are you talking about?"

"That's why you're here, isn't it? To tell me you've finished the store and you're leaving."

"The store is finished," he agreed, aware of how protectively her arms were crossed over her loose pink shirt. "But I still have the bandstand to do."

"I thought you might have decided not to bother with that."

It was defeat he heard in her voice. Not insult. Still, Cal couldn't help the defensiveness that lowered his voice to little more than a growl. "I've never voluntarily walked away from a job in my life, Lindsey, and I have no intention of doing it now. When I say I'll do something, I do it. This isn't even about the job." Frustration warring with guilt and a truckload of other feelings he was so lousy at dealing with, he rubbed his hands over his face and blew out a breath. "I don't even know how in the hell to do this."

Had it not been for his agitation, Lindsey might have wondered more at the little inconsistency that had just arisen. Cal's remark about having never walked off a job didn't jibe at all with what she'd heard the day after she'd hired him. She clearly remembered Gramps telling her how Cal had walked off his job at the gas station, giving the proprietor no notice at all. Gramps was a gossip, but he didn't make things up. Yet she didn't for a moment believe that the man who'd just turned from her was lying.

There was something Cal needed to say. Needing to hear
it, she forgot the little inconsistency. Her only concern was
what Cal had on his mind. The man was wound as tightly
as the anniversary clock on her mantel.

His edginess fed hers. "Don't know how to do what?"

"Apologize."

The admission, so simply spoken, put a hush in her
voice. "That's a start."

He didn't deserve her generosity, but he needed it.
Hoping for more encouragement, he turned to see her
standing ten feet away. Her stance was even more protective than it had been moments ago. She'd glued her back
to the post by the steps. It was as far as she could get from
him without leaving the porch.

"I'm sorry for what I said to you. In the apartment," he
added before she could ask which transgression he was re-
ferring to. "I had no business saying what I did when I was
here the other day, either. About the way you live your
life."

Beneath soft, thin cotton, one shoulder lifted in a tight
shrug. "It's okay. You were right."

"That doesn't mean it was my place to criticize it."

She didn't argue with that. She said nothing else at all as
the seconds began to tick by, and Cal found himself faced
with the rest of what he had to say. Finally, he turned to the
rail, searching the huge gardenia bush poking through the
porch slats as if to find the words he needed in the dark,
glossy leaves.

All he found were flower buds.

Fingers splayed, he clamped his hands on the waist-high
railing, his shoulders hunched beneath the white T-shirt
tucked into his faded jeans. "I shouldn't have come down
so hard on you about Logan, either," he told her. "I don't
think I was looking for anything concerning my brother

like you said, but you weren't pushing me the way I made it sound. It was just that some of the things you'd said brought back a lot of what I didn't want to think about. I guess I just didn't know how to deal with it." His fingers flexed against the rail. "I still don't."

That was all he'd come to tell her. At least, that was what he'd thought before he heard the soothing sound of her voice reach toward him.

"I'm sorry, Cal. I really am. I never meant to make it harder."

"You didn't." She'd actually made it so much easier, until he'd lashed out and denied himself that comfort. "It's hard just being here."

The admission hadn't come easily. She seemed to sense just how difficult it had been, too—as she'd seemed to sense so many things about him.

"I imagine it is," she said, venturing from her post to move toward the railing. From the corner of his eye, he saw her stop an arm's length away, her attention on the orange glow fading from the striated clouds that caught the sunset's color. "It probably doesn't help that everything still looks so much the same. There's no escaping where you are."

"Yeah," he muttered, more relieved than he'd imagined he'd be that she was talking to him again. More relieved still that she understood. "I can't believe how little has changed." He slowly shook his head. "Even that old metal fruit stand is still out on the highway. You'd think someone would have torn it down by now."

"The one you ran into?"

He hesitated. "Actually... my father did that."

She looked toward him, her hair lifting around her face in the gentle evening breeze. Cal kept his glance trained on the gardenia bush as he reached out and snapped off a twig.

"I'd heard you had."

"Yeah. Well, that's what I had to tell the sheriff. One more DUI and old Ben would have lost his license. Since we couldn't get the truck out of the ditch, I was sitting behind the wheel when the sheriff got there."

"How old were you?"

"I don't know. Sixteen, seventeen. I had my license." His brow lowered, his jaw working. "I must have been seventeen," he amended, as if he'd just allowed himself to delve a little deeper into the memory. "That's when I started trying to earn some money to get Jett and myself out of here. The only problem was that Ben figured any spare time I thought I had should be spent working on the ranch. I'd gotten a job in town, but Ben didn't like that idea, so he came in to haul me back to the RW."

The twig was methodically stripped of its leaves. Like the night he'd told her where he'd gone when he'd finally left the ranch, his voice betrayed no emotion. He simply recited the incident as something that had happened years ago, an event of no more personal significance to him than the Great Flood or the Fall of the Roman Empire. Only the tautness of his jaw betrayed his antipathy.

Acutely aware of that tension, Lindsey was even more aware of what he seemed to be telling her. "You were going to take your brother with you?"

"That was the plan."

"I thought Jett ran away on his own."

"He did." Cal felt his stomach clench. "Jett took off before I could get us out of there. Then Ben ran himself into a tree, Logan came home and I left."

There was a wealth of pain in that simplistic explanation. Lindsey felt it as surely as if it had been her own. The need to protect herself was strong. The need to keep him from feeling that pain felt infinitely stronger.

"You don't have to tell me this," she said, wanting to spare him. "Not unless it's something you want to do."

He did. He didn't know why, exactly. He just knew it was something he had to do. Maybe it was because he could no longer get the pain off his mind. Maybe it was because he wanted her to know he wasn't as bad a person as people had thought he was. He really wasn't sure. He knew only that there were things he couldn't resolve, resentments that wouldn't stay buried. And that when he talked to her, he didn't feel quite so... angry.

"Has Logan ever told you what kind of a man my father was?"

The question was posed offhandedly, but she could feel the agitation emanating from him. It was the need to ease that disquiet, and the fact that he had brought up such a subject, that drew her closer.

"Logan has never talked to me about his past, Cal. It's not the sort of thing he would do." As private a person as Logan was, it had probably taken just shy of forever for Sam to get him to open up. If he ever had. "Sam's never said anything about him, either. Your father, I mean. All I've heard is that he was a... difficult... man."

The corner of Cal's mouth lifted in a mirthless smile. "Difficult," he repeated, as if trying to see how the word fit. "I suppose that would be the polite way to put it."

The twig went over the edge, the agitation he'd masked finally surfacing in the abruptness of the movement.

His daddy was as mean a drunk as they come.

Remembering Gramps's words, Lindsey felt caution meet the chill of certainty. Sick at the thought of what Cal might be dealing with, hoping she was wrong, she almost let the question go. She couldn't. "When you said your father didn't like you working in town and he came to get you, what did he do?''

The muscle in Cal's jaw bunched. ''The same thing he always did when something didn't suit him. I was pretty used to it by then, though. Unless something felt broken, I didn't think much of it. The part I resented most,'' he added, ''was not being able to tell the guy at the gas station why I'd flaked out on the job.''

He'd been too embarrassed, too afraid, to admit that Ben was beating him up. That was why he hadn't gone back to the gas station and explained why he'd ''walked off'' that job, even though he knew he'd been called irresponsible because of it. He'd been a boy trying to be a man, because a man would never admit to the humiliation of being cowed the way he had been. At least, that was the way he'd seen it at the time.

Lindsey didn't see it that way at all. He hadn't been a man. He'd only been a boy. A boy who, even after all that, had been compelled, or forced, to cover for his father by taking the blame for bouncing their truck over a ditch. She couldn't recall the number of fights Cal was purported to have been in when he was young, but she did remember Gramps talking about how Cal would come into town with some of the ranch hands, looking as if he'd already been in some sort of hassle. From what she'd just heard, some of those fights he was supposed to have gotten into probably hadn't been fights at all. They'd been his father using him to take out his frustrations.

''I see now why you wanted to leave.''

For a moment, Lindsey didn't know if Cal was going to say anything else. Or if he'd even heard her. He'd drawn into himself, his thoughts as far from her as the horizon. He simply stood there, still and solid as a mountain, staring off beyond the field.

"I just wanted to get us away. Jett didn't have a chance when Ben would get drunk and start in on him. I got to where I could take care of myself, but Jett was this scrawny, quiet little kid...." His bit back his words, re-crimination darkening his noble profile.

"Oh, Cal," Lindsey breathed. She started to reach for him, only to draw back. As rigid as he was, as distant, she didn't know if her touch would be welcome. "You don't blame yourself for not being able to take care of him, do you?"

It was nearly impossible for her to picture Jett as Cal had described him. The man she had met at Sam and Logan's wedding was easily as powerful looking as Cal, though leaner in a raw, hungry sort of way. He was definitely a man who could take care of himself. Just like his brothers. And, she suspected, just as hard to reach.

The landscape finally lost its appeal. But the expression in his eyes when he met hers was one of self-reproach. "I was his older brother, Lindsey. That's what a brother is supposed to do."

"But you were just a boy yourself."

He didn't look as if that was any sort of an excuse.

"Where was Logan?"

"In college."

Logan hadn't been there.

Logan hadn't been there, Lindsey repeated to herself — and, as if a curtain had just slowly lifted, she finally caught a glimpse of why Cal had felt the way he had for so long.

He would only have been fourteen when Logan had left for school. Jett couldn't have been much more than eleven or twelve. Cal had looked out for his little brother. But there had been no one to look out for Cal.

Though it was impossible for her to picture the man beside her as a frightened child, she knew he must have been.

A frightened boy with no one but himself to turn to. He and Logan must have both felt that way.

"Was your father that way with Logan, too?"

"Did he knock him around, you mean?"

Inwardly, Lindsey flinched, so foreign to her was the thought of what Ben Whitaker had done to his sons. Outwardly, she only nodded.

"He did. But it got worse after Logan left."

After Logan had gone, life on the RW had gone from bad to barely tolerable. Logan had once told him that Ben hadn't drunk at all when their mother was alive. But since Cal had been only five years old when their mother had died, his only memory of her wasn't so much a memory as it was an impression of someone soft who'd baked cookies and smoothed his hair. He had no memory at all of a time when his father didn't start his day with a new bottle of whiskey.

He told Lindsey that, too, and as the sunset succumbed to dusk and the hush of evening settled around the porch, he also told her how he'd tried to fill his brother's shoes after Logan had gone. Not once did he say he blamed Logan for leaving him to cope alone. He told her only that no matter how hard he tried, he'd never been able to do the chores as well as Logan. He'd never been as good with the horses or the cattle. Points his father had repeatedly thrown in his face. Cal had known he wasn't as good as his brother. Even Logan had known it, which was why he'd helped him with his chores after his own were finished. Cal hadn't liked working with the animals the way Logan had. What Cal had liked to do was build things, work with his hands. Their father had expected his sons to be ranchers.

It was no wonder Cal was so angry, Lindsey thought as she listened, the hurt she felt for the boy as strong as the pain she felt for the man. Though he had said nothing specific against his elder brother—something that had struck her as very revealing—the resentment was there, the unspoken rivalry, the inability to please his father the way Logan had. And that was even beyond the abuse he'd suffered at the hands of a parent whose first duty had been to protect him from harm. But she didn't understand how complicated the problem was between the brothers until she asked Cal when he had left the ranch.

"I left about a week after Logan came back. He had the experience, and all the hands who hadn't quit were deferring to him, so there was no reason for me to stick around. I hated the place anyway."

She could understand why he would. But she also understood that while he might not have wanted to stay, it had hurt to have his position usurped. For four years he'd been "the oldest." With Jett having been gone for a couple of months by then and Logan back, Cal could well have felt . . . unnecessary.

She knew from Sam that when Logan came back, he'd been completely overwhelmed. "Did Logan tell you he hadn't wanted the ranch then, either?"

The thought appeared utterly foreign to Cal. "Why would he have told me that?"

"Because he didn't. At least, that's what he told Sam. He was studying to be a veterinarian, remember? And he had to give that up. He'd also been left with an infant son to raise."

Cal remembered the baby. The ranch foreman's wife had latched onto it the minute Logan had walked in the door. He remembered Logan being real uptight about the kid, too. Logan had been uptight about everything.

So had Cal.

"Didn't the two of you talk about any of this before you left?"

He didn't remember. It had been so long ago. Not that it would have mattered. It didn't change anything.

"You know," she began, unable to imagine the turmoil the brothers must have been going through, "you said you couldn't do anything as well as Logan could. You were four years younger than he was, Cal. When we're kids, that four-year gap makes a huge difference. You can't expect the same things of children when they're, say, eight and twelve or twelve and sixteen. You were barely into your teens when he moved away to school. Yet you were expected to fill a young man's shoes. By your father comparing you with him, you were being measured by a standard you couldn't possibly have reached at the time."

Cal knew next to nothing about children, about what to expect at any given stage of development. He knew only that there was some sort of absolution in Lindsey's quietly spoken words—and that forgiveness was something with which he wasn't terribly familiar. Especially when it came to himself.

"If I tell you something," she began, sounding a little uncertain, "will you please not get upset with me?"

The way you did before, she could have added.

He gave his head a tight shake. "What is it?"

"What you said about being compared with Logan," she said in preface, still cautious. "It almost sounds as if you resent him for something he had no more control over than you did. Maybe it isn't even Logan who brings the bad feelings," she suggested. "Maybe it's just what he reminds you of. The way I reminded you of things you didn't want to think about, so you got upset with me."

A deep frown swept his shadowed features. In the growing darkness, she couldn't tell if it was a frown of contemplation or disagreement. Wondering if he was closing her out, thinking it entirely possible, she hurried on anyway.

"What happened when you were kids wasn't your fault," she told him, because she had the feeling that he did blame himself somehow. He felt he hadn't been good enough. Or strong enough. Or capable enough. "It was the fault of an alcoholic father raising three boys alone. I don't imagine there's one of you who doesn't bear scars from everything that happened. But that was something that was done to you, not something you did to one another."

She drew a deep breath, praying she wouldn't alienate him again. She knew, however, that she would risk that over having him continue to hurt the way he was. She would suggest it once, then remain forever silent. "I know Logan misses you. Just give him a chance. Give yourself a chance. He's your brother, Cal. I can't believe that part of you doesn't miss him, too."

The sun had disappeared behind the hills, taking the warmth of the day with it. From the deep grasses beyond her yard came the steady call of crickets serenading each other. She was wearing only a thin T-shirt over her jeans, and the chill finally got to her. Or maybe it was just nerves that caused her to shiver as she crossed her arms. Cal hadn't said a word.

When he did speak, his voice was little more than a deep rasp. "I should let you go in." His hands slid from the rail. "I'm sure I took you away from something."

He'd said he wouldn't be upset. But she would rather have had his anger than his indifference.

She reached for him as he turned, her fingers curling around his forearm to keep him from walking away. But it wasn't indifference she saw when his glance skimmed from her hand to her face. It was pain. Even in the shadows, it caught her in its grip.

She'd never understood the empathy she had with this man, but that inexplicable understanding had her reaching up to curve her palm to his cheek before she could even consider what she was doing. Beneath her hand, she felt the hard ridges of his bones, the unyielding set of his jaw, the warmth of his skin. "Are you angry with me again?" she asked, aching for the loneliness he must feel.

A grim smile touched his mouth. "I told you I wouldn't be."

"That must mean that you are," she murmured, defeated, and started to pull back.

He caught her hand in midair. "I'm not," he told her, meaning it. "Not with you."

He didn't know exactly what he was feeling just then. But getting away had seemed like a good idea. His insides were knotted and every muscle in his body screamed for movement. The thought of pounding on boards held some merit, or dismantling something. At least it had before she'd touched him.

He still held her hand. She had curled it into his palm.

"Lindsey," he began, feeling the tension in his body undergo a distinct change in quality. She only had to touch him for his body to react. Sometimes all it took was the thought of her. "All I wanted to do was apologize. I don't want to have to do it again."

She stared up at him, taking in his chiseled features, his closed expression. "I don't understand what you mean."

He didn't get a chance to explain. Not that she thought he was going to. The muffled ring of her telephone filtered through the open door, the sound seeming far more welcome to him than to her.

"You'd better answer that."

She was about to tell him that the answering machine could get it, when she remembered where she was sup-

posed to be right now. With a disheartened groan, she
turned to the door. Only to turn right back.

"Don't go, Cal. Please?"

She didn't give him a chance to answer. She simply
pulled open the screen, holding it wide enough that he had
to catch it or get hit with it, and hurried through to the
kitchen to answer the insistent summons.

The living room was dark, but the light in the kitchen
was on. Because of that, Cal could clearly see her after
she'd picked up the wall phone in the kitchen and moved
back into the doorway to watch him step inside.

From what he could determine of her conversation, she
was supposed to be at a meeting. She was also supposed to
have brought something she apparently hadn't been able
to find in her search of the boxes of papers on the kitchen
table. All he cared about was that she'd just told her caller
that something had come up and she wouldn't be able to
make it tonight.

"You didn't have to do that."

"Yes, I did," she told him, hanging up the receiver under the cabinet. Pretending a calm she was far from feeling, she crossed her arms and leaned her shoulder against
the door frame. The light spilling from the kitchen cast
him in bronze, the proud angles of his face seeming
sculpted as he stood in the middle of her living room. "Do
you want some coffee?"

"Are you making it?"

"It's okay. It's instant."

He didn't want coffee. What he wanted was to know
why she'd canceled her plans for him. But as he studied her
in the doorway, her casual posture drawing his glance up
her long, slender legs to the pattern of the lacy bra faintly
visible below the neckline of her thin cotton shirt, he knew
he wouldn't ask.

A hesitant smile waited on her lips, her head tilting back as he moved from the shadows into the light.

"Sure," he finally said, his glance sweeping her face as he brushed her cheek with his fingertips. Her skin was so soft. Like the inside of a rose petal. "Sounds good."

She made no move for the coffee. She didn't move at all. "Regular?" she asked, her voice hushed. "Or decaf?"

"Regular." He followed the motion of his thumb as it traced the curve of her cheekbone, then slipped down to the corner of her mouth. "That way I'll have something to blame when I can't sleep tonight."

Her breath was expelled with a delicate shudder. "You're having trouble sleeping?"

"Yeah." The skin just below the hollow of her throat was every bit as soft as her face. "I tend to lie there thinking about this."

Lindsey felt her heart slam against her breastbone. His eyes were on hers as he carried his feather-light touch down to meet the vee of her shirt. The barrier of fabric didn't stop him when he reached it. Continuing past the band, he traced the faint outline of her bra along one scalloped cup, his finger burning through the cotton.

Following the strap up to her shoulder, he leaned closer. "And this," he whispered, lowering his head.

Warm and full, his mouth settled over hers in the sweetest of kisses. As big as he was, as tough as he was, that he should be capable of such gentleness never failed to astound her. But there was heat behind that gentleness, and his restraint had his whole body as taut as a bow. She could feel it when her hands settled at his waist.

He held so much inside. So much more than anyone ever saw. But he'd let her see, and she knew how hard that must have been for him. Easing forward, she slid her hands over the steely muscles of his back, drawing him closer. This was what he needed, she thought, aware of his body molding to hers as she tightened her hold. Though she doubted his pride would ever allow him to admit it, he needed a pair of arms right now. It was comfort he was seeking. She felt certain of that as he drew her up and tucked his face into the curve of her neck, holding her as tightly as she held him.

Are you in love with him? her sister had asked.

Her sister's words came back to her as she smoothed his hair, cupping his head as she would a child's. Lindsey had denied the possibility. What she felt was wild physical attraction and a sort of kinship she couldn't begin to explain. It was as if they were soul mates, though as divergent as their lives had been she couldn't imagine how that could be. But, then, she couldn't have imagined herself in love with him, either.

And she feared very much that she was.

The thought had her heart pounding. Or maybe what caused that erratic beat was the feel of his lips when they brushed the side of her neck—and the husky sound of her name rasped in her ear just before his mouth claimed hers once more.

She felt a shudder ripple through him at the contact. Or maybe the reaction had been hers. She couldn't tell. She knew only that the instant he slipped his tongue into her mouth, every sane thought vanished from her head. Fearing what she felt, needing him to make the fear go away, she leaned into him, seeking him just as he sought her.

He was no longer gentle. Need replaced tenderness while tongues and hands teased and searched. He shifted her against him, aligning her so she could feel how that need built. He grew harder—she softer. He rasped her name against her lips. She swallowed his on a moan.

Lindsey didn't remember him turning her, but he must have, because she felt her back against the doorframe. His hands slipped under her shirt and his fingers caressed the sides of her breasts. All the while, he was kissing her, making her want him, making her need.

His breathing sounded a little ragged when he pulled his hands from beneath her shirt and rested his forehead against hers.

"I didn't come here to take you to bed, Lindsey. But that's where we're headed if we don't slow down."

He dragged her hands from around his neck and clamped his fingers around her wrists. The thought of not making love with her was almost more than he could bear, but if he didn't let go of her right now, he wouldn't.

She lifted her manacled hands, pressing a kiss to the back of his. The touch of her lips was light, the merest sensation of skin against skin. "Is that what you want?" she asked, her voice little more than a whisper. "To slow down?"

"Lindsey," he growled.

"That's not an answer."

"No. That's not what I want."

A smile, beautifully feminine, amazingly innocent, touched her mouth. "Then don't."

Heat flared in his eyes as she turned her hand in his. He had never felt the need to possess as fiercely as he did at that moment. Curling her fingers through his, he let her lead him around the corner and into her room. Her hand was trembling. So were her lips when he turned her into his arms. He would make her tremble more before the night was over.

"Lift your arms," he murmured, sliding his hands under her shirt.

Lindsey did as he asked, and her top fell to the floor as he nudged her toward her bed.

The big four-poster was draped in swaths of white fabric, the white sheets and comforter still tangled from her battle with sleep last night. His admitted sleeplessness seemed terribly ironic to Lindsey, given how she'd fought her thoughts of him. Yet as she tugged the hem of his shirt from the waistband of his jeans, encouraged by the heat in his eyes as he watched her, she had no hope of denying what she felt for him. He had burned himself into her soul the first time he'd held her against him, and that feeling of having been branded by him had never gone away. It no longer mattered that he would be gone soon. Not the way it once had. That he would soon be gone was the very reason she reached for him now.

Splaying her hands over the muscles of his chest, she touched her lips to his nipples and the hard muscles of his abdomen. He would be gone soon and she might go her whole life without ever again experiencing what she felt with this man. With him she was whole, necessary.

The skin of his back was hot beneath her hands. Just as hot as his breath when he chuckled darkly, told her to "be careful" and pulled her up to nuzzle aside her bra. But he didn't touch her the way she wanted him to. With a caress as light as air, he trailed a path of liquid fire over her stomach to the underside of her breast with his fingers. She ached for him to carry that touch to its center. Yet, even after the lacy garment had joined their shirts, he only continued to tease her while he unfastened her jeans and skimmed them over her hips.

His jeans followed, along with her panties and his shorts. She hadn't turned a light on, but even in the pale illumination coming from the doorway, she could clearly see the beauty of his body. Magnificently strong, undeniably aroused.

She turned, suddenly conscious of her own nakedness.

"Don't," he told her, moving her hand from where it rested on her shoulder to cover herself. "You're even more beautiful than I'd imagined, Lindsey." He slid his hands over her ribs, cupping her breasts. Warm and moist, his breath feathered over her neck, his voice dropping to a husky whisper. "And I've imagined you a lot."

He showed her just what he'd imagined, too, tantalizing her with the images he'd created—until her knees threatened to buckle and he eased her back onto the bed.

Cal followed her down, covering her mouth with his and her hip with his hand. She was everything he'd imagined she would be. Sensual. Responsive. But she was something even more. She was what he'd gone his whole life without.

The thought was fleeting, lost in a wash of sensation as the demands of his body began exacting their toll. He'd wanted to take his time with her, to explore every nuance of her lovely body, to make her ache for him the way he ached for her. But when he felt her nipple bloom against his tongue and she pressed him closer, he began to wonder if his control would last. He was convinced it wouldn't when her small, soft fingers slid down his stomach and closed around him.

Air hissed as he sucked it in between his teeth. He wasn't sure if what he felt was pleasure or pain. He knew only that it was all going to be over in about six seconds if she didn't stop. He told her that, too. All she did was push her hands into his hair and lift her head to meet him in a kiss that threatened to obliterate conscious thought.

He eased himself over her, giving up the fight. The taste of her filled him, consumed him. He needed her. The thought jammed itself in the back of his brain as he slid his hand beneath her hips. Then she arched against him, and he was slipping into her, feeling her warmth surround him. Glorying in the feel of her, needing her as he'd never needed anyone in his life, he was aware of nothing but the sensations they created—and of something he'd never felt before.

A profound sense of . . . belonging.

Chapter Eleven

The gray light of dawn had faded the night, filling the room with its pale glow by the time Lindsey awoke.

Curled on her side, she fought the lulling fog of sleep, wanting to drift back, only to be pulled relentlessly toward consciousness despite her best efforts. Giving up, she started to stretch, then went perfectly still when her eyes opened and she found herself facing an empty pillow.

She didn't know what time it was. For an instant, she didn't even know why the sight of that pillow should cause such an anxious feeling in her chest. But with that feeling, consciousness kicked in, and memories of the night returned in a heart-stopping rush. Within seconds, anxiety turned to a vague, sinking sensation. But she was spared having to think Cal had gone when she shoved back the hair his hands had reduced to wild tangles and she turned from that empty pillow.

He was standing at her window.

Unmindful of his nakedness, he had his back to her, one hand clamped around his neck and the other braced on the frame beneath her eyelet curtains. With his dark head lowered, it looked as if his attention was on the window-sill rather than the thick foliage in her tiny, hedge-lined backyard. But it was hard to tell for certain. She couldn't see his face. She could see only his back. In the early light, the muscles in his broad shoulders, tight buttocks and powerful legs appeared sculpted by shadows.

Holding the lace-edged sheet to her, she slowly sat up and drew her knees to her chest. He'd made love with her again before they'd fallen asleep last night. Again when they'd awakened sometime in the wee hours of the morning. She knew the heaviness of his body, the strength of his arms. She knew the smoothness of his back, the hair-roughened texture of his legs. She knew the feel of his big, capable hands, and how incredibly, torturously patient he could be. But mostly she knew that right now something was wrong.

"Cal?"

At the sound of her voice, he lifted his head, his shoulders rising with his deeply drawn breath. Slowly releasing that breath, the effort a conscious attempt to relax, he pushed his fingers through his hair and turned from the window.

Beautifully, unashamedly male, he raised his eyes to hers.

The white percale clutched between her breasts gained a few more wrinkles when her fist tightened. She'd never seen him look so grim.

"What's wrong?"

"Will you come for a ride with me?"

A ride? "Now?"

"Now," he repeated flatly. "Before I change my mind."

"Where?"

"To the ranch."

A thousand insecurities had knotted themselves in Lindsey's stomach in the past sixty seconds. Yet in less than one, Cal had totally overridden her scramble for emotional cover. As she edged toward the side of the bed, her only thought was of what he had just decided to do.

"If that's what you want," she told him, knowing now was not the time to ask what had made him change his mind. "Of course I'll go."

He'd said he wanted to go now. Not wanting to hold him up, she slipped from beneath the blankets, thinking to get her robe on the way to the shower. He didn't let her get that far. She'd made it to the foot of the bed when she felt his fingers curl around her upper arm.

He didn't pull her to him as he would have last night. Tense, his thoughts distracted, he skimmed his hand over the curve of her shoulder, carrying his now-familiar caress to her cheek while he searched her sleep-flushed face.

His touch was sure. The look in his eyes was not.

"I don't know what to say to him, Lindsey."

They stood a foot apart, their bodies close enough to feel the heat radiating from each other's skin. At that moment, totally vulnerable to each other, Lindsey felt the intimacy between them to be as strong as anything they had shared in each other's arms. It was that emotional need that frightened her the most. Hers for him.

"The words will be there when you need them," she told him, soothing the furrows in his brow. "We can talk about it on the way out to the ranch, if you want."

His only reply was a tight nod.

"Do you want me to call Sam and make sure Logan is there? He could be out on the range somewhere already."

The alternative was for Cal to make the call himself.

He would do it if he had to, but she would make it easier for him if she could. With another nod, he pulled her hand from his face and pressed a kiss into her palm.

''Thank you,'' he said, and deliberately stepped from her to swipe his jeans and shorts up from the floor.

Logan wasn't on the range. When Lindsey phoned just before Cal left to get a shower and his truck, Sam told her he was working in the breeding barn and that she would call him as soon as she hung up to tell him his brother was coming. Sam had been getting ready for work herself, in between chasing down her son's homework and change for her kids' lunches, but she wasn't going anywhere now. She would be there, too, in case Logan needed her.

Sam didn't specifically say that. But Lindsey knew Sam's concern for her husband would prevent her from leaving. She was just as sure Sam knew she was coming with Cal for a similar reason. Being sisters—being women—there were times when explanations weren't neccssary.

It would have been nice, however, had Cal been a little less reticent. He didn't say more than three words when they got into the truck, and nothing at all as they headed out on the old highway. Though the silence provided more opportunity than she wanted to entertain her own anxieties, Lindsey didn't try to fill the quiet with reassurance or questions. She could well imagine the inner turmoil that had his jaw locked tight enough to shatter teeth. She had a knot the size of a fist in her stomach herself.

Cal wasn't talking, but he wasn't letting go of her, either. Except for when he needed to shift, he kept her hand trapped on his thigh for the entire twenty-two-mile trip. Not until they had turned off the old highway and the ranch compound came into view when they crested the last rise, did Cal let go. Once he did, she could almost see his emotions retreat.

It had been a lifetime since he'd last seen this place. Yet nothing in the somber set of his features revealed an impression or a thought as they passed the cattle lazing in the meadows beyond the fenced drive.

Lindsey had been to the RW only a few times herself. Each time she had been impressed all over again with the enormity of the place. This part of the property was merely the entrance. The ranch itself was spread out over hundreds of thousands of acres, most of it beyond the views of the peaceful, meadow-lined road. The Pedernales River wound to the north, miles of fencing disappearing into valleys and behind huge granite balds. The heart of the operation was a complex of barns and stables and outbuildings set back from a modest ranch-style house.

By the time Cal had pulled under the branches of the huge live oak near the walkway to the front door, his dispassionate inventory had forced his eyebrows into a deep scowl.

Lindsey watched in concern when he cut the engine. "Does it look the same to you?"

"I don't remember all those outbuildings. Just the one barn and the corral." His narrowed glance sliced toward the lovely, inviting home sitting in the middle of a spring-green lawn. "And the house never looked like that."

Lindsey didn't know about the rest of the structures on the huge property, but the house had undergone a few changes just since Logan and Sam's wedding. The white siding above the red brick had been freshly painted, flowers bloomed in pots on the long, pillar-lined porch and crisp, white priscilla curtains swayed gently behind gleaming, open windows.

It wasn't the house that held Cal's attention. It was the long, large garage that sat nearly a city block away. Several of the ranch's vehicles occupied the open-fronted space: Logan's pickup, a couple of Jeeps, a tractor and, at the far end, an old, dilapidated sports car.

Something about what he was seeing seemed to deepen his frown. At least, that was Lindsey's impression before he caught sight of the tall, dark figure that had just emerged from down by the metal bull pens.

She saw his hand clench around the steering wheel.

"I sure as hell hope you're right about family," he muttered, and pushed open his door.

Apparently he didn't believe in wasting time once his mind was made up. Or maybe he just wasn't going to allow himself time to sit there and change it. Whichever, Lindsey scrambled out her own side a split second later. She called a hurried "Wait!", sick at the thought that he might blame her if this meeting with his brother didn't work.

Cal didn't hear her. The closing of his door cut her off. Though he didn't slam it, the sound echoed like a rifle shot in the still, country air.

Quieter sounds immediately followed from behind her— the faint squeak of a screen opening and the tap of feminine shoes on the porch as Sam stepped out. It was the man ahead of her who had Lindsey's uneasy attention, though. She'd caught only a glimpse of Cal's hard profile before his steady strides carried him toward Logan's tall, formidable figure—a tall, formidable figure himself in a black T-shirt, jeans and the heavy boots that crunched ominously in the gravel.

That steady sound faded with distance, muffled further by the baleful bawl of a calf and the snickers and whinnies of the horses in their corrals. The peaceful sounds seemed incongruous to Lindsey, totally out of sync with the anxious beat of her heart in her ears as the hundred yards separating the brothers slowly disappeared.

Logan's stride was as sure as his brother's, his western boots sending up little puffs of dirt to be carried off by the morning breeze. From so far away, Lindsey couldn't have seen his face even if he hadn't been wearing the battered cowboy hat that inevitably shadowed his arresting features. She could see, though, that the sleeves of his chambray shirt were rolled to his elbows and that his jeans were as worn and weary looking as the old ranch hand scurrying off behind him.

There was no pretense here. No attempt on either man's part to impress the other. Each was what he was. And when they stopped, separated by five feet of ground and seventeen years of bad feelings, Lindsey couldn't begin to imagine what was going through their minds.

"How did you get him out here?" whispered Sam, who had hurried across the lawn to where her sister had rooted by the trunk's front fender.

"I didn't." Keeping her glance on Cal, Lindsey shook her head. She still didn't understand what had happened herself. "We were talking last night about what it was like for Cal growing up here. When we woke up this morning, he just said he wanted to come out before he changed his mind.

"It was so awful, Sam," she had to add, thinking of what he'd told her. Afraid to consider what he hadn't. "I can't imagine growing up the way they did."

As absorbed as she was with the brothers, Lindsey didn't realize what she had just revealed until she felt Sam looking at her. But when she met her sister's eyes, there was none of the concern or warning or worry she might have expected at having just said she and Cal had spent the night together. All she saw was the same understanding she heard in the quiet "I know" that Sam murmured before she looked back to where the brothers stood.

"I can't stand this," Lindsey concluded a few moments later.

"We can't just stay here staring at them."

"Could you leave right now?"

"Not if my life depended on it."

Standing so far away, neither could tell what either man said, if anything. Lindsey did see Cal tip his head in the direction of the garage, however, and, a moment later, saw Logan nod as if in agreement, before both men turned in step to walk toward the building.

They had just passed the shadow at the near end, when Logan drew up short. After what appeared to be a moment's hesitation, he offered Cal his hand.

Lindsey held her breath, her heart bumping in her chest as the men stood facing each other with Logan's hand outstretched between them. She knew how guarded Cal could be, and how distant. The way he paused now made her think he didn't quite trust the gesture. Or, possibly, that he hadn't expected the welcome it represented.

Take it, she silently begged, willing him past the barriers still so obviously in his path. *Please. Take it.*

He did; then, incredibly, he turned that handshake into a quick, fierce hug. Logan swung his arm up over his wide shoulder, hugging back. Within seconds, the men had clapped each other on the back in that stoic, matter-of-fact way men had of showing each other they cared, and stepped apart.

Whatever awkwardness they suffered appeared to go unacknowledged. At least, to each other. Like the two proud men they were, they kept their focus straight ahead as they resumed their distance and their course, moving steadily, if not a bit more slowly, toward the far end of the long, open metal structure.

"I think it's going to be okay," she heard Sam whisper.

For more reasons than Lindsey cared to consider, she prayed her sister's intuition was right. But all she did was murmur "I hope so," then headed for the kitchen and the coffeepot with Sam when the men disappeared from view.

When Cal appeared on the front porch thirty minutes later, Lindsey's nerves felt strung as tight as the tennis racket buried in the back of her closet. It was apparent that the meeting had taken its toll on him. Weariness was etched around his eyes and his firm mouth was pressed in a grim line.

He stood back from the door, his eyes distant and his hands jammed at his waist. "Are you ready?"

"If you are. Come on in while I get my purse."

"I'll wait for you in the truck. We're late enough as it is." His head dipped in a nod. "Sam," he said by way of acknowledging the woman behind her, and turned on the thick heel of his boot.

Looking no more encouraged than Lindsey felt at that moment, Sam snagged Lindsey's purse from the entry table. Handing it over, she said she was going down to talk to Logan and that she'd see her in town. By the time Lindsey stepped onto the porch, Cal was inside his dusty blue truck.

When she climbed in herself, he did nothing more than glance at her before swinging the truck around to head back out the drive. Searching his profile, Lindsey all but held her breath as she waited for him to tell her what had happened.

"So," she began, her nerves unable to bear the wait. *Are things worse? Better?* "Are you all right?"

His only response was to draw a deep breath and reach over to pick up her hand.

"It was a disaster," she concluded as he threaded his fingers through hers.

As if to check for himself, his ice-blue eyes flicked to the rearview mirror.

"No," he told her, his tone distracted. "It wasn't."

"Then everything's okay?"

It was hope behind the question. Cal seemed to hear it as naïveté, a quality he had apparently failed to realize she did not possess in abundance.

"I wouldn't go that far."

She shot him a look of extreme forbearance.

"How far would you go, then?" she asked, knowing he and Logan couldn't have delved into anything too deeply. Not in the short time they'd spent together. "Was it as hard as you'd thought it would be?"

There was more tension than certainty in his quiet "I don't know. It was okay, I guess."

Forbearance gave way to what felt suspiciously like annoyance. She understood that he would need to sort things out. She also understood that he would be a little stressed right about now. But he wasn't the only one feeling uptight. What he felt, she felt. It didn't have to make any sense. That was just how it was.

"Look, Whitaker. You got me out of bed and brought me out here before the sun was barely up to sit and worry with my sister about what was going on out there with the two of you. You're not going to get away with that cryptic nonsense you call answers. What happened? What did you talk about?"

His frown actually looked like incomprehension. "Not much of anything. We just ... talked."

She slugged him.

"Ouch!" Rubbing his biceps he glared at her. "What did you do that for?"

"Keep your eyes on the road," she muttered, actually feeling a little better as she settled back in her seat. She'd once been a reasonably contented person. One who had been relatively happy with her life. But that was before he'd worked his way into her heart and poked a zillion holes in her not so well-ordered existence. He deserved what he got. "Because you're making me crazy," she told him in response to his question. "I was *worried* about you."

Cal had no idea why it made him feel better to hear that, given the way she frowned when she said it. She wasn't very happy with him at the moment. But, then, he wasn't terribly happy with himself. A lot of old beliefs and feelings had been rudely shaken in the past fourteen hours, and he had no idea what to make of the feelings replacing them.

He didn't quite know how he felt about the lovely woman stewing beside him, either. Except that somehow she always managed to make things a little better.

He couldn't believe she'd slugged him.

"We talked about my car."

A little of the starch slipped from her shoulders when she turned to face him. "That old one in the garage?"

"You know about it?"

"Only because Sam told me while we were waiting for you. We were trying to figure out what you were talking about down there, and she decided it was that old car." Someone had dumped the old wreck on RW years ago and Cal had found it. According to Sam, one of the old hands had told Logan that Cal used to tinker with it, just to see if he could get it to run. "She said he saved it for you in case you ever came back."

"Yeah," he mumbled, the word edged with disbelief. "That's what he said. I couldn't believe he hadn't scrapped it."

The car had apparently been the catalyst, the safe subject around which the two men could talk. Lindsey had often noticed that men needed something like that, something nonthreatening—and, preferably, inanimate—around which to communicate. It didn't matter that Cal and Logan had spoken only of camshafts and pistons or whatever it was that made cars go—if that had been the direction of their conversation. What was important was that the brothers were talking again. Men didn't discuss feelings and hurts the way women did.

At least, that had been Sam and Lindsey's conclusion as they'd nursed their coffee while keeping an eye on the window. According to Sam, when a man bared his soul, it was almost always to a woman. But not just any woman. She had to be someone he trusted not to use his vulnerabilities against him. For to other men, he must be invulnerable. Every other male, even his own brother—especially his own brother—was, at some level, an adversary. Only with a woman could he allow his defenses to fall.

Watching Cal now, Lindsey wondered if he realized how much he had lowered his defenses with her. Or how much strength he had shown in facing something he had avoided for half his life. That indomitable strength had been a part of him since he was a young man, and it had drawn her from the moment they'd met.

"Was that all you talked about? Your car?"

"That and the ranch. He said part of it's mine."

The ranch was the largest and richest in the state. Yet he might as well have said he was part owner of a crescent wrench, for all the difference the information appeared to make to him.

Officially, half the ranch was his, he told her. Unofficially, a third of it was. Their father had disinherited Jett, but Logan had said he'd always thought of the brothers sharing equally. Though Cal had been amazed to learn he still had an interest in it himself, he agreed Jett belonged on the deed, too.

"Do you think you'd ever want to work it?"

There was no hesitation at all in Cal's decisive "No. I told Logan I've put some money down on my own wood shop. That's all I want. As far as I'm concerned, my part of the ranch is his. Having worked it the past seventeen years, he's earned it."

Few men would be so fair. Few others would be so true to the simplicity of their own needs. "The wood shop," Lindsey repeated, wanting to deny the betraying heaviness in her chest so she could be happy for him. He was finally getting what he'd always wanted. "You're buying the one you went to Austin to look at last week?"

The nod he gave her was a little distracted. "If they accept my offer."

She took that to mean that he hadn't yet heard. But she really didn't want to think about what he would be doing once his work here was done. "Are you going to see him again? Logan, I mean."

He said he would, the words sounding as preoccupied as he looked. "Probably sometime before I head back to Austin."

His left hand gripped the top of the steering wheel. Turning his wrist so he could see his watch, he frowned at the dial. "Do you want me to drop you off at your house or your store? I have to swing by the mill as soon as we get back to town."

He had to check on the shingles he'd special-ordered for the bandstand, he told her. The mill had made the originals.

The reminders of his impending departure from Leesburg had been far more subtle than the change of subject. But those reminders hadn't been as intentional. When he'd spoken of his shop, Cal had only been doing what she'd so charmingly insisted he do—answering her questions.

There were times when getting what a person wanted wasn't all it was cracked up to be.

"The house," she told him, because she hadn't dressed for work.

With his nod, they both fell silent.

Twenty minutes after that, he was pulling up in front of her driveway.

Cal had let go of her hand when he'd had to downshift at the junction. Since he hadn't taken it again, Lindsey thought he might reach for her when the truck rolled to a stop at the curb.

He didn't. He made no attempt to touch her at all. He just told her he'd see her later, then waited for her to climb out of his truck and open her front door before driving off. She didn't know if he'd kept his distance because he was preoccupied, if he was having second thoughts about letting her get so close or because her neighbor was out front watering her petunias and he was simply being discreet. With Cal, it was hard for her to tell—though it really wouldn't have surprised her had the latter been his intent. He'd been protective of her before, when he'd shown her his concern about how her standing up for him might affect her position in the community. There was a nobility about the man that he went out of his way to conceal. But there was also a reticence that sometimes made him impossible to reach.

* * *

Lindsey scarcely saw Cal the rest of the day. Because she was never late opening her shop, Essie had practically flown in the back door the moment Lindsey arrived at the boutique, wanting to make sure she was all right. Louella had noticed the store's dark windows, too, and within minutes of turning on the lights, the chatty but kind-hearted waitress had also appeared.

Fortunately, both women had no problem with the marginally truthful—and somewhat incomplete—expla-nation Sam offered about having gone out to the ranch to have coffee with her sister and losing track of the time. No mention was made of Cal. Essie merely remarked that she'd heard him leave early this morning, since he hadn't appeared yet, either, and had surmised he'd headed off for supplies as he so often did.

There was no mention of anyone having seen Lindsey and Cal together. And no one associated Cal's late start on the bandstand that morning with her late arrival at the boutique. Not that Lindsey would have denied being with him. It was just that it was no one's business why they had been out at the RW at the crack of dawn, even though it did make her feel good to know that her neighbors were watching out for her. Sometimes, living in a small town, it was hard to tell if the closeness she loved so much was a drawback or a benefit.

It was also hard to tell how Cal was tolerating the small audience he amassed while he worked in the square, brac-ing the bandstand so he could shore up its foundation. There was no opportunity to talk to him. Sam usurped the one logical opportunity Lindsey would have had, by tak-ing him a sandwich on her way over to the boutique. The gesture spoke volumes about how her sister felt about his appearance at the ranch that morning, and how much it meant to Logan to be speaking with his brother again. But between the people coming and going while he hammered and sawed and dug, her preparations for the grand re-opening of her shop, and a Fourth of July celebration committee meeting, she didn't see him alone until she got home that night.

He was waiting on her porch when she arrived.

He said nothing other than a quiet "Hi" before she opened the door and they stepped inside. He simply took her in his arms the moment he closed the door behind them. Aligning her body to his with a possessiveness that stunned her, he kissed her until her breathing had altered and she was clinging to the fabric at the back of his shirt to keep from sinking to the floor.

"I wasn't going to come here tonight," he whispered, his breath hot against her ear, "but I've wanted to do that all day."

Heat shot through her at the feral sound of his voice. Or maybe it was the feel of his hands that threatened to turn her blood to steam.

"Why weren't you going to come over?"

His eyes roamed her face, his hands shaping her sides as they drifted up her body. "Because I figured you needed your sleep. You didn't get much last night." His hand curved over her ribs, his thumb brushing the underside of her breast. "I didn't think it would be fair to keep you up tonight, too."

It was hard for Lindsey to tell which was stronger at the moment: the relief she felt that he hadn't withdrawn from her again or the strange sense of inevitability that moved her closer. She had precious few defenses where this man was concerned. At the moment, she couldn't muster up a single one of them. "That's very thoughtful of you."

"Actually, it was purely selfish. I figured maybe I could have you to myself tomorrow night and Sunday. We could go down to San Antonio."

A thrill of something she shouldn't have let herself feel darted through her as he drew her closer.

"You're letting yourself take a day off?"

"That job will be finished soon enough, Lindsey. I just want to be with you. Okay?"

The unexpected thickness in her throat made speaking risky. So she just gave him a quick little nod that probably betrayed her anyway and focused on the weave of his shirt.

With the tips of his fingers, he nudged her chin back up. The gleam in his eyes turned to something that looked strangely like regret. "I really don't want to leave now. But just say the word and I will."

She could no more have told him to go than she could have sprouted wings and flown to the moon. They both knew how little time he had left here. A week. Maybe two. Austin wasn't that far away. There were possibilities after he'd gone. Yet he was no more willing than she to question what would happen when his work was finished.

His dark head lowered, his breath feathering over her face as he kissed her once more. He meant only to kiss her good-night. And maybe just to hold her for a minute, because she had given him the courage to do something he'd never thought he could do. At least, that was his intention before it occurred to him that she wasn't going to ask him to go.

The realization hit Cal the moment he felt Lindsey lean into his kiss. Her slender, supple body flowed against his, fitting perfectly to his chest, his hips, the length of his thighs. She wound her arms around his neck, allowing him to draw her closer, fitting them together as if she were the other half of his body. The other half of his soul.

The thought shook him as deeply as the arousal coursing through him. Yet he didn't deny the feeling as he once would have done. Lifting her in his arms to carry her to her bed, he considered only the feel of her hands clinging to him and the soft sounds she made when he carried his kiss from the curve of her throat to the firm swell of her breast. Instead of wondering why he wanted to keep her from burying herself in this place, he thought only of how sweet she tasted, how soft her skin was against his and, long minutes later, how incredible it was to see her need for him shining in her eyes as he hovered over her. Then she arched against him and he didn't think at all. He simply let himself feel as they found their rhythm—until feelings slowly gave way to the unfamiliar sense of belonging he'd felt with her last night and she lay curled at his side.

It was nearly midnight when he left. It was Cal who insisted that he go, though Lindsey had to agree it was best. She told him that, too, standing in his arms in the dark of her living room. His staying last night had gone unnoticed, but Cal didn't want to risk having someone see him leave in the morning. Lindsey had to smile at that. He *had* been protecting her reputation this morning—something she found very endearing and, because a reputation truly could go down in flames in seconds in a place like Leesburg, something for which she was grateful.

Yet, as she closed the door softly behind him, what Lindsey considered far more important was what he allowed them to avoid by not staying the night—the intimacy that came with waking up next to each other in the morning. Of sitting across from him at the breakfast table. Not that she would actually cook breakfast. She cared far too much to inflict that sort of indignity upon him. But he was removing a circumstance that might only strengthen a bond that had already formed with far too much ease.

She appreciated that far more than he probably realized. She might have fallen in love with him, but she couldn't let herself wonder what it would be like to wake up next to him every morning. Or share every day with him. Or wonder what their sons would look like. She didn't want to need him. Or let herself count on him—only to have him walk out when she needed him most, like Annie's husband. Or die, like Sam's. Or just not be there most of the time, like her father. Or, like the man she'd almost married, simply decide she wasn't what he wanted after all.

Sam thought she was cheating herself. And maybe she was. But, then, her sisters were so much braver than she was. Sam was of the "better to have loved and lost" school of thinking—which, Lindsey was beginning to think, was a royal crock. It hurt like the devil to lose someone you loved.

So she wouldn't count on Cal to be there for her. And she would somehow ignore the bits of dreams that had crept into her heart—even though she already knew they would make his leaving so very much harder.

Chapter Twelve

"You calling it quits already, Whitaker? You usually don't go in until dark. We have a couple of hours to go before the sun sets."

It was the "we" that almost made Cal smile when he cast a tired glance toward the old man on the bench by the bandstand. He couldn't pinpoint exactly when Gramps had claimed partnership in the completion of the project, but there was no doubt that he did—along with a few other sidewalk supervisors.

At the core of the group that regularly gathered in the square to watch the metamorphosis of the bandstand were Gramps and Herb and, when he wasn't working, Jack. Jack was becoming a friend. Someone to talk with about basketball scores and grades of motor oil and where to find the best fishing holes. Gramps and Herb were, Cal supposed, becoming friends in their own way, too, cranky as they often were.

Most everyone had now departed for the day, though, including Herb, who was having dinner at his daughter's house. Gramps had stayed to critique Cal's paint job.

The brush Cal had used to finish the handrails was dropped into a bucket of water. "The only thing left to do is paint the floor and the stairs," Cal said in reply to Gramps's disgruntled question. "No sense starting that now. Shouldn't you be heading home pretty soon yourself?"

Scruffy gray eyebrows lowered in incomprehension. "What for? There's nobody there."

Cal didn't know what to say to that. But the pragmatic response seemed to strike a too-familiar chord as he turned to gather up the tarps he no longer needed. Gramps seemed totally accepting of the fact that there wasn't anyone waiting for him to come home. There had been a time when Cal hadn't thought all that much of sharing that circumstance himself.

It wasn't himself he was thinking of, however, when he saw Gramps slowly stand and straighten himself out. He was thinking only of an old man who had nothing to do but pass his days living through other people until it came time to go home to an empty house.

"Look, Gramps. I need to go wash up," Cal began, holding out his paint-spattered hands and forearms as if to prove his point, "but that won't take me long. How about I buy you some dinner? We've both got to eat."

He'd added the latter comment so Gramps, proud old duffer that he was, wouldn't think he was feeling sorry for him. It was the truth, though. Cal did need to feed himself at some point tonight. Though he and Lindsey had taken to pooling their limited culinary skills, she had another meeting tonight.

A remarkably wry smile deepened the creases in Gramps's wrinkled face. "That's right neighborly, Whitaker. But I think I'll just head on over to the Lone Star and listen to the boys lie to one another for a while. I'll take a rain check on that offer, though. Just be sure you make good on it before you pull out of town. You hear?"

Hitching up the straps of his overalls, he ambled toward the walk. Two steps later, he turned back.

"Speaking of which," he muttered, as if still in the middle of the conversation. "Are you going to take on that job for the mayor? Heard he asked you this morning to give him an estimate for doing up the market the way you did the dress shop over there. Hear Phil's going to ask you to do the drugstore, too."

"I don't know," Cal had to tell him. "I haven't decided yet."

Gramps's contemplative nod as he turned away seemed to indicate he could appreciate that the matter might require a little thought. After all, Cal had been in Leesburg for well over a month, and Gramps knew about the shop in Austin that Cal was to close on soon. It had been in escrow for weeks.

What Gramps had somehow failed to overhear was that Phil had already offered Cal the job. Both the mayor and the pharmacist had been dropping by all week, along with nearly everyone else who'd had business at the beauty or barbershop, the veterinarian's, the bakery, the library or the newspaper office. Or so it had seemed. In a place like Leesburg, the restoration of a structure in the middle of town constituted major entertainment. The two men Gramps had mentioned, though, had been as interested in the research Cal had done to make sure his restoration was historically accurate as they were in the painstaking work that had slowly transformed the round, weathered structure into the sparkling, white centerpiece bands had played in at the turn of the century. Cal had enjoyed those discussions of history almost as much as he'd enjoyed the work.

The bandstand would be finished tomorrow.

There had been a time when Cal would have felt nothing but relief at having finally finished what he'd been hired to do, relief that he was finally able to leave. Especially since he had his woodworking shop to get up and running. Yet now he wasn't nearly so anxious to go.

He wouldn't have bet a plugged nickel on the possibility before he'd arrived here, but he had actually gained the acceptance of people who once would scarcely meet his eye. More important, with the help of the woman who had made him step beyond himself, he had found something more than a sense of accomplishment in the work he had done. He felt a sense of contribution. With each sunrise, the old ghosts had faded a little more, and without realizing it, he'd slowly come to feel more a part of this place as he'd helped to renew it.

He was even getting to know his brother. He and Lindsey had gone out to the ranch last Sunday.

Cal headed across the street, nodding to the two boys who waved at him from down by the ice-cream shop. One was Sam's nine-year-old son, Michael, an incredibly inquisitive kid who must have asked a hundred questions about what he was doing and why when he'd first met him. He'd noticed the kid hanging around, but not until Sam had introduced him and her eldest daughter, Erin, to him a couple of weeks ago, had he known who he was. The only member of Logan's family that he hadn't met was his son Trevor, since he was away at college.

It seemed odd to think of himself as an uncle—even though "Uncle Cal" was always what little Amy called him when she'd come rushing through the square on her way from school to her mom's office. Having thought of himself as solitary for so long, it seemed odder still to acknowledge that he really was part of a family. But, then, that was what Lindsey had tacitly maintained all along.

There was something else Lindsey had been right about. Even though he'd practically taken off her head when she'd suggested the possibility. He *had* wanted to come back here. He'd just needed a reason.

But he needed a better reason than the offer of work to stay.

All he wanted to do was find out what time she'd be home tonight. At least that was Cal's thought when, having just washed up, he headed down the steps from the apartment. His timing couldn't have been better. Lindsey, clutching a thick file, was just backing out the door of her workroom. The moment she glanced up and saw him, her mouth curved in the smile that never failed to remind him of sunshine.

She met him at the bottom step, her soft scent drifting toward him, evoking memories of the hours they'd shared in each other's arms. The pleasure he'd taken in her. The pleasure he'd given. Combined with the warmth of her smile, its effect was positively lethal.

"How did it go?" she asked, as she so often did when their paths hadn't crossed all day. The late-afternoon sun shot streaks of gold through her hair as she tipped her head. "You look a little tired."

He told her he was, liking how it felt to have her notice something so inconsequential. Liking, too, that she was always interested in the more tedious aspects of his day. It was such a little thing. The small talk. Something that once wouldn't have meant anything to him at all. Now, with Lindsey, it made him feel . . . connected.

That intimate communication worked both ways. He was just a little slower than she was sometimes at picking up the clues.

The faint lines of strain behind her smile finally registered. "It looks like it's been a long day for you, too." Trailing his finger over her brow, he frowned. "What are these for?"

Her nose wrinkled in mild exasperation, reminding him a little of how Amy looked when told she couldn't do something. He'd bet Lindsey would have beautiful children.

"Camille just called," she muttered as his hand suddenly stilled, then quickly fell. "She's moving back to New Mexico, so now I have to find someone else to help me with the shirts. I just received three more orders."

Cal's glance fell to the folder she hugged to her chest. It was marked "Fourth of July." She was taking it with her to the city council meeting tonight.

"Have you considered giving up some of this other stuff so you'd have time to do them yourself?"

The arch of her eyebrows suggested he was playing two cards short of a deck.

"I just asked if you'd considered it," he said defensively.

"No, I haven't."

"Would you?"

"Would I what?"

"Consider giving up some of . . . all these things you do."

Her quiet "Why?" was laced with caution.

One shoulder lifted in a dismissive shrug. "I just wondered," he said, sounding far more indifferent than he felt. He hadn't intended to bring this up now. He'd thought to approach her tonight, when she wasn't having to rush off somewhere and he'd figured out what he'd wanted to say. But the answer would be the same no matter when or how the question was posed. Watching her now, he needed that answer.

"I assume you've heard what the mayor asked me to do this morning," he began.

"The whole town has," she conceded, looking as if she'd known he would bring it up when he was ready.

There had been a time when Lindsey's calm demeanor would have fooled him. It didn't anymore. Beneath the quiet inquiry in her eyes, he could see a hint of what looked very much like hope.

"Are you going to take the job?"

"That depends. I wanted to see what you thought of me sticking around for a few months longer before I gave him an answer. I have another job here, too, if I want it."

Her smile reappeared, soft, warm, encouraging. "I think it would be wonderful. You and Logan would have a chance to get to know each other better. And you could meet his son when he comes home for—"

"I'm not talking about Logan," Cal cut in. Because of her, he and his brother would work things out, whether or not he stayed. "I'm talking about you and me. What would happen to us."

The smile vanished like a ghost. "Why would anything have to happen? Can't we just go on the way we are?"

There were times when a question resulted in unexpected answers. And even more unexpected conclusions. All Cal had wanted to know was if their relationship was as strong as he was coming to feel it was, and if she wanted it to continue. Her response had, in its own way, given him the answer he'd hoped for. But it also made him realize that "the way we are" wasn't all he wanted from her.

"If I stay, you want our relationship to stay the way it is," he concluded, his voice deceptively mild.

Suddenly apprehensive, she searched his face. "Don't you?"

"Is that what you want?"

"Cal, if you..."

"Just answer me. Please. Is that what you want?"

"Yes."

He pressed his lips together, conclusions solidifying. "What if I'm not willing to settle for that?" He was a careful man. Inherently cautious. He always studied the grain before he worked a piece of wood, and he didn't make a cut without knowing which way the wood would split.

"What if I want more of your time?" he continued, needing to know where he stood with her. "More of you?" His voice grew pensive, his thoughts more certain as he caressed the downy softness of her cheek. "What if I want it all, Lindsey? What if all your talk about family finally got to me and I decided I wanted one of my own?"

His list of softly spoken hypotheticals clearly shook her. Her voice was scarcely more than a whisper. "What if you change your mind?"

Silence suddenly shimmered between them, her eyes pleading, his searching.

"Do you really think so little of me?"

Her whispered "No" came in a rush, her fingers curling over his wrist as if she feared he might pull away. "That's not what I mean at all."

"Then what do you want from me?"

"I want what we have. Please, Cal. I'm afraid to want more."

It was her admission that kept him from pushing. No one knew better than he how hard it was to let go of the defenses a person developed to protect himself. And Lindsey was hanging on tight. Had it not been for the way she'd leaned into his touch and the support she seemed to seek from him now, he might have believed he already had all she could give. But she was capable of so much more. He knew she needed more. Just as he did.

"Has anyone ever told you what a hypocrite you are?" His tone was gentle, like his touch. "You were so insistent about me giving my brother a chance. About letting the people here give me a chance. Yet you won't give me one." His heart felt tender at that thought. Like a bruise that had just been bumped. "Or yourself, for that matter."

His thumb brushed her bottom lip, then brushed it once more as he waited for her to tell him he was wrong. But the denial never came.

"Lindsey! There you are! I waited for you out front. Then I got to wondering if I'd misunderstood and was supposed to meet you back...here."

Essie cut herself off, her ample frame coming to a halt ten feet away. Eyes wide behind her silver-rimmed glasses, she could clearly see Cal's hand fall as he straightened, and the tension that had Lindsey hugging her file like a shield when she turned.

"I didn't mean to interrupt," she hurriedly explained, her expression somewhere between approval and chagrin. "Tell you what, Lindsey. I'll go on over to the library and set up for the meeting myself. You just take your time."

Cal was already shaking his head. "It's okay, Essie. I won't hold her up any longer."

Lindsey turned back to him, clearly uneasy. "Will I see you later?" she asked, her voice unusually hesitant.

Seeing her tonight had definitely been his intention when he'd started down the stairs. But his plans had changed. Drastically.

"Not tonight. I've got a lot of work to do in the morning, so I'm turning in early. And I'm going up to Austin tomorrow afternoon." Without thinking about how freely he touched her, he tucked back the wisp of hair curling at the base of her neck. "Have a good meeting."

He turned then, vaguely aware as he headed back up the steps of Essie's effusive apology to Lindsey for interrupting.

There was nothing more for him and Lindsey to say that wouldn't result in an argument he didn't want to get into. She hadn't denied a thing he'd said. She was holding back and she knew it. But he also knew she cared about him. Whether she was prepared to admit it or not, she trusted him, too. A woman as protective as she was of her heart would never have allowed their relationship to become as intimate as it had if she didn't. She would never have risked sharing herself. And he'd shared more of himself with her than he had with any other human being.

She'd been left at the altar once. He knew she would never allow herself to be in that position again. He couldn't blame her. That was why he wouldn't give her the opportunity to worry about having it happen a second time.

He'd been gone for two days.

Two days, twenty-two hours and, as near as Lindsey could figure, fourteen minutes. He was supposed to have been back six hours ago.

Not that she was counting.

Deliberately turning from the clock behind the boutique's jewelry case-cum-sales counter, Lindsey attacked a stack of blouses with her tagging gun.

Sam was late, too. Not that Lindsey was concerned about her sister's tardiness. It was just that Sam had called first thing this morning and made her promise she'd be at her store at three o'clock when she got back from some meeting. Meetings inevitably ran late.

And some days ran long. Especially days a person spent trying to not worry.

As idiotic as Lindsey suspected the thought would sound to anyone else, she would actually have felt better if she and Cal had had a real argument. But he hadn't said a word about the unsettling conversation they'd had the evening before he'd left. In a way, they might never have had the conversation at all. Just before he'd taken off after finishing the bandstand the next afternoon, he'd kissed her as he always had—as if he could never get enough of her—then told her he'd see her sometime this morning.

What bothered her, though, was that he had never committed to taking the jobs he'd been offered. And he'd seemed awfully tense when he'd finally walked away. What had put the perpetual knot in her stomach, however, had been her discovering that he'd taken his tools from her spare workroom.

There had to be an explanation for that. Cal was an honorable man. Though her logical mind kept insisting something wasn't right, her heart refused to believe he'd simply walked away.

The chime over the boutique's front door put a merciful end to her mental machinations. Sam walked in, smoothing the sleeve of her deep-pink silk suit.

Her sister's appearance caught Lindsey totally off guard. Sam's smooth, blond hair was caught with a pink rhinestone clip. Matching earrings, which also matched the raw silk of her suit, winked from her earlobes.

"Wow," said Lindsey, a grin surfacing. "What kind of a meeting did you attend?"

"Don't ask," her sister hedged, looking annoyed with whatever it was she'd gotten on her sleeve. "Do you have any spot remover? I think this is Gummy Bear. Or maybe it's gummy worm. It's hard to tell."

Tugging Sam's sleeve—and Sam—back to the counter, Lindsey contemplated the offending spot. Had it not been for the anxiety she was battling, she would have displayed a little more curiosity about where Sam had been. There wasn't anywhere in Leesburg a person couldn't go in denim.

After digging a small container of spot remover out from under the counter, Lindsey returned her attention to the sleeve. "Do worms come in grape?"

"Probably. It's Michael's favorite flavor." A swift frown darted over her features. "What's the matter?" Sam's hand touched Lindsey's, sudden concern replacing her seeming preoccupation as she finally met Lindsey's eyes. "Why are you shaking?"

Lindsey hadn't realized she was. She'd been aware of the feeling on the inside, but until she'd tried to dab at what her nine-year-old nephew would probably call "worm guts," she hadn't realized it showed.

So much for outward calm, she thought.

Pulling back her hand, she gave her sister a wan smile. "You first. You didn't say why you wanted to talk to me when you called. What's up?"

It wasn't until just then that Lindsey realized how uneasy her sister was. But the look on her flawlessly made-up face grew uneasier still when she said, "I'll get to that in a minute. I want to know why you're upset."

To anyone but her sister, Lindsey would have denied that she was. She was trying to deny a lot of things at the moment. But this was her big sister. What was more important at the moment was that her big sister knew what it was like to have been steamrolled by a Whitaker.

"Have you seen Cal?"

"Not today," Sam replied, suddenly interested in her sleeve again. "Why?"

"Because I don't know where he is. He said he had something he needed to take care of in Austin and that he'd be back this morning. But it's already after three . . . and he took his tools with him."

It only took seconds for Sam to understand her sister's apprehension. "And you're afraid he's not coming back," she quietly concluded.

"I didn't say that. I'm trying as hard as I can not to think that way," she hurried on before her sister could tell her there were certain things she really didn't need to say for her to know. "But I just have this awful feeling that something has happened. I have no idea where to find him or what's happened to him. What if he's lying in a ditch somewhere?"

It seemed extremely odd to Lindsey that much of the tension faded from her sister's expression just then. But it certainly seemed to as Sam reached toward a small carousel of earrings. "You really do love him, don't you?"

"What does that have to do with anything?"

"Don't you?"

Confused, anxious, she gave Sam a wary nod. She and her sister were usually on the same wavelength. Now, it was as if they weren't even having the same conversation. "Yes, I do," she whispered, thinking it rather unfair of her sister to force her to admit such a thing when she was so torn already.

"I was pretty sure you did. But I just had to make sure."

"Make sure?"

"He's not lying in a ditch," she quietly reassured her. "He's fine."

"How do you know? You said you hadn't seen him."

"I said I hadn't seen him today." Picking up a pair of pearl earrings, Sam idly toyed with the thumbnail-size teardrops. "He'll be here."

Taking the earrings with her, she headed to the small section of formal wear at the back of the shop.

Lindsey would have given her best dressmaker's shears for a tenth of her sister's confidence. She would have told her that, too, had a huge shadow not overtaken her doorway just then.

The chime sounded brightly as the door opened. Her heart skidded to a halt as shadow turned to substance and Cal walked in.

She'd never seen him dressed in anything other than a T-shirt or work shirt and jeans. Today he was wearing an open-collared, black silk shirt that made his shoulders look a mile wide and pleated, black dress slacks that broke perfectly above black, leather dress boots. His hair had been trimmed. Not enough to make anyone think him conservative by any means. But the dark hair combed neatly back from his strikingly handsome features now only covered his collar instead of hanging below it.

She scarcely caught a glimpse of his face, however. And he didn't see the relief that flooded hers that he'd finally shown up. His glance darted straight to Sam.

"How is everything?" he asked her, the question sounding to Lindsey like the casual greeting the inquiry often was.

"Good," she assured him, absently smoothing a sleeve of white lace. "Where's Logan?"

"Waiting over at the café."

With a nod, Sam turned back to her browsing.

Certain she was missing something, but not at all sure what, Lindsey watched Cal move toward her. He'd obviously been with his brother. But there was no time for her to piece together anything else before she felt him grasp her hand.

"I need to talk to you for a minute."

She thought she gave him a nod. She wasn't sure. She did know she let him lead her into the workroom that was now separated from her store by a door rather than a curtain.

"Are you all right?" she asked the instant he closed the door behind him.

The concern in her warm, brown eyes went a long way to relieve the apprehension Cal didn't want to admit to. Not wanting to consider what he would have done had his reception been less favorable, he dragged in a breath of gardenia-scented air. He was about to take the biggest risk of his life—and he hated how unnerved he suddenly felt.

"I'm fine," he told her, keeping her more or less trapped between the wall, the door and his body in case she decided to bolt. "But I've got some people waiting on an answer, and I need to get back to them as soon as I can."

"People?"

"I'll get to that in a minute." He took a step back, stalling. Now that it was time to say what he'd come to say, the words deserted him. It hadn't occurred to him how much courage this was going to take. "There's something I need to tell you before I do. Okay?"

She'd been right. He wouldn't just walk away. He'd tell her face-to-face that he was leaving.

It would have been easier if he'd been a coward. "Okay," she quietly agreed.

"Would you answer a question for me first?"

She gave him a nod, not sure if the disquiet she felt was hers or his.

"Do you remember the night I first came here?"

Of course she did. She remembered every moment they'd spent together. "Why?"

"Because we were talking about the town. We had a difference of opinion about it...about how I thought it was a place to move from rather than to, the way you had." He'd been so adamant about his position. So inflexible. "You told me that opinion depended on what a person was looking for."

She recalled that first night as clearly as she did another. The night he'd basically accused her of using the town as a place to hide from everything she'd once wanted. "I remember."

"Do you think a person can change his or her mind about a strongly held conviction?"

His phrasing gave her pause. His or her? "I imagine it's always a possibility. Why?"

"Because I've changed mine. Everything I want is right here."

The disquiet she felt collided with something that felt suspiciously like hope. "What do you mean by... 'everything'?"

"Just what I said." He curved his hands over her shoulders, his glance following the path of one as it slipped down to rub her upper arm. He'd needed to touch her. The words came easier when he did. They always had.

"You made me face a lot of things I had to get behind me, Lindsey. Stuff I'd never wanted to deal with." It seemed she had all but forced him to face his anger. Yet, just by listening to him, just by being there, she had lessened that anger somehow. Just by being, she made his life better. Her smiled healed. Her touch calmed, even as it excited. And he couldn't imagine another day of his life without her. "I couldn't have done it without you."

Her expression grew gentle. "You have always underestimated yourself, you know."

A faint smile pulled at the corners of his mouth, but he said nothing. He just continued to watch his hand move from her arm to her shoulder until the smile faded. It was almost as if he was looking for something in that soothing motion, but he was having no luck finding it.

Then the motion stopped. "There's something I want to give you," he said, sounding as if he'd been picturing whatever that something was. "Something you once told me you'd wanted."

"What's that?"

"Children."

Beneath his hand, he felt her go still.

"Children?"

With her seeming incomprehension, Cal's hesitation vanished. "You said you always wanted them."

"I know, but . . ."

"But you want them to have both a mother and a father," he finished for her. "I know. We can do that. You'd have to help me out until I get the hang of it, but it'll work. I love you, Lindsey. I've never said those words to anyone in my entire life, and in some ways, this whole idea scares the hell out of me. What scares me more is letting you go." The breath he drew sounded a little ragged. "Say something, will you?"

She looked up at him, at his newly cut hair, his freshly shaved face, his new shirt. Inside her chest, her heart felt strangely tender. "I love you, too," she quietly said. "I can't tell you how much." Quiet faded to a whisper. "But I'm scared, too."

Years seemed to wash from his features as he cupped her face in his big hands. His eyes, as clear as a summer sky, scanned her face.

"I'm not going to leave you standing at any altar, Lindsey. I'm not going to leave when you're sick, or senile, or when you burn the stew. I'm not going to leave you period. Or this town. I canceled the deal on the building in Austin and I've got enough work here to buy the one I've moved my tools into over on Main. I'd like a shot at restoring the library and the courthouse, too. I'd also like you to be my wife. Now."

"Now?" she choked.

"Now. I didn't want you worrying about me not showing up. So everything's ready, if you're willing. Logan's waiting with a justice of the peace and we've got the clerk to issue the license." Logan had said he'd be honored to help pull the ceremony together when Cal had stopped at the RW to ask him to be his best man. He'd even told Cal he wished he'd thought of the idea himself with Lindsey's sister. If he had, maybe he wouldn't have had to ask her twice to marry him. "He and Sam will stand up with us."

Though Lindsey was all but blocked by Cal's big body, the window at the end of the workroom was in clear view. In it, she saw her niece Erin, wearing her fuchsia prom dress, hurrying by. Amy was with her, dressed in hot pink organdy, with her blond curls held up by a huge matching bow.

Her flower girl.

"I'm being railroaded?"

"'Fraid so."

He didn't look the least bit contrite.

Sometimes the biggest risk was not taking one at all. Cal had taken those risks. With his brother. Now with her. Yet all he was really asking of her was that she believe in him, believe that, as far as it was in his power to control, he would be with her.

She had believed in him from the very beginning.

"Can I have an hour?"

"To think about it?" he guessed, looking a little ambivalent about that idea.

He already had her in his arms, the heat of his body flowing into hers. Looping her arms around his neck, she raised up to brush a kiss over his firm lips. "I've already thought about it," she told him. "You told me the other day I wasn't giving us a chance. It only took you being a few hours late today to make me realize I really need that chance with you. I need us. If you hadn't come back, I'd have come after you."

"Oh, yeah?" he growled.

"Yeah," she started to whisper, only to have him steal the word, along with her breath, when his mouth covered hers and he edged her back against the wall.

Her knees felt like melted wax, but a smile tugged at her mouth when he finally raised his head.

His eyes glittered over her face. "What do you need an hour for?"

Lindsey nudged him back, snagging his wrist when he released her. Turning his hand over, she glanced at his watch.

When she and Cal had left Sam, her sister had been checking out the wedding gowns. Sam knew exactly which one Lindsey liked the best.

She gave a smile as bright as the sun. "To get ready for my wedding."

Epilogue

"There's a wedding in the square!"

The wedding of Caleb Whitaker to Lindsey Hayes must have set a record of some sort in Leesburg. The only people in town who had known about it were Sam, Logan and Cal, since Cal had asked Sam to keep it that way in case Lindsey turned him down. Not that Sam had thought there was a chance of that happening. She knew her sister. And, as she told Lindsey while she helped her dress, she knew exactly how persuasive a Whitaker could be.

It wasn't long, however, before word was out. All it took was Louella overhearing Cal tell his brother, who was waiting at the café, that the wedding was on. Within the hour Lindsey had asked for, no fewer than fifty people had gathered around the newly refurbished bandstand in the square to wait for the bride. Essie was the only one not smiling at first. She grumbled to anyone who would listen that she really wished Cal would have confided in her so she could have baked him and Lindsey a proper wedding cake—though she did manage to add pink roses and a bride and groom to a sheet cake she had on hand. Someone had borrowed a folding table from the community church and draped it with a lace tablecloth, and that cake now sat on the table, in the square. Someone else had rounded up a punch bowl and cups for the punch the mayor donated from his market. Louella commandeered from the florist the single white roses Lindsey and Sam would carry and a small basket of daisies for Amy.

The birds singing from the sweeping branches of the live oaks and pecan trees in the square provided the music. The white and purple alyssum bordering the sidewalk through the square served as decorations on the "aisle." The bandstand itself, gleaming in the dappled afternoon light, became the altar. There were no candles or ribbons, no lavish floral displays. Yet when Lindsey stepped from the front door of her boutique, white satin rustling as she gathered the train of the pearl-embellished gown to keep from dragging it on the street, it never occurred to her to notice what was missing. She saw only Cal waiting at the bandstand's steps.

She didn't really recall who all she passed as Erin picked up her flowing train and she followed Sam and Amy up the alyssum-lined walk. It seemed as if all the townsfolk had closed their businesses early, though, because every shop owner in Leesburg seemed to be there. She vaguely remembered seeing Gramps, Herb and Jack, and Rita from the pharmacy dabbing at her eyes. Lindsey's friend Sue, the home-ec teacher, gave her a thumbs-up, along with a couple of girls Lindsey recognized from the prom dress class.

Beneath the lace and pearls on her bodice, Lindsey felt her heart give a little tug. Everything would have been perfect had her parents and Annie been there. She knew Cal had wanted his youngest brother there, too, because Sam had told her he'd tried to track him down. But Jett had moved on from the job he'd been working in Canada and no one had been able to find him. Cal had Logan, though. It had to mean a lot to have his brother beside him.

Oblivious to the murmurs drifting through the crowd, Lindsey stopped an arm's length from where Cal remained at the foot of the steps leading to the bandstand's canopied floor. Sam and Amy had already proceeded up the stairs. Logan and the justice of the peace were there, too, waiting.

The pressure behind her bodice seemed to increase. "Hi," she said to Cal, strangling the stem of her rose. "Ready when you are."

If she lived to be a thousand, she would never forget the expression on Cal's handsome face at that moment. He appeared proud and sure and just a little possessive as his glance moved from the shimmering gown and the filmy veil streaming behind her to the trust shining in her eyes.

"I love you," he whispered.

"I love you, too," she returned, just as quietly.

"It's going to be okay, honey. Honest."

"I know."

With the back of his finger he grazed her cheek, his hand brushing the teardrop pearl dancing from her ear. "There's just one thing I have to know before we do this."

"What's that?"

The look in his eyes was part desire, part affection, but mostly curiosity. "Do I really make you crazy?"

"Absolutely," she said, her smile certain.

Cal matched her expression. A moment later, knowing now how it felt to belong, he reached for the hand of his bride.

* * * * *

Don't miss *The Black Sheep's Bride*
by Christine Flynn,
book 3 in THE WHITAKER BRIDES—
coming in February 1997 from
Silhouette Special Edition!

WITHOUT A TRACE
Nora Roberts

Trace O'Hurley had turned his back on responsibility and commitment long ago. Now he lived as he pleased—but that was all about to change.

Gillian Fitzpatrick had responsibilities and commitments—her brother had disappeared and she was frightened and desperate. Trace was her only hope. He had the connections, the expertise...and the guts. But just what was Gillian going to have to do to convince him to help her...?

"Her stories have fuelled the dreams of 25 million readers."

Entertainment Weekly

"The versatile, brilliant Ms Roberts... constantly provides her fans with something refreshing and mesmerising."

Affaire de Coeur

MIRA®

COMING NEXT MONTH

THE BRIDE AND THE BABY Phyllis Halldorson

That's My Baby!

What was it that steered Mariah Bentley to the tiny orphan stranded in the blizzard? All Mariah knew was that a miraculous Christmas baby was now snuggled in her arms. But then ravishing stranger Aaron Kerr laid claim to his little nephew…and laid siege to Mariah's senses!

A GOOD GROOM IS HARD TO FIND Amy Frazier

Sweet Hope Weddings

Country doctor Rhune Sherman certainly met his match when Tess McQueen arrived in town. But she had a score to settle, and he didn't want to think about the raging attraction between them—until the townsfolk of Sweet Hope decided to do a little matchmaking!

MR ANGEL Beth Henderson

Kevin Lonergan didn't see himself as any kind of hero. But Rella Schofield's kids were eyeing him with something akin to worship. The look in Rella's eyes whispered something else entirely…

THE ROAD BACK HOME Sierra Rydell

He was the last person beautiful Siksik Toovak expected to see at her isolated cabin. Years ago, Billy had left her and the dreams she harboured far behind. Now Billy had grown into a confident, sexy stranger—and he needed her help…

DADDY CHRISTMAS Cathy Gillen Thacker

From the moment they'd met, Matt Hale knew Gretchen O'Malley was the woman he wanted to spend the rest of his life with. Now he was going to be a daddy, and marrying Gretchen was a New Year's resolution he was determined to keep!

A CHRISTMAS BLESSING Sherryl Woods

And Baby Makes Three

Widowed Jessie Adams was about to give birth, and she needed help—fast! Unfortunately, the closest ranch in the small town belonged to her charismatic brother-in-law, Luke, who was the *last* person Jessie wanted to be stranded with…

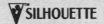

GET 4 BOOKS
AND A MYSTERY GIFT

Return this coupon and we'll send you 4 Silhouette Special Edition® novels and a mystery gift absolutely FREE! We'll even pay the postage and packing for you.

We're making you this offer to introduce you to the benefits of Reader Service: FREE home delivery of brand-new Silhouette® romances, at least a month before they are available in the shops, FREE gifts and a monthly Newsletter packed with information.

Accepting these FREE books and gift places you under no obligation to buy, you may cancel at any time, even after receiving just your free shipment. Simply complete the coupon below and send it to:

SILHOUETTE READER SERVICE, FREEPOST, CROYDON, CR9 3WZ.

No stamp needed

Yes, please send me 4 free Silhouette Special Edition novels and a mystery gift. I understand that unless you hear from me, I will receive 6 superb new titles every month for just £2.30* each postage and packing free. I am under no obligation to purchase any books and I may cancel or suspend my subscription at any time, but the free books and gifts will be mine to keep in any case. (I am over 18 years of age)

E6YE

Ms/Mrs/Miss/Mr _____

Address _____

_____

_____ Postcode _____

COMING NEXT MONTH FROM

▼™ SILHOUETTE®

Intrigue
Danger, deception and desire

WHITE WEDDING Jean Barrett
HANDSOME AS SIN Kelsey Roberts
HEART VS. HUMBUG M.J. Rodgers
TILL DEATH US DO PART Rebecca York

Desire
Provocative, sensual love stories for the woman of today

MIRACLES AND MISTLETOE Cait London
CHRISTMAS WEDDING Pamela Macaluso
A COWBOY CHRISTMAS Ann Major
DADDY'S CHOICE Doreen Owens Malek
EVAN Diana Palmer
GIFT WRAPPED DAD Sandra Steffen

Sensation
A thrilling mix of passion, adventure and drama

LOVER UNDER COVER Justine Davis
CALLAGHAN'S WAY Marie Ferrarella
FIVE KIDS, ONE CHRISTMAS Terese Ramin
A VERY CONVENIENT MARRIAGE Dallas Schulze